CW00661095

MURDER AT MIDWINTER MANOR

A MISS MERRILL AND AUNT VIOLET MYSTERY

ANITA DAVISON

Boldwood

First published in Great Britain in 2024 by Boldwood Books Ltd.

Copyright © Anita Davison, 2024

Cover Design by Head Design

Cover Illustration: Shutterstock

A CIP catalogue record for this book is available from the British Library.

Paperback ISBN 978-1-78513-341-1

Large Print ISBN 978-1-78513-342-8

Hardback ISBN 978-1-78513-340-4

Ebook ISBN 978-1-78513-343-5

Kindle ISBN 978-1-78513-344-2

Audio CD ISBN 978-1-78513-335-0

MP3 CD ISBN 978-1-78513-336-7

Digital audio download ISBN 978-1-78513-339-8

Boldwood Books Ltd
23 Bowerdean Street
London SW6 3TN
www.boldwoodbooks.com

1

MIDWINTER MANOR, SURREY, 21 DECEMBER 1916

Aunt Violet gunned her Sunbeam roadster through the canopy of trees that lined the drive of Midwinter Manor, took a sharp left turn and brought the vehicle to a skidding halt on the snow-covered drive.

'Not the most comfortable journey with the hood down the entire way,' Hannah grumbled lightly as she emerged from beneath the lambswool rug that had been her constant companion since leaving Chiswick. 'Why don't they make motor cars with heaters? I can barely feel my feet.' She planted her new high-heeled leather boots into slushy wet snow up to her ankles and groaned.

'Stop complaining. I promised to get us here before dark, didn't I?' Aunt Violet climbed from the low-slung motor car, pressed her hands against the small of her back and leaned into them. 'I'd welcome a hot bath right now, and maybe a scotch.'

Aunt Violet stared up at the symmetrical building constructed in a mock Georgian style, though it was less than twenty years old. The mansard roof was punctured with a neat row of dormer windows, the lower floors sporting full-height casements.

'It's grander than I imagined,' she observed without a trace of envy. 'What made Mycroft and Iris move here?'

'The house on the other side of the Atherton estate Mycroft inherited from his father was a relic from Queen Anne's reign and quite run down. When the War Office commissioned it for use as a military hospital, he jumped at the opportunity to move here. Midwinter Manor is only a mile away from the old house and close enough for him to still oversee his tenant farms. He hopes the government will repair the old place when the war ends, and he can move back.'

'How optimistic of him! What if they don't oblige?'

'Knowing Mycroft, he'll likely let it fall down in that case. Iris always hated the old house and boasts this one has modern plumbing and no draughts. I warn you she can be tedious about it so we must make encouraging comments about everything.'

'As if I would do anything else.' Her aunt's laugh was more a snicker, making Hannah frown.

'Why so tetchy, Aunt Violet? Is your arm troubling you?'

At Easter that same year, a murderess wielding a knife had injured her aunt during a confrontation. The wound had healed well, but residual nerve damage meant it sometimes ached in cold weather.

'A little. The driving didn't help. You might have offered to swap places for the last ten miles.'

'And risk Mama seeing me at the wheel? Can you imagine what she would say? She's going to be shocked enough when she sees my hair.'

'You can't keep it a secret forever. And as for your hair, I love it. I might even have my hair bobbed when we get home. Short hair is so... liberating.'

With the loss of Hannah's lady's maid to a munitions factory, Hannah's thick, waist-length hair had become a time-consuming chore to maintain. The decision to have it cut into a sleek bob had been terrifying, but after a week of brief regret each time she caught sight of herself in a mirror, what she saw there now made her more confident.

'Ah, here's Iris.' Aunt Violet nodded to where Hannah's older sister appeared from beneath the stone canopy over the wide front door, a grey shawl thrown over her deep burgundy gown. She was taller than Hannah's five feet five inches, but Iris Atherton was not so slender – the result of bearing four children in six years. She wore her glossy chestnut hair drawn back from her face in an unfussy chignon, which made her seem older than her thirty years.

'Now, Aunt Violet. Positive things.' Hannah summoned a welcoming smile as Iris approached.

'I'm so relieved you got here safely.' Iris leaned in for a kiss, her powdery cheek brushing Hannah's. 'Even if you *are* very late.'

'Couldn't be helped, Iris.' Aunt Violet slapped her gloved hands together, her breath forming a white mist in the icy air. 'I'm not responsible for the state of the roads.'

'Yes, well, you're both here now.' Iris sighed.

Two footmen emerged from the front door and, with identical polite nods to the new arrivals heaved the cases from the rear seat of the car.

Hannah waylaid the younger one, handing him a lidded basket. 'Would you take that to the kitchen? Somewhere warm and out of a draught would be preferable. Oh, and he's probably hungry.'

'Er, of course, Madam.' The footman backed away slowly, the basket held out at arm's length.

With the bookshop cat, Bartleby, safely delivered, she rejoined Aunt Violet who was showing Iris her new purchase.

'The engine is twenty-two horsepower and can go at thirty-five miles an hour,' Aunt Violet said proudly. 'It was one of the last off the production line as they have stopped making them until the war is over. Would you like to see beneath the bonnet?'

'No, thank you.' Iris grimaced in disgust. 'You're aware the speed limit is twenty miles an hour, aren't you?'

'Not that you'd notice,' Hannah said, though no one appeared to hear her.

'No one pays any attention to the speed limit.' Aunt Violet waved her off. 'Anyway, it's more a suggestion.'

'Indulge her, Iris. The motor car is still a novelty.' Hannah eased her sister to one side. 'Is everything all right? You seem... tense.' She chose the word carefully so as not to imply her sister was anything but radiant.

'Wouldn't you be with a houseful of guests who require constant attention, and only one nurserymaid?' Iris sniffed.

'What happened to Molly, or whatever her name is?' Aunt Violet looked up from the other side of her recent acquisition.

'Mabel,' Iris corrected her. 'She's taken herself off to Cumbria for Christmas. Her family have gone down with chest colds, so she's gone to take care of them.'

'How inconsiderate of them.' Aunt Violet's arch tone earned her another scowl from Hannah, which she ignored. Iris had a houseful of servants who managed her entire life with minimal effort from her.

'And Mother is being impossible.' Iris appeared determined to air every grievance. 'I thought she might help with the children, but she's never around when she's needed.'

'Mother was never at her best with small children, Iris. You know that.'

'They are her grandchildren!' Iris said as if that made a difference to Madeleine Merrill. 'I hoped you'd talk to her for me.'

The prospect of getting between her mother and sister made Hannah's stomach tighten, but Aunt Violet's strident response saved her from having to reply.

'You were the same at their age. I'm sure they'll calm down.' Aunt Violet spoke with all the authority of someone who'd remained stoically single.

'It's not the children, really. They are dears. But with supplies so scarce these days and fourteen people to feed, I—' She turned as the door banged open and a boy in tweed knickerbockers, long socks and laced-up black shoes came running towards them. His matching jacket had buttoned lapels and two oversized flap pockets. Ten feet away his foot slipped, causing him to stagger, but he righted himself at the last second.

'Do take care, Xander,' Iris admonished him. 'We don't want any sprained ankles. Not this week.'

'Auntie Han!' The boy launched into Hannah's arms and wrapped both legs around her waist.

'Ugh!' Hannah groaned. 'You can't do that any more, Xander, you're getting too big. How old are you now? Ten? Eleven?' Grimacing, she hitched the child higher on her hip.

Alexander Hugh Atherton, known as Xander, Iris and Mycroft's firstborn bore a startling resemblance to his mother – a sturdy child with floppy, toffee-coloured hair and a sprinkling of freckles across his nose.

'I'm eight!' Xander corrected her with childish disdain. 'I've been watching out for you all afternoon and now it's almost bedtime and we won't get to play.' He leaned back to focus on her face, swinging his booted feet.

'We're here until after Boxing Day, so there's plenty of time. Didn't Matilda and Laurie want to come and say hello?'

'Fiona said it was time for our bath, but I ran off, and she couldn't catch me.' His gleeful expression abruptly turned serious. 'Have you brought me a present?'

'Isn't that a job for Santa Claus?' Hannah rubbed her nose against his.

'Yes, but he's not coming for aaages yet. You're here now.' He rested his forehead against hers, his hair giving off a faint scent of liquorice and coal tar soap.

'Then you'll just have to wait and see.' Hannah lowered him to the ground. The boy's feet barely hit the gravel before he repeated his demands from Aunt Violet, who laughed and gave his hair a gentle ruffle.

The crunch of boots on snow brought their attention to a man approaching from the front gate, a military-style grey overcoat flapping around his ankles with each step. He had a muffler wound around his neck that hid the bottom half of his face, and a fur-trimmed hat pulled down over his forehead, so only his eyes were visible.

He halted a few feet away. A pair of penetrating brown eyes framed by arched eyebrows rimmed with ice crystals appraised them with bemused enquiry, giving no clues as to his identity.

A friend, a neighbour or a tradesman? Hannah couldn't tell. He had an open, enquiring expression and seemed to be waiting for an introduction.

'Mr Gates?' Iris stiffened. 'Where have you been? My husband was unaware you had gone out.'

'I went to collect a package from the village post office, Madam.' He nodded to a brown paper packet tucked beneath one arm.

'You walked there and back in two feet of snow?' Iris raised an eyebrow.

'I came across the fields, which was quite bracing, actually.'

His muffler slipped as he talked, revealing an amiable smile on a face younger than Hannah expected.

'You might have informed us you had left the house.' Iris seemed put out, but Hannah couldn't think why if he was on an errand for his employer, which seemed to be the case.

Hannah raised an eyebrow at Aunt Violet, who returned it in kind. Iris was rarely sharp with people, so this open hostility was out of character. Xander appeared confused. His head swivelled like a spectator at a tennis match.

'Apologies, Mrs Atherton.' Mr Gates inclined his head, but his tone conveyed no concern he might have offended.

'I'll take the envelope to my husband if it's so important.' Iris extended a hand towards him.

'Please don't trouble yourself.' Mr Gates settled the packet more tightly beneath his arm. 'I dropped it in the snow and need to check the documents are undamaged.'

'As you prefer.' Iris stiffened before she seemed to realise they weren't alone. 'Oh, um, this is my sister, Miss Hannah Merrill, and my aunt, Miss Violet Edwards, who are with us for Christmas. Anthony Gates, my husband's secretary.' Nods of acknowledgement and curt greetings were exchanged.

'Your aunts will come and see you later, Xander.' Iris smoothed her son's hair and brushed bits of fluff and pine needles from his jacket. 'Now go upstairs and apologise to Fiona and have your bath. I'll be up later to say goodnight. Mr Gates, would you escort Master Alexander back to the nursery?'

'Of course, Madam.' He placed a hand on Xander's shoulder, giving no sign he regarded the task being beneath him. 'Come along, young man.'

The pair approached the house, with Mr Gates nodding occasionally as the boy chattered excitedly, a wide smile aimed up at his companion.

'Xander seems to like him,' Hannah observed.

Iris's muttered response was inaudible.

'Could we go inside now?' Aunt Violet asked with the impatience of a toddler. 'It's bitterly cold out here, and I cannot wait to see the house.' She raised her eyes skyward to where a sudden flurry of needle-like snowflakes bit into her cheeks.

'Oh, of course, I forgot.' Iris led the way into the house. 'You've never been here before.'

'Had I received an invitation, I would have,' Aunt Violet muttered, returning Hannah's warning glare with a lazy shrug.

2

Having relinquished their outer clothing to the butler, Iris led them into an expansive hallway with high ceilings.

'This is all very elegant.' Aunt Violet's tetchiness dissolved as she turned full circle, her neck craned to take in a central cantilevered staircase rising to a wide galleried landing lined with doors on the upper floor. A large rectangular glass lantern set into the roof allowed daylight to flood the interior.

A massive marble fireplace dominated one wall, decorated with garlands of laurel and holly that adorned the fireplace, between which clusters of red berries peeked from glossy green leaves and artfully placed pinecones. A Christmas tree stood at the far end that reached up to the first landing, its lush branches packed with glittering ornaments, wrapped gifts and tiny white candles attached to the ends of the branches.

'You don't intend lighting those, I hope?' Aunt Violet stared at the tree with suspicion.

'Not until Christmas Eve, when they will be carefully monitored. The rest of the time they are for decoration only.' Iris laughed for the first time since they'd arrived. 'You've missed afternoon tea, I'm afraid, and the dressing bell for dinner will go soon, so I'll take you straight up.' She headed toward the staircase to the first floor, leaving them to follow.

'Now, Iris, refresh our memory about your guests.' With Hannah's weakness with names, she made an effort to get ahead of any embarrassing moments.

'Well, of course, Mother and Father,' Iris began. 'Then Mycroft's younger brother Selwyn, whom you know, along with his American wife, Norah. Their two daughters came with them.'

'I remember the Atherton twins. They have nursery-bookish names but I'm blowed if I can remember them.' Aunt Violet brought up the rear as they walked single file.

'They're not twins,' Iris corrected as if chastising her for not keeping a record of Iris's social calendar. 'Their names are Millie and Maura, and there are ten months between them.'

'Irish twins then.' Aunt Violet smirked. 'Though they might as well be with those names.'

Hannah suppressed a smile, recalling two fair-haired girls with high, breathless voices who liked to dress alike, then banished the image and concentrated on what Iris was saying.

'A neighbour of ours from the village will be here for dinner. A Mrs Dunleavy and her young daughter, but they won't be staying.'

'She must be a special friend for you to invite her to a family dinner?' Hannah said.

'Not really.' Iris sighed. 'She dropped so many hints about how she wanted to see the house in its full glory, so in a weak moment, I invited them.' She paused halfway up the staircase and glanced back over one shoulder. 'But only tonight. I don't think I could bear her company longer than that. Millie's fiancé is here too,' she said, continuing up the stairs. 'Captain Lynford Ellis, who is rather dashing actually. Though, for some unknown reason, Mycroft also invited his parents, Basil and Rose Ellis. He's something to do with the military, but I forget what. Captain Ellis is such a charming young man,' Iris gushed. 'Which you'll see for yourself. He's on extended leave from the army, but I warn you he's a little... unsettled at the moment. He was at High Wood, you know?'

Hannah didn't know. Her only knowledge of High Wood was that it had played a part in the Somme offensive the previous September. The term 'extended leave' however, was more familiar, indicating Captain Ellis had been granted a period of rest and contemplation to recover from the traumatic experiences at the front.

'I saw their engagement announcement in *The Times*, but we've not met.' Hannah repeated all the names in her head to commit them to memory.

'He's being awarded a medal for bravery,' Iris added, obviously impressed.

'A medal?' Hannah said archly. 'Oh, well, that will make everything all right then, won't it?'

'Don't be sarcastic, Hannah, it's a great honour.' Iris glared at her as she traversed a galleried landing lined with doors on all four sides that gave a panoramic view of the floor below. 'She sounds more like you every day, Aunt Violet.'

'She's my greatest achievement.' Aunt Violet met Iris's critical look with a triumphant smile. 'This is your room, Hannah.' Iris threw open the door of a room about twelve feet square containing a high brass bed piled with a satin coverlet, facing a six-foot wide mullioned window with a view of pure white that stretched for miles. Matching cushions in a calming sage green adorned the bed and two chairs; the walls were painted a deep gold with cream paintwork. A dark mahogany bureau with a mirror stood on one side, a chest of drawers on the other beside a matching three-door wardrobe. Everything in the room, down to the reading lamps on the matching side tables, was brand new, with no scratches or faded areas.

'Aunt Violet, you're next door,' Iris said. 'I'll send a maid to help you both unpack.'

'That's not necessary, Iris, really. I can manage perfectly well.'

'Whereas I would never be so churlish as to refuse such a luxury,' Aunt Violet beamed. 'Send her up.'

'Your bathroom is through there, Hannah.' Iris pointed to a door in the corner. 'You won't need to share because Aunt Violet's is also next to her room. I don't know how you both manage in Chiswick with just the one.'

Hannah held her sister's gaze but refused to react to this catty remark. She loved Iris, but she did like to flaunt her privileged lifestyle. One Hannah had never hinted she envied.

'How luxurious.' Aunt Violet peered inside. 'The one thing I've always hated about house parties was having to traipse down dark, freezing hallways in search of a communal bathroom. I might even come again, Iris.'

'I hope you didn't mind my asking you to bring food?' Iris's hostess smile faded into uncertainty. 'Only we're required to send quotas of produce from the tenant farms to the army for the troops, so we must be sparing.'

'Of course not. It was a practical idea.' Hannah removed her hat. 'We cannot expect you to feed everyone for an entire week.'

'Papa at least located a couple of well-fed geese. And no, I didn't ask where he got them.' Hannah caught her sister's mischievous smile. 'Even the Ellises raided their larder for us, but then they are staying until New Year, so it's only fair. Cook has been preparing for days, and I've had to hire extra servants from the village. It's all been quite stressful, and—Hannah! What *have* you done to your hair?'

'I had it cut off.' Hannah placed her hat on a nearby chair.

'I can see that. It's so – well, short. Like Irene Castle but without the curls.' Iris cocked her head to one side. 'Although it really suits you. What does Mama think of it?'

'Er... She hasn't seen it yet. And I'd rather you didn't say anything. I want to surprise her.' Hannah plumped up the sides of her hair that had been flattened by her hat.

'Oh, you'll do that, all right. Maybe it will take her attention off me and my failings for a while.'

'What *are* you talking about?' Hannah hauled her suitcase onto the bed and started unloading the contents into drawers. 'The house is beautiful, and everything will be fine.'

'It's not just the house guests.' Iris sank down onto Hannah's bed, her vivid eyes on her sister. 'Selwyn and Norah brought the Calhoun Ruby with them. It's ancient and therefore horribly old-fashioned as well as being heavy, and *such* a responsibility.'

'What's this about a ruby?' Aunt Violet reappeared from next door and joined Iris on the bed. 'Have you seen it?'

'Selwyn attempted to show us it briefly, but Norah insisted on locking it away immediately after they arrived. It's an heirloom and by tradition it's passed to the eldest daughter on her engagement, making Millie the custodian.'

'How antediluvian,' Aunt Violet muttered. 'Anyone would think they were European royalty! Though most of *them* are broke.'

'I think giving a gemstone a name is pretentious.' Hannah transferred a pile of underclothes to a drawer.

'Well, for goodness' sake keep your opinions to yourselves. Norah has announced we'll all see it at dinner tonight.' Iris scooted backwards on the coverlet. 'So I want you two on your best behaviour.'

Norah Calhoun was a native of New York, brought to England by her family. She was one of the women given the epithet 'buccaneers' because their mamas paraded them about London society in search of husbands with titles, in need of a fortune to bolster their impoverished estates.

But Norah had defied all expectations by falling in love with Selwyn, a third son and Mycroft's younger brother, who – barring a catastrophe – would not inherit the majority of their father's estate, one of which had gone to Mycroft. To show their disappointment, the Calhouns had awarded Norah a less-than-impressive allowance, though she still got the ruby.

Hannah suspected Selwyn frequently received reminders of her sacrifice during their marriage and wondered if he ever regretted his youthful decision.

'Mycroft said it would be fine, as they are only here for a week.' Iris was perilously close to tears. 'But Darius agreed with me, saying—'

'Darius is here?' Hannah halted on her way to the wardrobe, her arms falling to her sides, her best evening gown trailing the floor.

'Oh!' Iris's face fell in almost childish disappointment. 'I shouldn't have told you that. It was to be a surprise. Mama invited him. We had so many more women than men coming.'

'Did she?' Hannah stooped to retrieve the dress, hoping that no one noticed her sudden blush.

Emotionally bruised from former romances, both Hannah and Darius had danced warily around each other for over a year, unable to ignore their mutual attraction, but using their long-standing friendship as a convenient shield.

'It was only a small deception, darling,' Iris said, sounding unnervingly like their mother. 'We were only considering your happiness.'

Hannah clamped her mouth shut so as not to disparage her mother or sister, and snapped shut the empty suitcase and slid it under the bed. Madeleine Merrill had firmly set her sights on Darius as a future husband for her younger daughter, unaware that her determination actually made Hannah want to feel less inclined towards Darius.

'I want to hear more about this ruby.' Aunt Violet bounced on the mattress as if she were testing the bed springs.

'It's extremely valuable.' Iris wriggled closer, her arms wrapped around an upraised knee. 'A Calhoun ancestor apparently brought it back from Burma over a hundred years ago. There's some mystery surrounding its origins, something about it being stolen from a holy temple and smuggled out of the country.'

'Really? Are we to expect a mysterious Asian gentleman in a turban to come knocking on Christmas Night to claim it back?' Aunt Violet said.

'I never thought of that. Maybe it carries a curse threatening to exact a terrible vengeance on all the Calhouns?' Iris leaned conspiratorially closer to her aunt as the pair erupted into gleeful giggles.

'It would mortify Norah since she's so proud of it—' Iris broke off as Hannah glared at her.

'Would you both mind taking your stories of curses somewhere else?' Hannah propped her hands on her hips and split a look between them. 'The dressing bell sounded a few minutes ago, and I need to change.'

'Oh, sorry, darling.' Iris eased off the bed. 'Come on, Violet, we'll leave her in peace.'

'Now who's being tetchy?' Aunt Violet turned at the door with a knowing smile. 'Just because Darius didn't tell you he was coming.'

'Will you both understand that he's my—'

'Closest friend,' the pair chorused. 'Yes, we know.'

Hannah threw a hairbrush at the closed door, but it fell short, dropped onto the floorboards and rolled under the bed.

3

Hannah studied her reflection in the cheval mirror, trying to decide if her gown was suitable for the occasion or if she ought to change into something simpler. Her dressmaker had created it for her the year before, but as the war dragged on, such extravagance had become unpatriotic.

The pinch-waist gown was of aquamarine silk, the bodice decorated with seed pearls. A sheer overskirt floated to her calves and swirled around her like water when she moved.

An image of Darius Clifford floated into her head, and she changed her mind. She had known him for as long as she could remember – from a skinny boy to a gawky, self-conscious youth who tended to clumsiness and blushed in company, to how he was now. His strong, symmetrical features, amiable smile and lively midnight blue eyes combined with a low, rolling laugh made her pulse race simply thinking about him...

Fastening her wristwatch, she checked the time and gasped. She was late. Again. She tweaked the ends of her bobbed hair, grabbed her beaded evening bag, and blew a fleeting kiss at the mirror before hurrying downstairs.

Soft golden light spilled from the dining room below her, along with the clink of glasses and the inaudible murmur of chatter as she reached the hallway. She rapidly stepped back to avoid colliding with a heavy-set man who strode past her. He marched down the corridor away from the dining room, his curt, 'You, there!' aimed at a retreating figure.

Andrew Gates, looking smart and very handsome in a dinner jacket and crisp white shirt turned towards him with an enquiring frown. 'Is there something you require, Mr Ellis?'

'I know you, don't I?' The man looked to be in his sixties, possessed of the arrogant mien of a man accustomed to ordering others about. 'I've seen you before. Never forget a face.'

'I'm Mycroft Atherton's secretary, sir,' Gates said. 'We met when you and your wife first arrived.'

'Don't be facetious, man, I—'

The rest of his words were lost as Hannah's brother-in-law loomed towards her from the dining room, his arms outstretched.

'Hannah!' He enfolded her in a brief but firm hug that made her grunt as her ribs protested. 'I had no idea you'd arrived.' His candid grey eyes crinkled at the corners behind a pair of horn-rimmed spectacles he quickly removed and swung in a circle by one arm.

Mycroft Atherton, at forty-two, was his wife's senior by more than a decade. He was a tall, well-built man with a permanent smile and kind eyes who wore his ruinously expensive clothes as if he had thrown them on in the dark.

'I'm sorry not to have been here to greet you, but I see you are all settled and look splendid.' His gaze hovered somewhere above her eyes. 'Have you done something to your hair?'

'I have, yes.' She left him to work out what for himself. Mr Ellis and Gates continued their conversation further along the hall, but she could not hear what they were saying.

'We're so glad you and Violet could come,' her brother-in-law said with obvious pleasure. 'Iris has been so excited about her family being together. It's been a rough year for all of us.' His frown faded and was replaced by a delighted smile. 'I believe Iris has arranged a surprise for you this evening.'

'If you mean Darius, Iris let it slip earlier, so I'm fully prepared. I would, however, appreciate not being seated too near my mother at dinner.'

'Hah! Yes, she and Iris appear to be in cahoots.' His gaze shifted past her and he groaned. 'Oh, Lord! She's invited that wretched Dunleavy woman.' He nodded towards a woman in her early forties whose frizzy brown hair was gathered into a dated, untidy pompadour on top of her head. She wore a red silk shawl adorned with palm-sized white roses that billowed behind her as she approached the dining room, waving to someone inside.

'My darling Iris has no armour against her at all.' Mycroft lowered his voice, although the woman was too far away to hear. 'She's a socially aware widow on a permanent lookout for a new husband. Ah, well, it's too late now.' He nodded to where a footman stood to attention outside the dining room with two maids carrying silver tureens and ladles. 'You go ahead, Hannah. I'll see you in a tick.'

Hannah nodded, aware the two men she had been eavesdropping on earlier had parted and she was alone in the hallway, leaving her to wonder what it had all been about.

The Wedgwood-blue room boasted full-height windows along one side, and a double set of French doors installed at the far end led onto a wide terrace. Lanterns containing candles hung from the stone balustrade throwing tiny beams of light onto the snow beyond the bevelled glass.

Thick laurel branches twisted over and around the windows and archways to the floor, with red holly berries and spiky ferns interspersed throughout. Another Christmas tree, larger than the one in the hall, bristled with glass ornaments of red, gold and green intermingled with wide red ribbon, white Christmas roses and red poinsettias.

She had barely stepped inside the door when Darius appeared at her side. 'I've been told your sister cannot keep a secret, so the surprise is spoiled,' he whispered close to her ear. 'Or did you prise it out of her?'

Standing over six feet tall and broad-shouldered with a build gained from years of playing rugby at boarding school, he wore his thick brown hair unfashionably long. His strong, symmetrical features gave him a striking appearance and he had a penetrating gaze that could unsettle on the first meeting. However, his amiable smile brightened the silvery flecks in his midnight-blue eyes, and an unusual rolling growl of a laugh endeared him to everyone.

'I admit it. I used thumbscrews.' She stared into his eyes, annoyed to find she was blushing, and wished she had a fan she could hide behind. 'By rights, I should be annoyed with you for deceiving me.'

'I'll make up for it later, promise.' His soft breath on her cheek made her bite her bottom lip. Despite what she had told her family, Darius Clifford had a startling effect on her she could not control. 'When did you arrive?'

'Yesterday, and unfortunately your sister asked everyone to choose their seats at dinner and Mrs Dunleavy claimed the chair next to mine.'

'Did she indeed?' Hannah arched an eyebrow. 'Perhaps you could keep a place for me in the sitting room for coffee?'

'Damn coffee.' He leaned closer. 'Meet me in the music room after dinner. I'll explain everything and apologise for my deception then.'

'That sounds like an assignation.'

'It was intended to,' he said, just as the woman in the silk shawl – whom Hannah assumed must be Mrs Dunleavy – clamped her be-ringed hand tightly onto Darius's arm and dragged him towards the table. Hannah felt suddenly invisible, though Mycroft's reference to 'that wretched Dunleavy woman' was now adequately explained.

'There you are, Hannah.' Iris advanced on her. 'I did say eight, didn't I?'

'You did, Iris.' Hannah watched with regret as Darius walked away. 'And I promise to do something about my timekeeping. I must say, you've outdone yourself. This is quite magical.'

'I'm so glad you like it.' Iris exhaled a long breath as if she had been waiting for her sister's approval. 'Most of the greenery came from the grounds, as it's so hard to buy these things now. The ornaments are from previous years and Mama lent me some, which I'm sure you'll recognise.'

'It's beautiful, Iris. And I've not seen anything like it since before the war.'

Urns stuffed with more greenery, red berries and pinecones sat at intervals on the long dining table, where polished gilt candelabra sported white candles, their yellow flames providing a subdued light which bathed the entire room in a soft golden glow.

'It's an informal dinner and as everyone has already chosen their seats, you'll have to sit here.' She paused in front of an empty chair and shot Hannah a 'serves you right' look, then sauntered to the far end of the table.

Madeleine Merrill, resplendent in lilac and black, occupied the chair next to the one Iris had indicated, like a youthful dowager duchess ready to accept homage from anyone prepared to offer it.

'Good evening, Mama,' Hannah sighed, her head dipped to accept her mother's proffered kiss only to be instantly engulfed by a cloud of floral perfume as her rear end made contact with the upholstery.

'Why are you so late, and what *have* you done to your hair?' Her mother delivered her greeting with customary criticism.

'Which question do you want answered first, Mama?' Hannah inhaled slowly and silently counted to ten.

'Don't be facetious.' She peered closer at Hannah's face and gasped. 'Are you wearing make-up?'

'A little Maybelline is hardly scandalous these days, Mama. And as for this...' She stroked her hair with her free hand. 'It's a bob cut. I love it, and I no longer get headaches from all those hairpins.'

'Aren't bob cuts what they do to horses?' She sniffed. 'You look like a boy.'

'Leave the girl alone, Madeleine. She doesn't at all.' Hannah's father leaned to speak from his wife's other side, his chin almost touching the table. 'She looks like that actress, but prettier. What's her name now. Ire—'

'Irene Castle, but without the curls. Yes, Papa, that's what Iris said. And thank you for noticing.'

'You see? *Actress*,' her mother hissed.

Her father's dinner jacket fitted without a wrinkle on his muscular frame, his salt and pepper hair leaping thickly from a low forehead. His eyes, the same hazel-green as her own, took in her face. He had eschewed the fashion of thick side whiskers and full beard which in his own opinion made him resemble either a badger or a retired army colonel.

'Well, *I* like it.' Hector smoothed down both sides of his moustache in a characteristic gesture that made Hannah smile.

'So modern and youthful. Well done, Hannie,' he added, using her childhood nickname.

'Your darling Hannie can do nothing wrong in your eyes.' Madeleine tutted, and with an exaggerated gesture adjusted the gossamer shawl she wore draped over her shoulder. 'Had she run away to the circus you would have applauded her spirit.' She gave Hannah's head a final, critical glance. 'I suppose I could get used to it.'

'I'm so relieved, Mama.' Hannah pressed a hand to her throat and fluttered her eyelashes. 'I've been frantic with worry all week.'

Giving a final tut of disdain, her mother turned to a couple further along the table. 'You remember Mycroft's younger brother, Selwyn Atherton, and his wife, Norah, don't you, Hannah?'

'I do. Mr and Mrs Atherton, it's so nice to see you again.' Selwyn was shorter than his brother, and less substantial, but with similar features to Mycroft. They had the same eyes, but Selwyn wore his tuxedo jacket and white silk waistcoat with a presence Mycroft could never achieve – even had he tried, which was doubtful.

Mycroft's brother left his chair and approached Hannah's, plucked her hand from her lap and pressed his lips against her knuckles like a courtier. 'We're family, so there's no need for formality. And indeed, I'm impressed with the way Iris has brought all this together. One can almost forget there is a war on.' He leaned back to reveal the lady beside him. 'Norah, dear, you remember Iris's sister, Hannah?'

'Of course I do, Selwyn.' Leaving her chair, the lady enfolded Hannah in an awkward hug, since she was still seated. 'My dear, you're all grown up.'

'Good evening, Norah. Um... Yes, it happened a few years ago now.'

'Oh – er, yes. Quite.' Norah released her and stepped back, her close-set eyes filled with confusion. Too late, Hannah remembered the woman had no sense of humour. Always thin, Norah had become scrawny to the point of emaciation, her small round eyes reminding Hannah of a ferret. 'Such a shame about Gerald,' she spoke at an octave too loud. 'Maybe it's for the best, though. Clearly, he wasn't the right man for you.'

'He didn't jilt me, Norah, he was killed.' Norah's expression froze in shock for a heartbeat and she looked about to dart away.

Regretting her quick tongue, Hannah changed the subject, 'How are Millie and Maura? I haven't seen them for... Gosh, two years, at least.'

'Three. You'll not recognise them.' Norah's bony fingers gripped Hannah's forearm. 'Maura is over there talking to Sissy Dunleavy and Millie is the charming creature beside Mycroft.'

Hannah's gaze found Millie – an attractive girl in a forest green gown – seated next to Mycroft, her fair hair pulled back from her face and piled on top of her head in large curls. An old-fashioned style, but one which showed off her long, elegant neck and the heavy gold chain around it. A cabochon ruby of deep crimson, as large as a robin's egg, hung just below the hollow in her throat.

Norah's face loomed close to Hannah's, revealing a thick layer of face powder that clung to the tiny creases beside her eyes. 'We thought this Christmas was the perfect occasion for her to show off the Calhoun Ruby. Isn't it divine?'

'Millie is really lovely,' Hannah said truthfully. Then, at Norah's stare, added, 'The ruby is, um... unusual too.'

A flash of disappointment crossed Norah's face. She dropped Hannah's arm abruptly and returned to her seat.

'I appear to have offended Iris's sister-in-law,' Hannah observed to her mother. 'Am I doomed?'

'No more than the rest of us.' Madeleine's sly smile mirrored Hannah's own. 'That ruby's an ugly old thing, isn't it? They should at least have had the stone cut to make it more attractive.'

'So,' Hannah began. 'Iris talked me through who was here. But remind me... I assume the young man about to sit next to Millie is her fiancé?' Hannah was determined not to apologise again.

'Correct. Captain Lynford Ellis.' Madeleine shifted sideways to allow a maid to serve her a brown liquid that smelled better than it looked.

A dark-haired young man hovered over Millie's shoulder, before taking his own seat. He was tall, maybe an inch or two shorter than Darius, which marked him out as unusual, since Darius towered over most people. He was thin, maybe a little too gaunt, and clean-shaven; a new trend among army officers who were no longer required to grow moustaches.

'Then the couple sitting opposite us must be Lynford's parents?' Hannah asked. They were the only people in the room apart from the Dunleavys that she did not recognise.

'A pleasant couple, if a little provincial.' Madeleine applied her spoon to her soup.

Hannah bit back a retort and broke a bread roll on her plate. Her mother's insistence on mixing with the 'right' people was both restrictive and elitist. 'Perhaps they're just shy?'

Between Hannah's role as a bookshop proprietor and her volunteer work at the military hospital, she encountered people from all walks of life, which gave her a perspective and humility her mother could not understand.

'Darling, shyness is no excuse for being unsociable. Do you want me to introduce you?'

'Not necessary.' Hannah caught the male half of the couple's eye. 'It's Mr and Mrs Ellis, isn't it?' she said, ignoring her mother's critical snort. 'I'm Hannah Merrill, Mrs Atherton's sister.' The table was too wide to offer her hand, so she made do with a bright, welcoming smile.

'Oh, er... Basil Ellis.' He blinked in surprise and waved vaguely at the lady beside him. 'My wife, Rose.' He was a portly man in his late fifties, with a pinkish complexion and the same gruff tone she recalled from his conversation with Mr Gates in the hall. His dark hair formed a two-inch halo around a shiny bald patch that gave him the appearance of a disgruntled monk.

Rose Ellis wore a shapeless saffron yellow gown that did nothing for her sallow complexion, though her expression was open and welcoming, unlike her husband, who wore an anxious, surly expression which Hannah suspected was permanent.

'Have you come far?' Hannah leaned back, startled by a passing maid who removed her unfinished soup bowl, then moved along the table, piling the crockery noisily into the crook of her arm, dripping brown soup onto the polished floor.

'Brought in from the village,' Madeleine observed, not caring if the maid heard her. 'Untrained. All the best ones have gone into the factories.'

Hannah did not respond, then tried not to smile as a second maid dumped an entrée of roast lamb in front of her with a loud clunk.

'We live near Woking, which is about fifteen miles or so.' Mrs Ellis spoke in a high, childish voice. 'It was a fairly straightforward journey by motor car.'

'Not as easy as it should have been,' her husband scoffed, his focus on his plate. 'My wife insisted we stop for refreshment at an inn not three miles down the road. A total waste of time.'

'I wanted to feel rested when we arrived, not worn out and

dishevelled,' Rose said in her defence. 'I don't like to give an unfavourable impression when meeting new people.' Rose accepted a portion of roast lamb, but as soon as the maid left, she transferred half of it to her husband's plate.

'I promise you, that was not the case,' Iris assured them graciously from her place at the bottom of the table. 'I'm really glad you could join us for our simple family Christmas.'

'If you can call a gargantuan tree and enough lights to signal a Zeppelin, simple!' Aunt Violet said in a stage whisper from Norah's left.

'Positive things, Aunt Violet,' Hannah muttered from the corner of her mouth.

'That *was* positive,' her aunt replied, one eyebrow arched in challenge.

'Had you attempted to be on time, Hannah,' Madeleine said, her voice tight, '*you'd* be sitting over there with Darius, and not Mrs "it's Dianna with two n's" Dunleavy,' she said in a sing-song voice. 'She's been fawning over him all afternoon.'

'Speaking of Darius.' Hannah stared pointedly at her mother.

'Were we?' Madeleine's eyes, so like her own, rounded. 'Yes, well, I'm surprised you didn't invite him yourself. Anyway, if he didn't wish to be here, he would have declined my invitation. Which is fortuitous, as there is a distinct lack of gentlemen around this table. Though there would have been an equal number, had that vulgar Dunleavy woman had not inveigled a last-minute invitation for her and her frumpy daughter.'

'Don't be cruel, Mama. Who is she, though?' Hannah nodded to where Mrs Dunleavy sipped delicately from a fluted glass, her free hand laid flat on Darius's forearm.

'She's a widow who owns a property on the other side of the village. A terrible flirt, which is embarrassing in a woman past forty,' she added unnecessarily, taking a bite of glazed carrot from the end of her fork. 'Before Darius arrived, she made a fool of herself with Mycroft's secretary, but I doubt he's interested.'

'I was surprised to see Mr Gates here.' Hannah recalled Iris's hostility towards the man and wondered what she thought of it. But then it wasn't unusual for a trusted member of staff to be invited to eat with family.

'Iris invited him to make up the numbers for tonight. Incidentally, are you and Darius betrothed yet?'

'Mama!' Hannah glanced around the table, relieved when no one else appeared to have heard. 'If the situation changes, you'll be the first to know.' She crossed the fingers of her right hand under the table, her gaze shifting to Darius, who caught her eye and winked.

A warm flush crept upwards from her toes, and to cover it she accepted a portion of vegetables she did not want from the maid who appeared at her shoulder.

'Captain Ellis?' The girl Norah had identified as Sissy Dunleavy called across the table, her voice slicing through the chatter. 'It must be wonderful being a war hero.'

An uneasy silence settled over the table, broken only by the click of cutlery on china as the room held its breath awaiting his response, while Sissy appeared unaffected by the sudden drop in temperature and stared guilelessly at her target. She must have been at least sixteen but dressed in a frilly pink gown more appropriate for a younger girl. Her dark hair was worn down in soft ringlets.

'In my view, Miss Dunleavy, heroes are overrated,' Lynford Ellis replied, easing his shoulders inside an evening jacket slightly too large for him. 'No soldier picks up a rifle in the pursuit of heroism. Those newspaper reports you're reading are mostly propaganda, embellished for the sake of those at home.'

'If I didn't know better, I'd say that bordered on sedition!' Mr Ellis interjected, diluting his words with a loud guffaw.

'Basil, really!' Rose destroyed a bread roll on her side plate into inedibility. 'Lynford didn't mean it like that.'

'Can't a fellow make a joke these days?' Mr Ellis said, unrepentant. 'No need to be prickly.'

'And why aren't you wearing your uniform, Captain?' Sissy persisted, demonstrating she was either socially unaware or simply didn't see her desire for answers inappropriate.

'I'm on leave, Miss Dunleavy,' Lynford replied with an amiable smile, seemingly unaffected by her questions. 'And my uniform got damaged during a bombardment, so I had to order a new one.' He looked up and addressed the table. 'Yet another drain on my officer's pay.'

'And what about you?' Sissy turned her candid gaze on Mr Gates, Mycroft's secretary. 'Why aren't you in the army?'

'If only I could.' Mr Gates's regretful, flirtatious smile made Sissy blush prettily. 'I'm asthmatic. Have been since I was a child, so the army rejected me.'

'Oh, what a shame.' Losing interest, Sissy focused her attention on the captain again. 'My brother received his conscription papers last week and he's joining the army in the New Year.'

'Then may his experience of war be better than mine,' Lynford murmured, keeping his gaze fixed on his plate.

'Sissy!' her mother hissed, her eyes like flint. 'Stop interrogating people.'

'I'm merely being sociable, Mama.' Pouting, Sissy poked desultorily at her food. 'Only, you don't see many young men not in uniform these days.'

'*I'm* not in uniform,' Darius said, bringing all eyes towards him, especially Hannah's.

'He works for the War Office.' Iris's answer encompassed the entire table. 'Only he's not allowed to tell us what he does.'

'Perhaps we don't wish to know?' Hannah's father raised his glass to Darius in salute. 'As long as it helps us win, eh?'

'That's enough questions, Sissy.' Dianna glared at her daughter while twisting the stem of her wineglass. 'Though, if you want *my* opinion, I disapprove of this conscription law,' Dianna announced. 'It's outrageous to force young men to join the army. It shouldn't be allowed.'

'A war cannot be won without soldiers, Mrs Dunleavy.' Darius's calm tone conveyed an underlying frustration. 'Kitchener's enlistment campaigns had some success, but we need thousands more men to truly make an impression.'

'Huh!' Hector waved his fork in the air. 'No one's listening to Kitchener any more.'

'That's because he's dead, Hector.' Madeleine sighed.

'I know that, woman. Blown up at sea, poor chap. Terrible way to go.'

'As is drowning, which is what the newspapers said happened to him,' Madeleine muttered under her breath.

'Never found his body though,' Lynford said, drawing everyone's attention just as a maid passed behind his chair to serve him a portion of glazed carrots. She tipped the dish too far forward and lost her grip on the oversized serving spoon which crashed noisily against the tray before landing heavily on the polished floor.

Lynford leapt to his feet with a sharp cry, knocking his plate to the floor with a flailing hand. His chair toppled backwards into the maid, unbalancing her.

A footman sprang forward, and with an impressive feat of agility, caught the maid before the contents of the dish ended up on the floor.

'I'm so sorry, sir.' The girl blushed furiously, still holding on to the dish.

The butler, Venables, gestured to the maid to continue her circuit of the table while the footman repositioned Lynford's chair.

'It's n-not your fault.' Lynford resumed his seat, but his hand on the table shook visibly. 'Sorry about that,' he addressed the room brightly. 'Thought I was somewhere else.'

An uneasy ripple of bemused laughter circled the room, but quickly faded and conversation resumed.

Millie covered his hand with her own, her eyes dark with concern, but he reclaimed it with a shake of his head.

'Dashed fuss to make over a spoon.' Basil jammed his napkin into the top of his waistcoat as if the linen had offended him. 'It's not even as if he was badly injured. Not like some.'

'Basil dear, injury doesn't always require losing a leg or an arm.' Rose applied her knife to a slice of lamb but changed her mind and pushed the plate away.

'Don't know what that's supposed to mean, I'm sure,' Basil muttered sourly, oblivious to the sudden stares and cutlery that halted in mid-air.

Iris instructed the footman to refill the empty glasses and to serve the dessert. The footmen and the maids rushed to obey, and little by little, the conversation resumed.

'It's started to snow again,' Dianna said with a sigh. 'My Sissy and I are bound to catch our death going home in the snow in a dog cart.' She motioned towards her empty glass, signalling the footman to fill it.

'A couple of miles isn't too arduous.' Madeleine shot a knowing look at Iris.

'It's all right, Dianna.' Iris gestured to Venables, who appeared instantly at her side. 'Would you kindly have a room made up for Mrs Dunleavy and Miss Sissy?'

Bowing his assent, the butler backed away.

'Just the one room?' Dianna glanced up from her glass, not bothering to hide her disappointment.

Mycroft cleared his throat and massaged his brow with one hand. Norah tutted, and Aunt Violet muttered something inaudible.

'I'm afraid so,' Iris said without a trace of regret. 'All the guest rooms are occupied, but I'm sure you won't mind sharing with Sissy.'

'I suppose we'll manage.' Dianna's claw-like fingers closed around the last petit four Selwyn was about to claim from a plate in between them. He slumped back in his chair with a disappointed pout.

4

Hannah discreetly repaired her make-up and checked her hair before descending the long staircase into the hall just as the butler approached from the end of the corridor bearing a silver tray loaded with a full decanter and several brandy glasses.

'Mr Venables.' She halted him as he drew level. 'Might I have a brief word?'

'Of course, Miss.' He switched the tray from both hands to one. 'What is it you require?'

'I sent a... basket to the kitchens with a footman when my aunt and I arrived earlier.'

'The provisions, Miss?' His pale blue eyes crinkled at the corners. 'The cook is extremely pleased with the contribution.' He leaned closer and whispered, 'Goodness me, Fortnum's chocolates. It's been a while since we've seen those.'

'Actually, I was referring to the other basket.' She waited for the penny to drop, but when he only looked puzzled, added, 'The one with the, um... livestock?'

'Ah, yes.' He gave the empty hallway a swift, almost furtive glance. 'The... er... livestock has consumed an entire tin of sardines, taken some water, and the last I saw was dozing in front of the fire in the housekeeper's room. Mrs Weberly has taken quite a shine to him.'

'Thank you so much, Venables.' Hannah released a relieved breath. 'I knew you wouldn't let me down. I simply couldn't leave him all alone at the bookshop for a week. Our assistant lives on the premises but he has gone home for Christmas and his mother won't have a cat in the house. Especially not a black one.' Since the war began, black cats had declined in popularity, considered the bringers of gloom and disaster. After an unfortunate start and near drowning in a rain barrel, Mr Bartleby had transformed from a half-feral bag of bones to an overweight, self-satisfied feline and had completely given up mousing.

'Don't you worry, Miss, he'll be fine with me. Does he have a name?'

'Mr Bartleby. But he never answers to it unless food is involved.'

'How literary, but then that shouldn't surprise me, considering he's a bookshop cat. May I say what a pleasure it is to see you again. Now, if you'll excuse me, I need to take this brandy to the billiard room ready for the gentlemen's game.' With a slight bow, he moved away just as female voices and footsteps on the stairs announced the ladies were on their way to the sitting room. To avoid being coerced to join them, Hannah made a dash for the music room and slipped inside.

The room's generous proportions and high ceiling dwarfed the Steinbeck grand piano that took pride of place in front of French windows hung with cream, gold and white brocade curtains to complement the similar colours of the room. Several standard lamps on side tables at intervals gave the space an almost cosy, welcoming feel despite its size.

Through the bevelled glass, the blanket of snow covering the sloping lawn glowed, and the border of ancient oak trees still visible beyond the terrace was lit by yellow flames in ornamental lanterns strung along the balustrade.

Darius stood at the piano, head bent as his fingers trailed the ivory keyboard, creating soft but discordant notes.

He looked up as she entered, smiled and raised both arms towards her and she walked into his embrace to accept his kiss; her eyes fluttered closed as her pulse quickened. 'Did you ask to meet me in here to show off your musical skills?'

'Hardly.' He pulled back slightly, his chin resting on her head, a pose easily accomplished due to his imposing height. 'I haven't played since my mother was alive. And I'm sorry I was unable to join you at dinner. I tried to explain to Mrs Dunleavy that I expected you, and she agreed to—'

'Move the second I arrived, then miraculously forgot?'

'How did you know?' He pulled back again and stared down at her.

'One of the things I love about you, Darius Clifford, is that you haven't the first idea how a woman's mind works.'

This was a man who had once woken up to an uninvited woman in his bed and, fearing the worst, had become engaged simply to preserve the woman's reputation. Though that was now – thankfully – a distant memory.

'What are you doing here, anyway?' She punched his bicep lightly and smiled when he pretended it hurt. 'Aren't you supposed to be spending Christmas with your father?'

'I was, but your sister offered me something far better.' He tucked in his chin, feigning disappointment. 'Aren't you pleased to see me?'

'Of course, I am. It's a lovely surprise, although you realise my mother has manipulated you? Iris is only her mouthpiece.'

'Ah, I suspected as much.' His gaze hovered on her fringe with a mixture of admiration and bemusement. 'How did the family react to your new hairstyle?'

'One cautiously approving, while the other is aghast, but she'll get over it.' She snuggled closer, relishing the sheer maleness of him. 'Now, what were you saying about music lessons?'

'Mother insisted I learn to play piano, but after her death, Papa lost interest in most things, including my education. If I played right now, I'd embarrass myself. I heard Selwyn's younger daughter, Maura, practising this afternoon though. Not that my musical knowledge extends far enough to recognise the piece.'

'Is she a talented pianist?'

'Exceptional, I would say. Never mind her, I have something I need to ask you.'

'Oh dear,' she frowned up at him in mock worry. 'Awful things happen when you say that.'

'Not this time. It occurred to me that with your entire family gathered in one place, which never happens, it'd be the perfect moment to announce our engagement.'

'Really?' She blinked, disarmed, as first excitement and delight, then foreboding welled. 'I thought we agreed to wait because of your job and, well, we still don't know what will happen with this war?'

In his position with the Secret Service Bureau, Darius was privy to exclusive information on the progress of the war, which was not going well despite optimistic newspaper reports intended to uplift public morale. In the event of an invasion, a group of intelligence staff planned to move abroad to fight the Germans from within. Darius had intimated he might be among them.

'I'm tired of waiting. And now the Americans are certain to join the allied forces in the spring, we cannot lose the war. It might take a while, but I'm fairly confident. What do you say we make it official?'

'What, tonight? But the evening is almost over.'

'No, silly – I thought over dinner on Christmas Eve would be ideal. I even came prepared.' He removed a blue velvet jeweller's box from his pocket and flicked open the lid revealing an exquisite cushion-cut diamond flanked by two emeralds on a yellow gold band.

'That's your mother's ring!' Hannah gasped.

'Um, yes, it is. It was.' A confused frown appeared between his brows. 'I recall you admired it once, but if I've got it wrong and you don't like it, I could buy you a new one.'

'That was delighted surprise you saw, not criticism.' She sighed, amazed how someone with so much to offer the world could be so lacking in conceit.

'I thought it was pretty, and the emeralds match your eyes.' He bent his head slightly and ran a finger along her jawline, his eyes locked on hers.

'Pretty? I'd say that's a three-carat stone, Mr Master of the Understatement. It's the most perfect thing I've ever seen.' She clamped her lips together hard, fearful she might cry. He was the most unexpected man, whose romantic impulsiveness made him irresistible. Her only regret was it took her so long to realise it.

A thought struck her, and she snatched her hand back. 'Does my mother know about this?'

'What? Not from me, she doesn't. I promised to keep our engagement secret, and I have done. Except, I confess I told Papa.' She opened her mouth to speak, but he forestalled her. 'He promised on his labrador's life not to utter a word to anyone – for now.'

'Really, Darius.' She flashed him a teasing smile. 'As if I would shoot his dog if he reneged.'

He returned the box to his pocket and took her in his arms again. 'Actually, I've always liked your mama.' He rested his chin on the top of her head, a gesture that always made her feel small and safe next to him. 'She was very good to me when my mother died. Did you know she took me to get kitted out for university when Papa could not handle it?'

'She did that? Really?' She leaned her cheek into his shoulder, inhaling the smell of expensive wool and equally expensive cologne. 'I didn't know that, but actually, it doesn't surprise me. For some inexplicable reason, she likes to keep her more human side hidden.'

'Only from you, which I've been told is not unusual between mothers and daughters.' He stepped back and planted a kiss on her nose. 'You're fortunate to still have her. I would give anything for mine to be here to see me marry.'

Her throat closed with a mixture of emotion and remorse at her own thoughtlessness. Darius had lost his mother when he was still at school, but Hannah remembered her vividly. 'Your mother was the sweetest woman I ever met.'

'She was, but I didn't say that to make you feel guilty. Mothers can be infuriating creatures, but they deserve to be appreciated.'

'Well, you did. Make me feel guilty, that is. And that sounded horribly like the beginning of a lecture.' She frowned. 'There won't be too many of those in the future, will there? Because I'm a ridiculously contrary person.'

'Of course you are. Unpredictability is one of your more interesting qualities.' His gaze roved her face with the same intense look he'd used when he'd proposed in a railway carriage on the way back from Lowestoft back in Easter, a mixture of hope and excitement. 'Christmas Eve, then. Agreed?'

'Agreed.' Hannah slid her arms around his neck, their lips

almost touching. 'I will even let Mama tell everyone it was her idea.'

Darius glanced towards the door as the sound of doors opening and closing in the hallway reached them, followed by footsteps and male voices.

'It sounds as if the other gentlemen are making their way to the billiard room. I'd better join them before someone notices my absence.'

'Do you have to?' She locked her arms tighter around his neck, sensing him weakening as he bent his head and ran light kisses across her jaw. 'No one knows we're here.'

A noise like glass breaking made Hannah stiffen. 'What was that?'

'A domestic accident, I expect.' Darius raised his head, frowning. 'Perhaps Venables has imbibed too much sherry at the party?'

'The staff are having a party? Iris didn't mention it.'

'Iris wanted to thank them for all their hard work.' He unhooked her arms from around his neck and checked his watch. 'It's after ten, and much as I regret it, I'd better go. Wait here briefly to avoid drawing attention. We don't want to spoil the surprise, do we?'

They shared a final, slow kiss before he left. The door had only just closed on him when a rattle sounded from the French doors across the room. Imagining some animal had found its way onto the terrace, she gingerly lifted the heavy curtain aside, just as the handle turned and the French door slowly opened.

* * *

Mild panic rushed through her as Aunt Violet's comment about an Asian gentleman returned but vanished as a familiar face appeared in the glass. She had scarcely got the door open halfway before a figure shoved herself roughly inside, sending Hannah back a pace.

'Maura?' Hannah pulled the door to, shutting out a wave of icy chill wind. 'What were you doing out there in the dark?'

'I wondered if you would recognise me.' Maura Atherton – the younger daughter of Selwyn and Norah – stamped her feet, shedding snow onto the polished floor.

'Of course, I know who you are.' Hannah bit back the 'you have grown' speech constantly aimed at the young. Maura's sharp, childish features had matured into youthful prettiness. 'Who could forget those garden parties at your grandfather's house when you were younger?'

'They were memorable, weren't they?' Maura blew into her clasped hands, her nose red from the cold. 'Love the new hair-style, by the way. Mother would never allow me to do anything like that.'

'My mother wasn't enamoured either, but I don't have to worry about it. And you haven't answered my question.'

'It was so stuffy in the dining room I needed some air, so took a walk on the terrace, only I didn't realise how cold it was.' Shivering, Maura hugged her cloak tighter around her.

'There's probably a roaring fire in the sitting room. Why don't you warm up with some coffee?'

'Er, no – Mother will be in there and I don't need another lecture about the Calhoun Ruby. Besides, Millie and Lynford are probably waiting for me in the drawing room with Sissy.'

'She likes to bring attention to the ruby, doesn't she?' Hannah pursed her lips in sympathy. 'Millie didn't seem comfortable wearing it at dinner. She kept touching it and easing her neck.'

'It's quite heavy, and not well balanced, so not the most comfortable thing to wear. But it's not that, more the responsibility attached to a family heirloom. Suppose she and Lynford never have children?'

'Then it would go to you, wouldn't it?' Hannah shrugged. 'Anyway, Millie's a young woman, so why worry about something that might never happen?'

'Don't misunderstand me. I'm happy for Millie, but we aren't alike. I don't want the ruby any more than I want domesticity and babies for my life. I want to travel, to explore my talents as a pianist. Mama says I'm being ridiculous, as she cannot imagine why any woman would want anything other than marriage and children.'

'At your age, no doubt the idea of marriage seems daunting, but you might change your mind when you meet the right man. How old are you now?'

'I'm twenty, and disappointed to hear you say that, Hannah. I thought you, of all people, would understand, what with you being a businesswoman yourself.'

'I apologise, I didn't mean to be condescending. If you're determined not to marry, it's completely up to you. I would never condemn you for it. I had to fight for my independence, too. But don't cut yourself off from what life offers when it might make you happy. And as for being a businesswoman, I jointly own a bookshop with my aunt, which hardly makes me a captain of industry.'

'Your suffragette aunt.' Maura's eyes rounded at her use of the word. 'Violet Edwards is an amazing woman. I've kept all the newspaper reports of her marching on the Commons and protesting at Downing Street. But don't tell my mother, it would horrify her. I hope to be as beautiful as she is when I'm that old.'

Hannah winced, glad her aunt was not there to hear, but Maura continued, oblivious. 'Is it true you and Aunt Violet caught a murderer and a spy at Easter?'

'Not on our own. We had help,' Hannah replied. 'It wasn't something we set out to do, but I'm very nosy and don't like to be told I cannot do something.'

'It must have been so exciting. Your mother told me you also volunteer at a military hospital.'

'Did she?' Hannah raised an eyebrow. 'You surprise me. She usually makes a point of voicing her disapproval. In her eyes, I'm a disgrace. An unmarried girl who left a perfectly respectable home to live alone and work in a bookshop. I've quite ruined my marriage prospects.'

'That wasn't the impression I got. She might criticise you in public, but I'm confident she is secretly proud of you.'

Hannah frowned, bemused. Perhaps she should give her mother more credit.

'Hannah?' Maura rested her hands on the keyboard. 'Have you seen many soldiers like – like my sister's fiancé, Lynford, at the hospital where you work?'

'What do you mean, like him? He's fit and healing well, so what exactly are you asking?' Deep down she knew but was reluctant to give Maura false hope or doom-laden prophesy. Lynford wasn't nearly as disturbed as some of the men she had seen at Endell Street.

'You know. Can a mind heal, like a cut or a burn?' Maura chewed at a cuticle on her thumb, then realised what she was doing and clasped both hands together.

'With care and understanding, I believe so. And Lynford has Millie, who seems more than capable of giving him what he needs.'

'She's devoted to him, but it's not going to be easy on her. He's going back to France soon and who knows what will happen there?' She smiled as a thought struck her. 'Perhaps I could take care of them both when I become a professional pianist, and I'm performing in famous concert halls to enraptured audiences worldwide.' She shrugged. 'Well, attentive ones, anyway.'

'That's quite an ambition,' Hannah said. 'I'm impressed.'

'I wish my parents were.' Maura pouted. 'In their opinion, I'm unrealistic and fanciful.'

'I'd be the last person to discourage you, but you won't be able to travel freely until the war is over.' *If then.*

'I know.' Maura's face fell. 'Lynford's letters to Millie said France was once such a beautiful country and is now fast becoming a wasteland. All he wanted was to come home. But now he's here, he jumps at every loud sound, like earlier at dinner. And he sits staring into the fire when no one is watching.'

'That must be difficult to witness. How does Millie cope?'

'She believes that he's overtired after so much fighting and saddened by the death of so many of his friends. But it's more than that. Sometimes, it's as if he wishes he hadn't survived.' She rubbed her upper arms through the cloak, her head cocked as a lively jazz tune started up from next door. 'Sorry, I don't mean to be so miserable. I'm sure everything will be all right. And listen! It sounds as if they've got the gramophone working. Why don't you join us? There's going to be dancing.'

'Thank you, but I've had a long day and I'm exhausted, so I plan to go to bed early.'

'Please don't mention I was outside this late. Mama will only fuss and spend until Christmas searching for signs of pneumonia.' She giggled, opened the door to the hall a crack and looked both ways, then back at Hannah. 'I'm off to learn the foxtrot now, so I'll see you at breakfast.'

Hannah followed her out but turned in the opposite direction and was halfway up the first rise of the staircase when she heard a low, frustrated moan.

Pausing, Hannah glanced over the handrail and saw Rose

Ellis standing in the now-empty hallway below, an anxious frown on her face.

'Mrs Ellis?' Hannah descended the stairs and approached her. 'Is there something I can help you with?'

Rose glanced upwards, clutching her bag tightly against her midriff. 'Ah, no, dear. I'm fine. I went to my room to fetch a shawl, but the maid must have put it away somewhere. Then, can you believe it, I got lost on my way back. These hallways are so similar.' She stared around, bemused, as if she had forgotten where she was. 'I hoped to join the ladies for coffee, but I seem to be—'

'The sitting room is that way.' Hannah pointed to a door at the far end of the hall to the right of the front door.

'Oh, of course it is. Thank you.' Her pale blue eyes met Hannah's with mild puzzlement. 'Aren't you coming?'

'Not this evening. I'm off to bed. Goodnight, Mrs Ellis.'

'Goodnight, er, dear.'

Hannah smiled as she watched her totter away in what were clearly new-heeled shoes.

5

Hannah woke the next morning to a rattle of brass rings as the maid opened the curtains, revealing fat snowflakes drifting past the window and gathering into the corners of the panes.

'I'll run your bath now, shall I, Miss?' She swiftly vanished into the bathroom, the whoosh of running water was followed by rapid footsteps in the hallways as the servants awakened the house.

With no incentive to leave the soft bed, Hannah dozed and thought about how easy it would be to fall back into the idle luxury she had experienced at her parents' house as a younger woman. When running baths, styling her hair, or fastening her own clothes were tasks performed by other people. Days when she was incapable of making a cup of tea or baking a cake; simple accomplishments she was now proud of, even if her mother regarded them as menial and unnecessary.

Her work at her aunt's bookshop had taught her she could function away from a world of social barriers where female children were groomed for marriage and nothing else. Sharing her modest house on the Thames at Chiswick with Aunt Violet had been a condition of living self-sufficiently, but one she would never regret; a haven where she could freely express her opinions and make her own choices without judgement.

Would marrying Darius bring her back to the life she fought to leave behind? Was what he offered her worth relinquishing her precious autonomy? One Aunt Violet swore was never to be given up no matter what the prize?

Darius always said he admired her independent spirit and even encouraged her to work with her aunt in the bookshop. He had also thrown himself into the murder investigations she and her aunt had become involved in, concerned for her safety but never critical. But would he demand she take on a more traditional role for her as his wife?

She pushed the thought away, unwilling to entertain conflict between herself and Darius when there was so much uncertainty about the outcome of the war. Was Darius's confidence in the Americans joining the allies well placed, or was victory still uncertain? Imagining the worst was unthinkable, but all they could do was be patient and hope. Everyone would.

For now, she stowed that thought in a box inside her head, threw off the covers, and went to laze luxuriously in a hot bath and decide how to spend a lazy day with nothing to command her time.

An enticing smell of cooked food reached her as she entered the dining room where she issued a general 'Good morning' to the occupants. Dropping a kiss on the cheek of each of her parents as she passed their chairs, she nodded to Norah and Selwyn Atherton, smiled at Rose Ellis and acknowledged Dianna Dunleavy, where an empty chair and a plate which held the remnants of a breakfast suggested Sissy had already been and gone.

Darius interrupted his conversation with Lynford Ellis to watch her progress to the sideboard with a smile as she noted neither Maura nor Millie had yet to make an appearance. Rejecting the cooked meats as being too early in the day for rich food, Hannah took an empty seat beside Aunt Violet at one end of the table and helped herself to a bread roll from the nearest basket.

'Where were you last night?' Her aunt cradled a cup of black coffee in both hands, a habit she had gained on her trip to New York some years before. 'You disappeared straight after dinner. Did you and Darius have a secret rendezvous?'

'If you know, then why ask?' Hannah poured herself coffee from the pot on the table as if it required her full attention.

'Not even a denial? Not that it isn't about time. Does Madeleine know?'

'I sincerely hope not.' Hannah shot her mother a swift look, relieved to see she was busy chatting to Rose Ellis. 'Her disappointment in my spinsterhood is one of the few ways I still have to annoy her.'

'You're becoming quite wicked in your maturity, darling. I wholeheartedly approve.'

'I apologise for breakfast being a little late,' Iris said, adopting her hostess role from the sideboard where she filled a plate with everything the bain-maries offered.

'Servants overdid it at their party last night, eh?' Hannah's father looked up from his plate, grinning.

'You could say that.' Mycroft snapped open his napkin with one hand and laid it across his lap. 'I've been informed Mrs Weberly and Venables continued drinking into the small hours in the housekeeper's sitting room and discovered this morning by a housemaid, both snoring loudly in armchairs.'

'I hope you intend to reprimand them.' Dianna's upper lip twisted into a sneer.

'Actually, no.' Mycroft set the saltshaker down with a thump. ''16 has been a rotten year for everyone with this dreadful war. Several families in the village have lost sons and Mrs Weberly's nephew died in the fighting.' He aimed a brief nod in Lynford's direction, which was returned. 'I shan't punish anyone for a little overindulgence at Christmas.'

'Hear, hear.' Hector slapped the table with the flat of his hand, as more murmurs of affirmation circled the table, leaving Dianna sour-faced.

'I hope everyone slept well?' Iris returned to the table and slid the heaped plate in front of Mycroft.

'My room was a little musty, so I suspect not properly aired.' Dianna focused on her plate of eggs, bacon and sausages, apparently determined to have the last word and make it a complaint.

'Iris dear,' Madeleine said, slathering a triangle of toast with blackberry jam. 'This conserve is exceptional. Where did you get it?'

Iris's hurt expression dissolved, and Hannah experienced a rare pang of affection for her mother.

'The maids organised a blackberry hunt in the hedgerows and brought back enough for Cook to supply the entire village with jam. We had a crop of redcurrants this year too, so we'll have relish to go with the leftover cold meat on Boxing Day.'

'You've done so well with this party, darling, but you should relax more.' Madeleine narrowed her eyes at Dianna. 'You're working too hard. I noticed you checked on the children twice last evening. That young nursery maid seems competent. Why not leave her to it?'

'Her name is Fiona,' Iris replied on her way back from collecting her own breakfast. 'She cannot do everything with Mabel away, especially with the baby.'

Mycroft got to his feet and held her chair for her as she placed her plate on the table. 'You might offer to help occasionally, Mama.'

'Why don't you do that for me, Hector?' Madeleine nudged her husband.

'Do what, dear?' He did not look up from his newspaper that lay flat on the table and forked up a slice of sausage.

'Hold out my chair for me like Mycroft did for Iris.'

He dragged his eyes from the paper and squinted at the floor. 'Whatever for, when you're sitting on it?' He caught Hannah's eye and winked.

'Hector, really! You can be so oblivious. I was just saying—'

The loud boom of a shotgun sounded outside the French windows, creating a flurry of surprised gasps.

'Goodness!' Madeleine's hand jumped, her toast falling onto her plate, jam side down.

Hannah covered her ear with her hand against the sudden uncomfortable pressure.

Rose gasped and flattened her hand against her chest while Dianna muttered something under her breath that likely was a complaint. Lynford's chair toppled sideways as he threw himself to the floor, sweeping a toast rack with him that scattered its contents in all directions.

'That was close.' Mycroft swung around in his chair. 'Nothing to worry about, everyone. Most probably the gamekeeper shooting rabbits.'

Darius scraped back his chair and bent to help Lynford up from where he lay, his eyes squeezed shut and both hands covering his head.

'Come on, old chap.' Mycroft approached him slowly, but despite his gentle encouragement and Darius's help, he seemed reluctant to get up.

Hannah clamped her lips together, fighting an urge to go to him, one her Aunt Violet also appeared to share as she scraped back her chair and started to rise.

'Best stay here.' Hannah laid a restraining hand on her arm. 'It will only make things more embarrassing for him.'

Aunt Violet nodded and sat down again as between them, Darius and Mycroft hoisted Lynford to his feet, while Selwyn settled him into his chair and brushed crumbs from the younger man's jacket.

Lynford nodded, and though shaken, returned their sympathetic smiles while murmuring thanks and stammered apologies.

Darius righted Lynford's chair and a maid sprang forward to clear up the slices of toast and the plate that had rolled beneath the table.

Iris busied herself compiling a fresh rack of toast. 'We all knock things over,' she said, setting the plate beside his half-eaten breakfast; an unnecessary task but one which she needed to perform.

'Ah, see there, the rug's scuffed, see?' Mycroft pointed vaguely at the floor. 'Must have tripped him. I'll have to see to that.' His valiant, if unnecessary, effort to put Lynford at ease only made things more awkward.

'What could be keeping Basil?' Rose's voice was overly loud. 'He never misses a meal, even when he's poorly. Lynford, have you seen your father? Indeed, has anyone seen him this morning?'

'I would have thought you were in the best position to answer that question, my dear Mrs Ellis?' Dianna issued a girlish laugh that sounded forced. 'I imagine he was the rather noticeable bulge beneath the coverlet beside you.' If this was aimed to amuse, it failed miserably.

'Basil's a poor sleeper, but Iris was most understanding and allocated us separate rooms for our visit.' Rose smiled triumphantly at her.

'Really?' Dianna shot a hard look at her hostess.

'I'll get a footman to give Basil a knock, Rose.' Iris stood, pointedly ignoring Dianna's disgruntled face.

'Please don't trouble, Mrs Atherton.' Lynford pushed the untouched toast away and stood. 'I'll go up and see what's keeping my father.'

The tension in the room dispelled like an exhaled breath and conversation resumed, accompanied by clicks of cutlery on plates as the contents of the bain-maries were attacked with relish.

'As I was saying, Hector.' Madeleine nudged Hannah's father. 'Iris ought to get more help managing the children. She's finding it hard to cope.'

'I never said that, Mama.' Iris sighed. 'Only I hoped you might take more interest in them while you are here. Four are quite a handful.'

'Have you considered you might stop having the little buggers?' Hector muttered, popping a slice of sausage into his mouth and chewing with relish.

'I heard that, Papa.' Iris bridled. 'Why would you say that about your own grandchildren, when we all know you adore them? Pity Mama doesn't feel the same way.'

'He was only joking, Iris,' Aunt Violet interjected. 'Though Hector, your sense of humour is a little suspect.' This remark was met with a slow wink from Hannah's father that totally lacked contrition.

'Darling, you know I've never been comfortable with small

children,' Madeleine protested. 'Their conversation is banal, to say the least, and they make such a lot of noise and mess.'

Hannah stirred milk into her coffee, recalling how she and Iris had spent most of the time with their nanny while Madeleine Merrill had attended every social event in London. At least Iris seemed to be more involved with her own brood.

'Anyway, Mama,' Iris began, clearly irritated. 'It's not as if the countryside is littered with young girls searching for domestic jobs.'

'Isn't it?' Hector glanced briefly up from his last piece of bacon. 'It was that way when we lived in town.'

'There's a war on.' Iris repeated the mantra to excuse every shortcoming. 'Most of them seem to prefer working in munitions factories.'

'You cannot blame them.' Darius joined the conversation. 'They earn more money there than their fathers did before the war. Although those factories are dangerous places. There have been some dreadful accidents with people killed.'

'There are even women bus conductors in London now,' Hannah added to show solidarity with Darius. 'And our former housemaid is making aircraft components in Acton.'

'We cannot all abandon our daily lives, Hannah.' Iris turned limpid eyes on her sister, a tiny tremble to her bottom lip.

'I'm not suggesting you should.' Hannah tried not to let her frustration show. 'I appreciate children can be difficult.' Her sister's four-year-old daughter, Matilda, came to mind – a self-possessed child with a strident personality. 'I'll give you a hand tomorrow.'

'Thank you,' Iris murmured, her eyes cast down in feigned martyrdom.

The click of the door announced Venables, who hurried to Mycroft's chair and whispered urgently in his ear.

'Are you sure?' Hannah's brother-in-law straightened, tossed his napkin on the table and, whispering something to Darius, scraped back his chair. Without another word, both men rose and followed the butler from the room.

'Whatever that was about, it wasn't good.' Hannah watched them retreat over the rim of her coffee cup.

'A crisis in the kitchens, perhaps?' Aunt Violet plucked a pastry from the table and took a bite, leaning back in her chair to view the hallway through the open door. 'Whatever it is, appears to be going on in the study.'

'I'll see if the girls are up yet,' Norah explained vaguely, as she too rose and made for the door.

Madeleine pushed back her chair and hurried after her.

'Where are you going?' Hannah's voice halted her mother at the door. 'Whatever it is, it's none of our business.'

'Nowhere, dear,' Madeleine replied, turning a guilty look on her daughter then addressing Dianna. 'Didn't you say you were going to check where Sissy had got to?'

'I did, didn't I?' Dianna scrambled to her feet and, still clutching a jam pastry, set off after the others.

'Where is everyone going?' Iris stared after them as the room emptied, a coffee pot held in mid-air. An oblivious Rose nibbled at a triangle of toast while staring out of the window.

'No idea and not interested,' her father muttered crossly from behind his newspaper. 'Can't be doing with female drama.'

'Nor me.' Selwyn snorted. 'Probably a dashed fuss about nothing.'

'I wonder if we should—' Hannah broke off as her aunt brought a hand down on her forearm.

'Don't.' Aunt Violet shook her head. 'There are enough nosey old biddies involved already.'

Five minutes passed, during which Hannah nibbled at another bread roll without enthusiasm.

Doors banged and multiple footsteps sounded in the hall until her curiosity got the better of her and she fidgeted. 'Aren't you in the least bit curious?'

'Are you suggesting we join the nosey biddies?' Aunt Violet raised an eyebrow.

'Yes.' Hannah nodded vigorously.

Aunt Violet's lips puckered as she considered the idea. 'Perhaps you're right.'

As one, the pair scraped back their chairs and rose.

'Wait for me!' Iris called, hurrying after them.

6

Out in the hallway, the women had assembled at the open study door.

'I'll ask that you stay outside please ladies,' Mycroft implored, his arm braced against the doorjamb to prevent entry. 'There's nothing anyone can do.'

'What's happened?' Hannah's gaze went to Darius, but before he could answer, she craned her neck to see into the room, her pulse racing.

Mr Ellis occupied the study chair, the upper part of his body sprawled across the vast desk, his arms spread. His head faced towards the window so only the back of his head was visible, displaying the full extent of his baldness like a round saucer on his head. The evening jacket he wore at the previous night's dinner lay over the back of his chair. Lynford stood on the far side of the figure in the chair, his face a mask of shock and indecision. Pieces of broken glass lay on the floor and were spread beneath the desk in a trail of irregular pieces.

'Oh, no!' Aunt Violet's tone showed she now regretted her 'old biddies' joke.

The crystal vase that once occupied the corner of the desk was no longer there. For a moment, Hannah thought Mr Ellis might have fallen onto it, losing consciousness as it smashed onto the floor. Was that the sound she and Darius had heard when they were in the music room the previous evening?

A half-smoked cigar and a glass of brandy containing a half inch of amber liquid were both within a hand's reach. Other than that, the desk was clear, with no indication of what he was doing there. Did he just choose a place for some private time, a smoke and a nightcap?

'Is he dead?' Madeleine voiced the question Hannah had not dared to voice, though the answer was obvious.

'I'm afraid so.' Darius looked up and met Hannah's eyes. 'Where's Mrs Ellis?'

'What happened?' Rose demanded, bustling forward. The group parted to let her through, but Mycroft held firm. 'What's wrong with him? Has he fainted? Just tell me, is he, is he...?'

Lynford circled the chair and approached her, his face rigid with a mixture of dread and regret. 'I'm so sorry, Mother, but he's gone. We can't let you in until the doctor has seen him. And we don't know what happened. This is exactly how I found him.' He placed a protective arm around Rose and attempted to draw her away from the door. 'Venables has gone to telephone for the doctor.' An announcement greeted with silence, as it was obvious that nothing could be done for the man now.

'Has he been there all night?' Rose brought a veined hand sprinkled with brown spots that resembled oversized freckles to her face; an image Hannah felt would be linked to this moment forever in her head, although she observed the scene with detachment, like a spectator at a play, her overriding emotion neither sadness nor shock, but curiosity. Her lack of emotion made her uneasy, for despite not knowing the man, shouldn't she still feel something for a life cut short?

A maid carrying a tray piled with used breakfast dishes had halted a few feet away, a shocked but curious gaze fixed on the small group huddled outside the study door.

Rose gasped, and clapped her hands to her cheeks, swaying against Lynford as if boneless. Had Lynford not been holding her, she would have dropped to the floor. Her lips moved but only one whispered word was audible. 'Basil.'

Madeleine wrapped an arm around the smaller woman's shoulders. 'Leave her to me.' She wrestled her from Lynford's hold with the confidence of one who reacted well in a crisis. 'I'll take her to her room.'

'Thank you, Mrs Merrill.' Lynford released Rose with obvious relief, leaving Madeleine to guide the distraught woman up the stairs, murmuring encouragement and promises of a nice cup of tea with each slow step as they disappeared onto the upper landing.

'Mads can always be relied upon when things fall apart.' Aunt Violet followed Hannah's proud gaze.

'It appears she can. And thank goodness for her,' Hannah replied, conscious she had come late to this realisation. What Aunt Violet saw as competence and compassion, Hannah had always seen as fussing.

'I'm so sorry, Lynford.' Iris squeezed his arm in sympathy, but he barely reacted.

'Do you know what happened?' Hannah asked, her gaze going from Mycroft to Darius.

Darius shook his head sadly. 'I'd say the poor fellow had a heart attack, or maybe a stroke, but I'm no doctor.'

'Did he have some underlying illness that might have caused it?' Aunt Violet asked, ever practical.

'It's possible.' Frowning, Darius approached Lynford who stood with his back to the wall as if he needed something firm to keep him upright. 'I can only imagine what's on your mind, Captain Ellis, but I must ask. Did your father have any known heart problems?'

'Call me Lynford, please. And not as far as I was aware. Mother might have more knowledge of his health than me. Although surely if he was feeling ill, wouldn't he have said something last night at dinner?'

'Not necessarily.' Mycroft sighed. 'Heart attacks can come on suddenly. And – Sorry old man, but it looks as if he's been dead for a while.'

'I know what death looks like,' Lynford said, but without rancour. 'Now, you'll have to excuse me. I must go to my mother.'

'Of course.' Darius nodded. 'We'll do what's required here.' But Lynford was already halfway up the stairs and probably didn't hear him.

'Where's Norah?' Iris asked, evidently remembering her sister-in-law had left the dining room before them. 'She was here a few moments ago.'

Hannah stared around the hall, her gaze snagging on Dianna, whose face paled, and she swayed slightly. 'Are you all right, Mrs Dunleavy?'

'Er. Yes, I—' Dianna blinked and backed away. 'My smelling salts are in my bag that I left...' Her voice tailed off as she turned and fled back the way she had come.

'I think Norah went to wake the girls.' Madeleine answered Iris's question. 'What's wrong with Dianna?'

'Squeamish, probably. Trust her not to offer any help.' Iris's resentful gaze followed Dianna as she disappeared into the dining room.

'She seemed genuinely shaken,' Hannah said. 'Not everyone is comfortable looking at dead bodies, Iris.'

'Sorry, that was harsh, and I do feel awful for Mr Ellis, but why did it have to happen now?' She looked about to burst into frustrated tears.

Hannah exchanged a glance with her mother, who shrugged, neither of them offering sympathy in case it opened the floodgates.

Mycroft gestured to a footman who had appeared through the baize door at the end of the hall. 'I assume word has reached below stairs that we have a death in the house?'

'Er – I heard a guest was unwell, sir, but—'

'Never mind. It was bound to get out. I'll instruct Venables to telephone for the doctor, but in the meantime, no one is allowed into the study. The door is to stay locked. Is that clear?'

The footman nodded and backed away the way he had come, most probably to spread rumours and speculation in the servants' hall. If Dianna didn't get there first.

Rapid footsteps along the corridor announced Mycroft's secretary, who skidded to a halt beside the door, his neck craned to see what was going on inside. He looked to have dressed in a hurry. His hair flopped over his forehead, and his tie twisted to one side of his collar.

'I've only just heard, sir.' Mr Gates split a worried look between his employer and Darius, ignoring the two women. 'Is it true a guest has died?'

'I'm afraid so.' Mycroft nodded. 'Now no one may enter the study until the police approve.'

'Is that really necessary, sir?' Gates's agitation increased. 'I need to collect some files to finish the accounts today. It was to be my last task before the holiday, so I would rather not delay it.'

'Can't be avoided, I'm afraid. Go back to what you were doing,

Gates. But if you could make sure that gossip in the servants' hall is kept to a minimum, I would appreciate it.'

Mr Gates eyed the study door for a few seconds as if he were about to argue, but changed his mind and backed away just as Hannah's father arrived with Selwyn.

'Is it true what we just heard?' Hector asked, reaching them. 'That Dunleavy woman came rushing in a few minutes ago shouting that Mr Ellis is dead. Is the woman drunk or insane?'

'Neither I'm afraid,' Darius replied. 'She told the truth, although I can understand the assumption. Mr Ellis appears to have collapsed and died sometime during the night.'

'In the study?' Hector gave the door a long, accusing look.

'Mycroft said he asked to use it after dinner, but it appears he never came out.'

'And no one checked on him?' Hector shook his head slowly and muttered under his breath. 'Bad show, that.'

'Good Lord, what happened?' Selwyn's eyebrows had risen in disbelief. 'Was it an accident?'

'It's doubtful. It looks like some sort of attack, but—' The chime of the doorbell muffled his next words and when Hannah looked to where Gates had stood a moment before, he had gone.

Venables admitted a man in a tan raincoat that flapped around his knees. His sparse hair combed over a bald patch was revealed when he removed his hat. His features were unremarkable other than his round horn-rimmed spectacles that had bottle lenses which made his eyes look huge. The presence of his black leather doctor's bag was the only hint he was in the medical profession.

'Thank you for coming so promptly, Dr Eames.' Mycroft strode forward to greet him. 'My apologies for calling you out during a holiday.'

'I live close by and, between you and me, I needed an escape from the in-laws.' He removed his glasses, which instantly reduced his eyes to a much smaller size, making him look like a mole. He pulled a handkerchief from a coat pocket which he used to wipe his glasses fastidiously before replacing them. 'A death in the house rather puts a damper on the festivities.'

'Quite.' Mycroft gestured Hannah forward and introduced her and Aunt Violet. 'And this is Mr Clifford, one of my guests who works for... the, um, the War Office.' He raised an enquiring eyebrow at Darius, who responded with a curt but reassuring nod.

'A pleasure to meet you.' Darius shook the doctor's hand.

'The War Office, eh? I hope you don't expect anything unto-ward to occur.' Chuckling at his own joke, Dr Eames swept his bag beneath one arm. 'Now, where's the body?'

'Allow me to show you.' Mycroft extended an arm in a 'this way' gesture, a swift smile aimed at Hannah before leading the doctor towards the study.

'Venables, have you seen my wife?' Selwyn stared around, puzzled. 'I thought she would be here.'

'Mrs Atherton went upstairs to see your daughters, sir. They haven't come back down yet.' The butler threw a swift glance at the upper landing from where the sounds of angry female voices reached them. 'It's been a most distressing morning.' He bowed and retreated, without waiting to see if he was further needed.

'It has indeed.' Selwyn rubbed the back of his neck with one hand. 'I'd better go and see if Norah and the girls are all right. I imagine this news must have come as a shock. Especially to Millie.' He took the stairs at a run, leaving the three of them in the now-empty hall.

'Well.' Hector rubbed his hands together. 'There's nothing left for us to do, so we might as well return to the sitting room to await developments.'

'What's happening up there?' Aunt Violet tilted her head back to view the ceiling as the sound of rapid footsteps crossed the landing, followed by a high-pitched cry she recognised as Norah's. Then a lower, more serious voice she identified as Maura.

'Mr Ellis is – *was* Millie's future father-in-law,' Hannah reminded her. 'She's bound to be upset.'

'Yes, I suppose so.'

Hector held open the sitting room door, poised to wait for them. 'That Gates chap seemed a bit miffed he was being kept out of the study.'

'He probably keeps his cigarettes in the desk and is peeved to be denied access.' Aunt Violet's attractive laugh and her father's low chuckle echoed along the hall.

Hannah started to follow but turned back when she saw Darius had paused outside the study door, one elbow propped on an arm he held across his midriff.

'Are you coming, Darius?' She wandered back to join him. 'You look worried.'

'I didn't want to say anything so as not to cause panic.'

'About what? If you mean the broken vase on the floor, I saw it too. That's what we heard last night, wasn't it?'

He nodded slowly. 'Yes, but it wasn't that. I think Mr Ellis was attacked.'

'You do?' Hannah's pulse raced. 'What brought you to that conclusion?'

'The fact he has an indentation in his skull.' He tapped his left temple. 'Right here. It wasn't visible from the door because of the way his head was turned towards the window.'

'What sort of indentation?'

'It's sort of curved. Deeper at the centre than the edges, but the skin wasn't broken. I didn't spot it last night at dinner, and I think I would have, so it's definitely recent.'

'If you spotted it, I'm sure the doctor will.' Hannah lowered her voice to a whisper. 'Darius, that means someone murdered him.'

'Come on, you two.' Aunt Violet waved to them from the sitting room door. 'Stop eavesdropping. You can wait for the doctor's verdict like the rest of us.'

'Don't say anything yet,' Darius said, squeezing Hannah's arm.

7

'Oh, excellent!' Aunt Violet strode to the sideboard where trays of both tea and coffee had been laid out. 'Someone must have had the same thought as me.'

Hannah poured a welcome cup from the coffee pot set over a paraffin flame, keenly conscious of Darius's shoulder touching hers.

He held up the milk jug and met her gaze, making her blush as she accepted. The air charged as they shared yet another secret.

'Poor Mr Ellis.' Hector retrieved his newspaper from one of the two wing-back chairs he had clearly occupied. 'Though I can't say I'm surprised. He ate three portions of lamb at dinner last evening and the way he demolished the chocolate mousse, it's a wonder his arteries didn't surrender years ago.'

'Papa!' Hannah carried her coffee to an empty sofa. 'The poor man's dead.'

'My darling girl, at our age that sort of thing is to be expected. Doesn't mean I don't feel sympathy for him and sadness for that poor downtrodden wife of his. He didn't even get to enjoy Christmas.'

'Even so, Papa.' Hannah wiggled back on the soft squab and tried not to spill her drink. She too had cast Rose as downtrodden and wondered if the woman's grief might be tinged with relief. Though even those who had resigned themselves to a life of being bullied and taken for granted became dependent. Perhaps she was more like her father than she imagined; not so much flawed, but pragmatic.

Her gloomy thoughts dissolved as Selwyn entered the sitting room with Norah, who clung to her husband while sobbing into a handkerchief. He escorted her to a sofa and gently lowered her into it. 'Now you sit right there, my dear,' he murmured, taking the space beside her.

From the sofa opposite, Hannah looked back over her shoulder to where Darius stood, a bone china cup and saucer dwarfed in his hands, a sardonic eyebrow raised in response to Norah's overt display of grief.

A few seconds later, Dianna ushered Maura and Millie ahead of her like a mother hen. Maura was still fastening her hair with a pearl clip, and Millie wore slippers, a top button of her dress undone. Their dishevelled appearance showed both girls had just woken up.

Iris, accompanied by Mycroft's twin springer spaniels, tails waving from side to side in anticipation of excitement or food, completed the small entourage.

'Oh, Selwyn.' Norah sobbed into the crumpled piece of cloth, her face buried in her husband's neck. 'It's gone. It's really gone.'

'What's gone?' Aunt Violet skirted the sofa and plopped down beside Hannah.

'The ruby pendant!' Dianna hovered over Norah, her eyes wide with a mixture of horror and excitement.

'Millie was supposed to return it to the study last night but left it in her dresser. Now we can't find it.'

'Are you sure?' Aunt Violet stared from Hannah to Darius and then back at the pair huddled together opposite.

'Of course, I'm sure!' Norah stiffened, then slumped back against Selwyn.

'Was the house broken into?' Hannah placed her cup on the table between them. 'Is anything else missing?' She was about to ask if it had anything to do with Mr Ellis's death, but Darius's firm hand on her shoulder kept her silent.

Selwyn shook his head. 'Mycroft is still with the doctor, so I asked Venables to check, but we don't know anything for sure yet.'

'I don't know where Sissy has got to.' Dianna slapped both hands to her cheeks. 'You don't suppose whoever took it has kidnapped her?'

'I hardly think so, Dianna,' Iris snorted. 'She's probably in the stables or chatting to the cook in the kitchens. She'll be back when she's ready so there's no need to start imagining things. We have enough drama going on here as it is.'

'That's true,' Hector muttered sagely. 'Poor Mycroft's got a lot to deal with without flighty girls making it worse.'

Dianna looked about to counter this remark, but Maura's hand on her arm quieted her. 'I'm sure she isn't far away, Mrs Dunleavy. She probably has no idea what has happened.'

'No, I suppose not.' Dianna fidgeted. 'Do we know yet what happened to Mr Ellis?' She squeezed into the space on Selwyn's other side, ignoring a hard look from Norah.

The door opened again, but instead of Sissy, Mycroft strode into the sitting room with an air of distraction oblivious to the tension in the air.

'Dr Eames, please come inside, I feel you ought to be the one to explain the situation.' Mycroft ushered the smaller man into the room, now denuded of his overcoat and hat.

'What situation?' Hector demanded. 'We were told Ellis suffered a heart attack.'

'All in good time, Father-in-Law.' Mycroft shot him a warning look before gesturing the doctor into an upright chair between the sofas.

Mycroft's surprised gaze went from the two subdued girls to Hannah and finally his wife before focusing on Norah. 'I'm dreadfully sorry this has happened, everyone, but Norah, dear, surely it's no cause for tears?'

'Calm yourself, Mama,' Millie spoke from the sofa opposite.

'Don't criticise me! And this is your fault for being so careless!' Norah snapped back at her, then rounded on Mycroft. 'How could you let such a thing happen?'

'I could hardly prevent it,' Mycroft began, defensive. 'It's a tragedy, but there was no way I could have known—'

'Mama.' Maura laid a tentative hand on her mother's shoulder, which was roughly shaken off. 'I don't think Uncle Mycroft was talking about the ruby.'

'What?' Mycroft jammed his hands into his pockets and glared at a still sobbing Norah. 'What's this about the ruby?'

Norah dropped the handkerchief in her lap and held up a jeweller's box, opened to reveal an indentation in the blue velvet where a necklace had been. 'Someone has stolen it!'

* * *

Mycroft opened his mouth, but no sound came out, and he closed it again. Confusion filled his eyes as if he was unable to comprehend yet another crisis.

'Has there been a burglary?' Dr Eames jerked his head at

each occupant like a nervous squirrel. 'You didn't mention that, Mr Atherton. It might have an impact on what happened—'

'I'm aware of that, but if you wouldn't mind, doctor, might we deal with one thing at a time?' Mycroft halted him with a raised hand before moving towards Selwyn and Norah. 'My dear girl, I-I'm not sure what to say.' He massaged his forehead with one hand. 'I don't understand. I was just in the study and the Chinese Cabinet has not been disturbed. At least, it looked that way. I didn't actually try the door. Are you sure it's not there?'

Selwyn repeated his account of how Millie had left the pendant in her room the night before, but this morning it was found to be missing, leaving the empty jeweller's box behind.

'Maybe the necklace got mislaid, somehow?' Mycroft attempted to defuse a situation that seemed ready to escalate. 'Have you completed a thorough search?'

'Of course we have! And it's not *mislaid*, someone stole it!' Norah's face flushed with anger as her frustration grew. 'Millie, you were explicitly told to return it to the study.'

'And I would have, Mama,' Millie pleaded. 'But it was so late when we left the drawing room, and I was tired. I thought it wouldn't hurt for one night.'

'From what I see, you didn't think at all!' Norah snapped, enraged.

'Mama, please don't be angry.' Maura wrapped an arm around Millie and pulled her closer. 'Can't you see she's upset?'

'*She's* upset? What about me? Her carelessness has lost me a family heirloom.' Norah rounded on Mycroft again. 'I demand this entire house be searched, starting with the servants' rooms.'

'How dare you!' Iris insinuated herself between her husband and sister-in-law, their faces inches apart. 'I appreciate you're upset, Norah. But you have no right to imply my staff aren't trustworthy. Are you sure Millie didn't put the pendant somewhere else and forgot?'

'Are you accusing my girls of lying?' Norah spat.

'I'm certain I put it in the dresser, Aunt Iris,' Millie began, then paused. Her eyes clouded and she brought a thumb and forefinger to her lips. 'At least – I thought I did. I, er, had some champagne at dinner last night.'

'You had a couple of glasses after dinner too,' Maura reminded her.

Millie started to cry, her brown eyes scanning the room. 'Where's Lynford?' Her voice, though high-pitched, was surprisingly composed considering the circumstances.

'He's with his mother in her room.' Mycroft cocked his chin at the hall. 'Madeleine is with them.'

'Pity. Mads is missing all the fun,' Aunt Violet said under her breath, earning herself an elbow in the ribs from Hannah.

'I must go to him.' Millie rose from her perch on the arm of the sofa where her parents sat.

'Stay with me, Millie. I need you!' Norah snagged her arm, holding her down. 'It's unfortunate about Mr Ellis, but—'

'Unfortunate?' Millie wrenched away from her. 'The man is dead, Mama. And my darling Lynford has just lost his father. How could you be so unfeeling?'

Norah's cheeks pinked in ugly patches. 'You don't have to be rude.'

Millie tutted angrily and stormed from the room, letting the door slam behind her.

'Mycroft, you cannot allow the house to be searched,' Iris insisted. 'We have guests!'

'If someone has indeed stolen the ruby, I shall have to, my dear.' He splayed his harms helplessly. 'The police are bound to insist.'

'What? Even the nursery?' Iris's eyes widened in horror.

No one seemed to notice Sissy Dunleavy clatter into the room until the spaniels began a series of warning barks.

'What's all the noise? I could hear you all the way to the front door. And what's wrong with Millie? She brushed past me just now without a word.' Sissy's outdoor coat was slung over one arm while she unwound a scarf from around her neck with her free hand, ruffling her long brown curls sprinkled with snowflakes that sparkled in the overhead lights, her nose and cheeks red from the cold.

'Where have you been, Sissy?' Dianna demanded.

'I went for an early morning walk.' Sissy frowned, confused at her mother's unreasonable question about something so prosaic. 'I didn't leave the grounds if that's what's worrying you. Why is everyone acting so strangely?'

Norah leapt from her seat and made a grab at Sissy's arm, sending her muffler to the floor. 'Did you see anyone lurking about on the grounds?'

'No. Well, not really.' Sissy jerked in her chin away from Norah's leering face. 'Perhaps the gamekeeper. The milkman. Oh, and there was this chap on his way into the village who waved. Why, is it important?'

'Unhand my daughter, immediately!' Dianna ushered Sissy away from Norah. 'You have no right to interrogate her.'

Dianna raised her chin and squeezed her not-inconsiderable backside onto a sofa next to Hannah and Iris, forcing them to shift sideways to make room.

'I don't understand it.' Norah clutched the handkerchief to her nose, despite the absence of tears. 'We only took the ruby out of the bank a few days ago. How could anyone know we brought it here with us?'

'Norah, you've been talking about that blasted jewel since we got here.' Hector rolled his eyes. 'I'll wager everyone within three miles of Midwinter knows about it.'

'How am I going to tell my family that I've lost it?' Norah started sobbing again.

'It's called a wireless telegram service if I'm not mistaken.' Hector snapped open his newspaper before disappearing behind it.

'Don't worry, Norah.' Selwyn patted her hand absently. 'I doubt the loss will even register with your Calhoun relatives.'

'What *do* you mean by that?' Norah demanded between sobs. 'It's a family heirloom.'

One dog growled deep in its throat until Maura stroked its head and made soothing noises until it stopped. The other was busy chewing Selwyn's copy of *The Times* into shreds.

'Abraham Calhoun is three thousand miles away.' Selwyn wrestled the remains of his newspaper away from the dog. 'I doubt he'll board the first ocean liner bound for England in a panic. He thought he had seen the last of it on our wedding day.' Selwyn confirmed the assumption that Norah had been given the pendant more to show the Calhouns' disappointment at her choice of husband as part of their family heritage.

A maid who had slipped in unnoticed to replenish the coffee tray, giggled.

Iris turned on her. 'What are you doing eavesdropping? Get on with your work!'

'Yes, Madam.' The girl started, dropped a swift curtsey, and darted away, most likely to carry tales to the servants' hall that would keep the staff entertained for the rest of the holiday.

'Well, Mycroft? What are you going to do about it?' Norah's face suffused with angry red, her ferret eyes blazing.

'There's not much I *can* do, so I intend to leave it to the police.'

'Huh!' Norah scoffed. 'What can the police do? The ruby

could be out of the country by now! And where did Millie go? She should be here with me. Doesn't she care how I feel?'

'Millie is where she's most needed. With her fiancé,' Maura said.

'I gather you require me to wait until the police get here?' Dr Eames's tentative question indicated he assumed he had been forgotten during Norah's outburst, confirmed by the startled looks turning his way. 'I assume they are on their way?'

'Er, yes, they are.' Mycroft rubbed his hands together and stared at the floor.

Hannah glanced at Darius, whose expression suggested his thoughts aligned with hers and Mycroft, now aware of the circumstances of Mr Ellis's death, dreaded having to tell the company.

'Pardon me, but I'm a little confused,' Hector interjected from his wing-back chair beside the fire. 'Why do you need to see the police? You've pronounced death and summoned a coroner's van. What else do you need to do?'

'It's the law,' Dr Eames announced firmly. 'All cases of sudden or violet death must be reported to the authorities.'

Darius cleared his throat, placed his empty coffee cup beside Hannah's on the low table and joined her on the sofa, throwing her a guarded look.

Before anyone could react to this announcement, the door clicked open and Madeleine appeared, one arm supporting a frail but composed Rose Ellis, followed by a subdued Millie and a solemn-looking Lynford.

'She insisted on coming down,' Madeleine said by explanation with an air of having lost an argument, and settled Rose onto the empty sofa opposite the fire, where Millie and Lynford joined her.

'I need to know how my Basil died,' Rose announced, her shoulders stiff as if braced for bad news.

Mycroft waited until everyone had resumed their seats, chose an upright chair for himself, his forearms on his knees and resigned the floor to the doctor.

'My first impressions,' Dr Eames began, 'are that Mr Ellis died sometime late last night. Possibly of a heart attack or a stroke. However, only a post-mortem will give a complete picture of what really happened.'

'Then what's all this about a violent death?' Hector demanded.

'What?' Lynford straightened, his gaze going from Mycroft to the doctor. 'What are you talking about?'

'I also said *sudden*, sir.' Dr Eames fidgeted. 'During my examination, I observed an indentation to the deceased's left temple. But it was impossible to say what caused it.'

Rose gasped, regarding the doctor with wide eyes.

Millie grabbed Lynford's forearm, her fingers gripping so tightly that he winced.

'Could he have fallen?' Lynford asked, sounding almost hopeful.

'I very much doubt it.' Dr Eames removed his glasses then put them back on again. 'He was seated and there were no signs of a struggle. However, I'd rather leave the official conclusion to the pathologist.'

'You mean, you don't really know how he died?' Lynford eased his collar with one hand and drummed his fingers on his thigh with the other.

'I suggest the injury occurred not long before he, uh, succumbed. He was seated and probably lost consciousness. I would rather not speculate any more as that will have to be confirmed.'

'I'll show you out, Dr Eames,' Darius ventured when Mycroft sat unmoving, his hands hanging loosely between his knees like a man who had no idea what to do next.

'Thank you, er, young man.' The doctor gave Darius a grateful look and accompanied him to the door.

Silence engulfed the room, broken only by the crackling of the fire and an odd cough as everyone absorbed this information.

Having replenished her coffee cup on the sideboard, Aunt Violet absently dropped a lump of sugar into it and sat down again beside Hannah. 'Did you know about this?' she demanded in a fierce whisper.

'Sort of.' Hannah chewed the corner of her bottom lip. 'Darius told me he noticed an injury of some sort but couldn't tell if it was serious or not.'

'You might have said.' Violet stirred the dark liquid vigorously, her spoon making sharp ticks against the china. 'I don't enjoy being the last to know.'

'There was no chance to tell you, honestly. And Darius thought it best to wait for the doctor to see if he thought it was relevant or not.'

'Who wasn't much help, to be honest. He created more questions than he answered. Do you think Mr Ellis's death had anything to do with the theft of the ruby?'

'It does seem odd, both things happening on the same night.' Hannah threw a swift look to where Norah and Iris seemed to have patched up their spat and were talking quietly. 'But you heard Norah. The pendant wasn't in the study and Mycroft said the cabinet where it was kept hasn't been disturbed.'

'It's a bit fishy if you ask me.' Aunt Violet took a sip of coffee and grimaced. Her cup hit the saucer with a firm click. 'Ugh. This tastes awful.'

'I'm not surprised.' Hannah smiled wryly. 'You don't take sugar.'

Aunt Violet discarded the cup with a frustrated snort and folded her arms.

'Poor Mrs Ellis.' Hannah watched her mother retrieve a blanket from the window seat which she draped over a silent Rose's lower half, despite the room being comfortably warm. 'Imagine leaving home for a holiday with your husband and having to return without him.'

Craving something practical to do in the doom-laden room, Hannah got up and poured Rose a cup of tea. The lush laurel garlands draped over the mantlepiece and bunches of holly arranged around the room seemed to mock them all with false cheerfulness, making Christmas seem like an irrelevance.

'Oh, how kind of you, dear.' Rose offered her a wan smile as she received the bone china cup. 'Just what I needed.'

'I'm so sorry, Mrs Ellis,' Hannah said, unable to think of anything more inspirational to say.

She looked up as Darius returned. He pressed Mycroft's shoulder as he passed his chair and went to join Lynford who had left his seat and was standing by the fireplace, staring moodily into the flames.

Millie sat with Maura but broke off their conversation at intervals to give Lynford a supportive smile which he barely seemed to notice.

Rose nodded silently, her lower lip trembling. 'I knocked on his door to say goodnight on my way to bed, but he didn't answer. I thought he was either already asleep or still downstairs in the study, so I continued to my own room.' She inhaled a shuddering breath and fought to remain calm. 'He must have been there all night, and I had no idea.'

The awkward silence descended again, broken by a faint

tearing noise as the spaniel returned to demolishing Selwyn's newspaper.

'Rose, please accept my condolences,' Norah began. 'I would have come to you when I first heard, but then I received some devastating news, and—'

'Norah,' Selwyn drew out the word in warning.

'Oh, yes, well.' Norah's complexion turned unbecoming red. 'Not the time. Of course. As I said. My—*our* condolences.'

Rose whimpered her acceptance and Lynford placed a protective hand on his mother's shoulder.

'What happens to my father's... body now?' He directed the question at Mycroft. 'I mean, we cannot leave him in the study like – like that.'

'That won't happen, I assure you. At least, not for long.' Mycroft's gaze flicked over Rose and settled on Lynford. 'Dr Eames has organised transportation to have him taken—' He stumbled on the next word, perhaps reluctant to use the words 'mortuary van'. 'He hopes this will take place sometime today, weather permitting.' He cleared his throat before speaking again. 'A Detective Sergeant Roper is on his way and—'

'A sergeant?' Norah interrupted, in a tone Lady Bracknell might have used in *The Importance of Being Earnest*. 'Is that all the local constabulary can spare for a valuable jewel theft? I would have expected an inspector at the very least.' She displayed no trace of tears, only righteous indignation.

'I've been informed most senior officers are on leave for the holiday and those on duty have to travel distances in atrocious weather.' Mycroft massaged the bridge of his nose with a thumb and forefinger. 'We're hardly in the wilds of Scotland, so it's not as if we're completely cut off. However, last night's snowfall has made some of the minor roads impassable. Of course, he's not been made aware of the missing ruby as yet. I assume he'll instigate a full search of the house to confirm the ruby is indeed missing. Although I imagine the more serious crime will be his first priority.'

'The Calhoun Ruby *is* a priority.' Norah drew herself up and faced Mycroft. 'I expect the loss of my necklace will be thoroughly investigated without delay.'

'No one is refuting your claim, Norah, but there are ways of doing these things,' Selwyn said reasonably, but Norah harrumphed noisily and slumped in her seat, dissatisfied.

'What's this about a search?' Dianna clutched at her neckline. 'I'm not having some common policeman rooting through *my* belongings.'

'You don't have any, Mama,' Sissy said from the armchair she shared with a Welsh springer spaniel, the animal's brown and white head in her lap. 'We borrowed everything from the Athertons last night.'

'Be quiet, Sissy,' Dianna huffed, annoyed. 'And I hope you aren't getting dog hairs on that dress?'

'*My* dress,' Maura muttered under her breath, but there was no genuine feeling behind it.

'Has anyone checked to see if someone broke in last night?' Iris asked. 'We've been so busy with Mr Ellis it might have gone unnoticed.'

'I've already asked that question, Iris, but no one seems to know,' Hannah said.

'I had a word with Venables when I showed Dr Eames out.' Darius stood with one foot braced on the fender, looking more like the lord of all he surveyed than his host. 'There have been some comings and goings already this morning. The postman and a couple of tradesman's vans got through. A footman had the morning off and walked into the village to visit his parents. Two maids who don't live in arrived on foot to help Mrs Weberly.

Venables says he cannot detect any tampering with the outside doors either as by the time he looked, they had all been unlocked.'

'I don't suppose anyone spotted a man in a turban wandering about the house or grounds recently?' Aunt Violet asked.

'What was that?' Norah turned on her, but Aunt Violet held up her hands in surrender.

'Must you?' Hannah widened her eyes at her, only for her aunt to cross her eyes and grin.

'Are you saying—' Selwyn enunciated each word '—that it's impossible to tell whether it was an intruder or one of us who took the ruby?'

'That appears to be the case,' Darius replied.

8

Luncheon was a subdued affair, with the houseguests occupied with their own thoughts. Dianna Dunleavy was the most restless and snapped at Sissy over minor infractions, while Norah pined over the loss of her ruby, refusing apologies or pleas to cheer up.

Maura withdrew to the music room, leaving Millie to hover over Lynford, who, as expected for someone in the first stages of grief, appeared troubled, sad and angry by turns.

Rose was shown attentive respect by all for her fragile state, and to distract her, Iris had asked Cook to prepare a dish tailored to her liking.

'I don't know why you are spoiling me like this, I'm quite all right, really,' Rose simpered as Iris set the plate before her, though she seemed to enjoy the attention.

Once the meal ended, everyone drifted away, some to do last-minute present wrapping, rest in their rooms, or read in the library, while the younger members ventured out for walks in the grounds or to stage snowball fights on the sloping lawn.

By mid-afternoon, the guests had reassembled in the sitting

room, which had become the centre of operations, gathered around the fire to exchange views and create scenarios.

Madeleine took Rose back upstairs for a lie-down, leaving Hector in a wing-back chair he had commandeered on one side of the mock-Adam fireplace. Its twin was occupied by Selwyn. The pair resembled bookends with their matching newspapers, while the brown and white Welsh springers stretched in front of the fire, and yawned, bored as everyone else with the wait for the police.

The sound of hoofbeats on the snow brought Hector's head up from his newspaper. 'That'll be the peelers, no doubt.'

Hannah rose and approached the window in time to see a footman help down a figure from a dog cart. He was garbed in winter clothing, his shoulders hunched against the icy wind, hat pulled down low, beneath which sat a thick muffler. The newcomer stomped across the snow-covered drive towards the house, stopping every couple of paces to shake snow from his shoes. Behind him, a footman unloaded a bicycle from the rear of the cart and wheeled it around to the back of the house.

'Shouldn't he use the tradesman's entrance?' Dianna tutted. 'Surely he won't expect to be admitted through the main door?'

'Perhaps you'd like to mention that to the detective sergeant personally, Dianna?' Madeleine said acidly.

Dianna chose not to argue just as Venables appeared leading the newcomer.

'Detective Sergeant Roper, sir. Here to investigate the death of Mr Ellis,' he added, should there be any confusion about the policeman's presence.

'Thank you, Venables.' Mycroft bit his bottom lip to prevent a smile.

Of medium height and build, the senior detective's asymmetrical features made his face appear lopsided. His moustache, most likely cultivated to disguise a non-existent upper lip, was waxed.

Having established a fractious relationship with Detective Inspector Aidan Farrell on their first meeting, Hannah had been prepared to dislike Roper, but his greeting was warm, almost friendly. 'Good morning, ladies, gentlemen,' he said, offering an obsequious bow.

'Are you alone?' Mycroft interjected before he could get any further. 'Surely a suspicious death and a serious theft require more than one man to investigate?'

'I agree, sir. And normally that would be the case. However, we only have a small complement of officers at the local police station and the roads are too bad for anyone to come from further afield at short notice.'

Uneasy looks and a muted clearing of throats prompted him to add, 'I hope to receive some backup officers later when the roads are passable, but can assure you I have experience in investigating serious crimes.'

'I notice he's not mentioned anything about having solved any murders,' Aunt Violet said, attracting a critical look from Iris.

A brief silence ensued during which the policeman cleared his throat before continuing, 'I've also been appraised of the theft of a valuable jewel, which will also be looked into.'

'*My* valuable jewel,' Norah corrected him.

'I thought it was mine now, Mama,' Millie observed cryptically.

'You know what I mean.' Norah glared at her daughter. 'It's been in my family for over a hundred and fifty years.'

'I'm more interested in where the item is now, Mrs...?' Detective Roper placed his arms behind his back and rocked on his heels.

'Atherton. Norah Atherton. This is my husband, Selwyn, and our daughters Millie and Maura.'

'My apologies, I usually have a—' He rummaged through several pockets. 'Ah yes, here it is!' He held up a pristine notebook and a newly sharpened pencil.

The pencil engendered Hannah's confidence, as those Inspector Farrell used were always short, stubby and had chewed ends. 'I was informed that until last evening, the pendant was kept in a locked cabinet in the study?' Roper continued.

'It was. However, the butler informed us the cabinet had not been touched,' Selwyn ventured.

'Where exactly was the necklace when it was last seen?' Detective Roper poised the pencil over the page of his notebook and waited.

'I wore it to dinner last night,' Millie responded. 'I left the dining room at around nine fifteen and went to my room. That is, the room I share with my sister. I placed it inside the case and left it in my dresser drawer.'

'And which of the ladies is your sister?' His gaze darted around the faces and paused on Sissy.

'Oh, not me.' Sissy giggled and pointed to Maura. 'That's Maura.'

'Thank you.' Detective Roper smiled, scribbled in his notebook, and went back to Millie. 'What did you do next, Miss Atherton?'

'Well.' Millie twisted her hands together in her lap. 'We, that is Maura, Miss Dunleavy and Mr Ellis and I met in the drawing room where we played the gramophone and danced.' She turned to Lynford for encouragement, which he gave by placing his hand over her clasped ones. 'The ruby is heavy and unsuitable for dancing, which is why I took it off.'

'And when the dancing finished, and you retired, did you check to see it was still there?' Roper asked.

'Er, no.' Millie swallowed, self-conscious. 'I realise now I should have. But I was so tired, and, well—'

'I understand, Miss Atherton.' Roper nodded dismissively. 'And the next morning you realised it was missing?'

'Yes, that's right.' Millie nodded. 'I didn't notice straight away, but when I opened the drawer to fetch my stocki... something, The clasp on the box was open when I knew I had closed it. That's when I realised it was gone.'

'And you, Miss Atherton.' He turned to Maura. 'Did you witness your sister put the necklace away?'

'Not exactly, no. We came upstairs separately after dinner, so I wasn't aware Millie had left the necklace in our room. I was in bed and asleep when Millie came to bed.'

'We came upstairs together, but I was saying goodnight to Lynford,' Millie blurted, blushing, then added to ensure there was no misunderstanding, 'He's my fiancé.'

'What time was this exactly?' the detective asked.

The two girls shared a quick, nervous glance before Millie answered. 'It must have been almost midnight.'

Maura nodded, her arms clasped around a dog's neck as if she sought comfort. 'That's right. We must have been the last to go upstairs, as the house was quiet, and only the hall lights were still on.'

'What about the rest of you?' The policeman's glance scanned the room, pausing briefly on each person as if gauging their reactions.

'The party split up into various locations after dinner,' Mycroft explained. 'The ladies remained in the sitting room over coffee, the young people were in the drawing room listening to the gramophone and the chaps adjourned to the billiard room where we remained until around midnight. That is, except for Mr Ellis, who was in the billiard room with us, but after a few minutes, he requested to use the study. I assumed he had retired when we all did, but apparently not.'

'And no one looked in on Mr Ellis during the evening?'

'Er, I didn't,' Mycroft said sheepishly. 'Did anyone else?' This question was greeted with shaken heads and low murmurs.

Hannah frowned, recalling Rose's claim she thought he was still in the study when she went to bed. If Basil went to the billiard room after dinner, how would she know he was in the study? Or did he stop by the sitting room to inform her? Was that why she was in the hall when Hannah went up to bed? But if she had seen or spoken to him, wouldn't she have said so?

'Miss!' Detective Roper's sharp tone made Hannah jump, indicating he had repeated himself. 'Were you in the sitting room between dinner and the end of the evening?'

'Er, no.' She fought not to let her gaze drift to Darius, conscious she was about to lie but could probably put it right later. In private. 'I went straight to bed after dinner.'

'I see.' He nodded, losing interest. 'And the ruby pendant remained locked in a cabinet in the study at all times until last evening when it was taken out for dinner?' he summarised, most likely for his own benefit.

'That's correct,' Mycroft nodded. 'When Mr Ellis was discovered this morning, I instructed the study be locked. From what I saw, the cabinet was untouched, but at that stage we knew nothing about the theft.'

'I'll have the cabinet examined for signs of tampering and take fingerprints in the study.' He returned the notebook to his pocket, nodding in self-congratulation. 'That's enough for now, but we've made a good start. I'll need to speak to each of you individually, of course, and in the meantime, no one leaves the premises. Now.' He clapped his hands together. 'I think it's time I examined the body.' He turned away and instantly the entire room seemed to release a combined breath, but when he halted and turned back it tensed again. 'One thing. Who found the body?'

All eyes instinctively sought out Lynford.

'I did,' Lynford said, swallowing. 'When he didn't come down to breakfast, I went to find him.' Then anticipating the policeman's next question, added, 'I'm Captain Ellis, Mr Ellis is – was – my father.' Beside him, Rose uttered a low sob, then fell silent. 'I went up to his room first, but the bed had not been slept in, so I came downstairs.'

'So, Captain,' Detective Roper spoke carefully. 'What made you look into the study?'

'I, uh...' Lynford faltered.

'Because...' Roper drew the word out meaningfully, 'if your father went to the billiard room after dinner and you were in the drawing room with the young ladies, what made you think he was in the study?'

'I told him, sir,' Venables spoke up. 'I met Captain Ellis on the stairs where he asked me if I had seen his father. Last evening I was on my way back from the billiard room when I observed Mr Ellis enter the study. No one appears to have seen him leave, so it was the first place I suggested.'

'I see.' Roper thanked the butler with a nod. 'I would like to see the study now, if you please.'

'Oh, yes, of course, Detective.' Mycroft turned to Venables. 'Please would you show Detective Roper—'

'Actually, sir,' Detective Roper interrupted, 'I would prefer you showed me yourself.'

Mycroft and the detective traded a stare that lasted several seconds, until finally, Mycroft inclined his head.

'If you insist, Detective.' Rising, he accompanied the policeman into the hall while the butler scurried away, presumably to get the key from the butler's pantry.

'That was awkward,' Darius commented.

Hannah agreed, but which encounter was he referring to. Mycroft or Lynford's?

* * *

Subdued by their first encounter with the police, Hector and Selwyn adjourned to the billiards room. Darius mentioned something about checking on his motor car in the garage, while Lynford and Millie disappeared somewhere they chose not to reveal. Rose announced a desire for a nap, prompting Norah to hold the door open for the older woman, then follow her out without an explanation.

'Is everyone leaving?' Dianna asked, mildly disappointed: probably because no one had asked her to go with them.

'To hide any incriminating evidence, I imagine,' Aunt Violet said from the window, where she stared moodily at the snow.

'Don't joke about it, Aunt Violet,' Iris said, hurt. 'I don't want to believe any of my guests is a killer or a jewel thief.'

'Did I hear the detective correctly?' Dianna asked when the room fell quiet again. 'That no one could leave the manor until he gave his approval?'

'Exactly that, Dianna,' Madeleine said in a tone she usually employed for one of her grandchildren. 'We are to remain here until the police are satisfied with our innocence.'

'But it's almost Christmas!' Dianna pouted.

'I'd rather stay here, anyway. It's more fun than The Laurels.' Sissy wrestled a ball from one of the dogs who climbed into her lap to retrieve it. She turned to Hannah. 'My brother, Freddie, is staying with friends in Abingdon until the New Year, so he won't even be there.'

'That's hardly the point!' Dianna rose and followed them from the room. 'Come with me, Sissy. I need your help with something.'

Sighing, Sissy untangled herself from beneath the springer and trudged behind her mother.

Maura issued an annoyed grunt as the door closed on Dianna. 'If Sissy Dunleavy thinks I'll lend her more of my wardrobe, she can think again. I hardly brought enough for myself, and Millie has already borrowed my spare stockings because she ruined hers.' She pushed to her feet. 'I'd better check she's not going through my things again.'

'Whatever's wrong with Dianna?' Hannah asked, her sympathy going out to Maura. 'She was keen enough to stay last night. Why the eagerness to leave now?'

'She always invites herself everywhere, but only on her terms,' Iris said. 'She'll likely change her mind tomorrow and then I won't be able to shift her if I wanted to.'

'What do you make of Detective Roper?' Iris asked.

'He seems to know what he's doing,' Hannah replied. 'But I'm no expert, despite my experience with policemen.' She flicked a sideways look at Aunt Violet, who was deep in thought and appeared not to hear her.

'Do you believe there's a connection between Mr Ellis's death and the stolen ruby?' Iris pulled a cushion onto her lap and wrapped her arms around it as if seeking comfort.

'I had the same conversation with Darius,' Hannah said, thoughtful. 'If so, it would be a remarkable coincidence, don't you think?' She discarded the copy of *London Illustrated* that had failed to hold her attention. 'How was the thief to know the necklace wasn't in the cabinet where it was supposed to be?'

'I hate to think he was in the house all the time.' Iris gave an exaggerated shudder. 'It makes me feel unsafe in my own home.'

'Iris, dear?' Aunt Violet turned from the window and strode to the table in the corner of the room. 'Might I use your telephone?'

'What? Oh, ye-yes, of course.' Iris aimed a questioning look at Hannah, who shrugged.

Aunt Violet plucked the earpiece from a candlestick telephone and jiggled the metal fork. 'Ah, operator. Could you put me through to Guildford 746?' She held the earpiece against her shoulder, her head turned to address Iris. 'Is there an empty room you can have prepared for an extra visitor?'

'I-I think so,' Iris placed her hand on the back of the sofa and turned to look at Violet. 'It might have to be in the attic because —' Aunt Violet waved her off in a 'one moment' gesture and replaced the earpiece to her ear. 'Ah, Aidan. You know you said Christmas was going to be tiresome this year? Hmm? Well, I've got a more interesting proposition for you.'

'Aidan?' Iris addressed Hannah. 'Is that the policeman Mama says is courting Aunt Violet?'

'Otherwise known as Detective Inspector Farrell, although that isn't quite how I would describe it. But yes.' Hannah kept her voice low. She had her own suspicions about her aunt's relationship with the handsome policeman, but discretion always stopped her from quizzing her aunt, whose frequent returns after dawn to their shared house and rapidly smothered laughter in corners spoke for themselves.

'He'll be here this afternoon.' Aunt Violet replaced the earpiece on the fork and returned to the sofa.

'Coming here, but what for?' Hannah shifted sideways as Aunt Violet plumped down on the sofa next to her.

'Who else do you know with such expertise in bodies and

jewel thefts? I'm willing to wager Detective Ripley's last post before promotion was to direct traffic.'

'His name is Roper,' Hannah corrected her. 'And you're being obtuse.'

'I just thought someone like Aidan could bring a new perspective to the case. Especially if Mr Ellis's death turns out to be murder.'

'No!' Iris jerked upright. 'I refuse to have anyone murdered in my house.'

Hannah was tempted to inform her she had no choice in the matter, but instead said, 'I doubt Detective Roper will be pleased to find a Scotland Yard man poking around in his investigation.'

'I hadn't intended on mentioning that part.' Aunt Violet smiled mischievously. 'Besides, it's not as if Aidan could be considered a suspect, can he?'

'I'm rather looking forward to meeting him,' Iris said, looking more cheerful than she had all morning.

'Sorry to disturb you, ladies,' Darius said as he put his head round the door. 'I forgot my book.'

The two spaniels raised their heads with interest from where they lay in front of the fire, lowering them again when they checked who the intruder was.

He approached a small bookcase from where he plucked a volume Hannah could have sworn was a random choice, as he didn't even glance at the spine. 'Ah! Here it is!' Skirting the sofa, he caught Hannah's eye and cocked his head in a beckoning gesture.

'Where are you going, Hannah?' Iris asked as Hannah started to follow.

'Um... I have something I need to do.' Giving each of the dogs a final rough hug and before her sister could protest further, Hannah joined the exodus.

9

Darius peered into each room along the ground floor, most of which were occupied. 'What about we try in here again?' he asked, pausing outside the music room.

'Maura might be in there,' Hannah said. 'I believe she likes to practise the piano.'

He leaned an ear against the door, then shook his head. 'Can't hear anything.' He opened the door a crack and stuck his head around the jamb. 'All clear.' He pulled Hannah inside and closed it again. 'Phew. In a house this size you'd think we could grab a few moments to ourselves.'

'By the way, thank you for the well-timed rescue.' Hannah coaxed Darius down onto the window seat beside her. 'Dianna is annoyed she has to stay here after all that wheedling to get a room last night, and Iris was becoming maudlin, though I cannot blame her. Her house party has deteriorated into a disaster.' She rested her back against the glass to allow the welcome coolness to permeate her woollen gown. 'That's better. Mycroft likes to show off how efficient the plumbing is, but I'm not used to being so hot all the time. I grew up with ice-rimmed bedroom windows first thing in the morning, and not daring to move four feet away from the fire.'

'Perhaps he's on a mission to eradicate chilblains altogether.' Darius laughed.

'What do you think of Detective Sergeant Roper?' Hannah asked.

'A typical country policeman, I would say. Big fish in a small pond. He made a valiant attempt to be pleasant.' Darius sprawled beside her, one knee raised onto the bench with its thin cushion, the other foot swinging two inches from the floor. 'However, I suspect he's the sort who's too stubborn to listen and believes to admit he's wrong is a weakness.'

'He's certainly determined that whoever killed Mr Ellis must also have stolen the ruby.'

'You disagree? Even when the two things happened on the same night?'

'But not the same location. Why kill Mr Ellis in the study when the ruby was in Millie and Maura's room? It doesn't make sense.'

'We aren't sure when Mr Ellis died, are we? No one saw him after he went into the study so maybe whoever took the ruby walked in on him. He challenged them and they killed him? I suppose it could be a coincidence, but is it likely?'

'You sound like Inspector Farrell. He doesn't trust coincidences either.'

'Speaking of Aidan, I'd be interested to hear his opinion on this.' He wrapped both arms loosely around his upraised knee.

Hannah had become acquainted with Detective Inspector Farrell two years before when he had investigated the murder of her best friend in her bookshop. The relationship between Hannah and the policeman had got off to a bad start, but after a trip to Lowestoft the previous Easter in pursuit of a killer, trust and mutual respect had developed between the two of them.

'You'll have the opportunity to ask him yourself as he's on his way here.'

'Really? Iris invited him to the house party?' Darius grinned, obviously delighted. 'No, Aunt Violet did. I don't think she has much confidence in Detective Roper.'

'Even so, I doubt he'll welcome the arrival of a Scotland Yard detective. He'll think he's being undermined.'

'I thought the same, but Aidan knows what he's doing. He'll be discreet. Interesting that he agreed to come with a single phone call, though. He must be missing Aunt Violet.'

Hannah's aunt always refused to discuss her burgeoning relationship with the handsome policeman, but their growing affection was obvious.

'What were we talking about before that?' Darius asked. 'Ah, I know. Did Mr Ellis encounter whoever took the ruby? And if so, why were they in the study at all when the ruby was elsewhere?'

'Exactly.'

'Try this one, then.' Darius seemed to be enjoying himself. 'Suppose the thief thought Millie had put the pendant back in the cabinet after dinner, but when he entered the study to take it, Mr Ellis surprised him?'

'Why would he kill him? If it were me, I'd say, "Sorry, wrong room" or "I was looking for someone," and just leave. We still don't know whether the thief was someone in the house or an intruder. If the latter, wouldn't Mr Ellis have raised the alarm?'

Darius gave this theory all of five seconds' thought, then shook his head. 'No. Mr Ellis knew Mycroft was in the billiard room, so if he had seen a stranger walk into the study, he would have told him straight away.'

'Unless he knew them and didn't want to make trouble?' Hannah suggested.

Darius nodded slowly. 'But the ruby wasn't in the cabinet, so how did the thief get his hands on it?'

'He might have seen Millie enter the drawing room, noticed she wasn't wearing the ruby and assumed she left it in her room. He had plenty of time to go up and take it.'

'A neat story, and fortunately, we don't have to prove it,' Darius said. 'That's Roper's job.'

'I wonder where the ruby is now?' Hannah mused. 'Is it still in the house or did whoever took it hide it somewhere? Or did an intruder make off with it? Not that there is any proof yet there has even been an intruder. Has your room been searched yet?'

He nodded. 'The gentlemen's rooms were the first ones Roper searched.'

'Ugh. Poor Iris. She has to endure the day knowing there's a body in her study.' She shuddered. 'The sooner the mortuary van gets here the better.'

'It's due later this afternoon, I believe. Venables cornered me in the hallway earlier to say the staff aren't too happy about having a detective in the house. That he'll assume they are automatically under suspicion simply because they're servants.'

'I hope that isn't true. Mycroft is unscrupulously fair, even generous towards his staff. Papa always says if he isn't careful, they'll rob him blind. I'm glad Mrs Weberly and Venables are exonerated anyway, though I would have given a lot to have been that housemaid who found them.'

'Nothing like a bit of drama in the servants' hall.' Darius laughed. 'Where would you hide a valuable jewel in this house? If you needed to, that is.'

'I'm not the best person to ask.' Hannah thought for a moment. 'Mycroft and Iris only moved here six months ago, and

I've only visited here twice before. I'm not familiar with all the likely hiding places.'

'There's another matter we need to deal with.' Darius held her gaze. When she failed to react, he added, 'Our engagement announcement?'

'Of course.' She clapped a hand to her face. 'We cannot possibly do it now. Not with a death in the house.'

'It does rather put a dampener on our plans. For the near future, anyway.'

'What about the ring? Detective Roper didn't find that, did he?'

'I thought of that, so kept it with me.' He patted his jacket pocket. 'Can't have him mistaking me for an international jewel thief.'

'International? That's ambitious. The Home Counties, maybe.' She chewed the corner of her lip as a thought struck her. 'Darius?'

'Hmmm?'

'May I see it again? The ring?'

He placed his finger against his nose and pretended to consider this. 'I don't see why you should. After all, we're not official, and no one knows about it but us. If you change your mind, I won't be able to give it to my next fiancée.'

'Next fiancée! How dare you!' She made a grab for his jacket pocket, but he was too quick for her and clamped his hand around her wrist. There ensued a tussle which neither seemed willing to win, combined with laughter and some close-quarter teasing.

Neither heard the door open nor did they notice Maura on the threshold, her arms folded and a wry smile on her face until she coughed to alert them to her presence.

'Oh, hello, Maura.' Hannah froze, one hand buried in Darius's pocket while he held the other above her head.

'Sorry to intrude,' Maura said, though she looked anything but. 'If you aren't using the piano, may I trouble you for the room?'

Darius promptly released Hannah's hand and took a step back. He cleared his throat and tugged down his jacket.

'We were just leaving.' Hannah scrambled to her feet and self-consciously smoothed down her ruffled skirt.

* * *

The afternoon dragged as everyone spent their time avoiding Detective Roper, who wandered the halls asking random and intrusive questions of the entire household. The family and guests gathered together again for afternoon tea in the sitting room, which now represented a refuge, as Roper was required to knock before entering.

No one appeared hungry for food, partly because five minutes after being served, a square black mortuary van swept up the drive and around to the back of the house.

'I don't suppose we can pretend we haven't seen it?' Selwyn asked, dropping an untouched fruit scone back onto his plate.

'Seen what, Mr Atherton?' Rose looked up vaguely from nibbling a biscuit. 'If you refer to that vehicle that passed the window, I'm glad my Basil won't have to remain in the study longer than necessary. I dread walking past that room.'

Lynford and Millie failed to show up for tea at all, and the strains of piano music revealed Maura was at the piano. Madeleine and a still fragile but composed Rose occupied the most comfortable sofa with Norah, leaving Hannah to wonder where Darius had got to.

The carefully prepared plates of finger sandwiches and scones were returned to the kitchens virtually untouched, and soon after, Mycroft, Hector and Selwyn adjourned to the billiard room for what they claimed was a debate over the progress of the war, unfit for female ears.

'Men are simple creatures,' Iris addressed the closed door. 'They're going for an uninterrupted smoke, which Mycroft knows I won't allow around the ladies.'

'Really, Iris?' Madeleine stared at her daughter with admiration. 'I would never get away with that.'

Their ensuing ripple of laughter was interrupted by Dianna's arrival with Sissy.

'Have I missed tea?' She surveyed the empty table, crestfallen.

'It's way past four, Dianna, so I am afraid so,' Iris said, relishing her guest's disappointment.

'It's your own fault, Mama.' Sissy bent to pet one of the spaniels. 'Had you not insisted on arguing with Detective Roper, we'd have got here sooner.' Sissy consoled herself with the remaining brace of almond biscuits left on a plate.

'Oh, well, never mind.' Dianna sighed. 'I'll order some delicacies sent up.' Iris appeared about to speak, but Dianna launched into an impassioned complaint. 'You will not believe how rude that Detective Roper was to me. I really didn't like his manner.'

'I imagine he pays little attention to drawing room niceties, Dianna, but that's his job.' Madeleine raised her feet onto the sofa and stretched its length, possibly to prevent Dianna from joining her.

'Did you answer all his questions?' Iris asked. 'He's more agreeable if you are honest.'

'I'm always honest!' Dianna plumped down on an empty armchair. 'He implied I was being deliberately vague!'

Hannah put down the book she had that moment picked up and prepared to enjoy the scene that was about to unfold.

Sissy hunkered down on a footstool, her feet turned in, so the toes touched, her waist-length dark hair hung loose down her back. How old did Iris say she was, sixteen? Far too young to be dressed like a child or to be dragged around the house by her mother.

'He couldn't grasp the fact my memories are sketchy.' Dianna clutched the neckline of a subtle gown of pale lilac evidently borrowed from Madeleine, though it did nothing for her.

'Which ones, Dianna?' Hannah asked. 'Perhaps we can help fill in the gaps for you?'

'Well, I couldn't remember exactly when I left the sitting room for a few minutes last night.'

'I can't remember either,' Madeleine said, thoughtfully. 'Was it before or after Rose left to fetch her shawl?'

'After, I think.' Dianna seemed unsure. 'Yes, it was after. And I recall Rose said she became lost and came back without the shawl.'

'That's exactly what happened,' Rose insisted, visibly hurt at what Dianna implied. 'Then Hannah found me and showed me the way to the sitting room.'

'You were gone for a while, actually, Dianna.' Madeleine frowned. 'Did you get lost too?'

'No.' Dianna fidgeted with a cuff on the dress as if she hoped the subject would be dropped. 'Anyway, it hardly matters. I told Detective Roper I had ordered Mycroft's motor car to take me and Sissy home, but he refused to allow it.'

'I'm sorry about that.' Iris enunciated her words carefully, her patience thin. 'Had you left last night, as expected, you wouldn't be stuck here with us.'

'How was I to know Mr Ellis would drop dead, and someone would steal Norah's ruby? Neither of which concerns me.'

Hannah kept her gaze on her book, staggered by how anyone could lack such glaring self-awareness.

'I'm certain he hears that a lot in his job,' Sissy said from the window seat, where she swung her feet idly. 'Doesn't everyone claim innocence at first?'

'He's audacious,' Dianna huffed. 'I will not allow him to order me about. I won't have it.'

'I think you'll find he can.' Aunt Violet left the sideboard and strolled to the sofa, cup in hand. 'None of us are free to leave Midwinter without his permission.'

'I cannot stay here,' Dianna insisted. 'It's almost Christmas and I've made plans.'

'What plans, Mama?' Sissy looked up from the contemplation of her feet. 'It's not as if the servants would care if we're there or not. I expect they'll be tippling the sherry in our absence.'

'Sissy, be quiet,' Dianna rounded on her. 'I have made arrangements I cannot change.'

'I know it's inconvenient, but we have no choice,' Iris reminded her. 'I'm sure the detective will eliminate you from the enquiry soon, and then you can go home.'

'I see I have little choice, but I'm not happy, Iris. I really am not.' She flounced out of the room but surprisingly did not slam the door as expected.

'Don't mind Mama.' Sissy crouched before the fire and rubbed her hands together, apparently delighted to have been left behind. 'She hates being told what to do.'

'She seems quite determined to leave,' Hannah said.

'Well, I'm not. I love it here.' Sissy hunched her shoulders in delight. 'Christmas at Midwinter Manor is going to be much nicer than The Laurels with only Mother and the servants to celebrate it with.'

'Then I hope we won't disappoint you, Sissy.' Iris summoned a smile, but the strain showed in her eyes. 'I'm afraid it won't be as exciting as any of us imagined.'

'It already is.' Sissy grinned. 'Mrs Atherton, please may I take the dogs out? I won't go further than the garden, as I've no wish to get myself arrested.'

'I'm sure the dogs would appreciate it.' Iris's smile was genuine this time. 'Mycroft will too, as he hasn't had time to exercise them.'

'She's truly a nice girl,' Iris observed when Sissy had gone. 'And she doesn't deserve Dianna for a mother.'

'We all agree on that,' Hannah said.

'Madeleine, dear,' Rose spoke from the depths of the sofa they shared. 'Would you mind taking me to my room? I feel quite fatigued after a stressful day.'

'I'm sure you do.' Sighing, Madeleine assisted Rose to rise, albeit with little grace, and escorted her out of the room.

'I'm aware this has been an ordeal for Rose,' Iris said. 'But she is treating Mama like her personal nurse.'

'I know.' Hannah smiled to herself. 'Mama wouldn't dare complain, but I bet Papa will hear about it nonstop tonight.'

'You are wicked, Hannah.' Iris tsked. 'Has anyone seen Norah this afternoon?'

'Yes, I have.' Aunt Violet said. 'She was with Detective Roper in the hall about thirty minutes ago. She was hounding him about why he hasn't found her ruby yet.'

'Poor Detective Roper.' Hannah sighed, though it was only politeness that prompted her. In truth, she lacked sympathy for the man. 'Unless he has found evidence of an intruder, the ruby must still be in the house. If so, he should have found it by now, no matter how well the thief hid it.'

A sharp knock on the door announced the arrival of the detective.

'Be careful what you say, everyone,' Aunt Violet said, summoning an ingratiating smile for the newcomer.

'Might I have a quiet word, Mrs Atherton?' Roper had discarded his thin overcoat and resembled a bank clerk in his plain grey suit and crisp white shirt, but without the subservient expression.

'Of course, Detective.' Iris summoned her best hostess voice.

'Your butler has informed me a room is being prepared for another guest expected to arrive later this afternoon. When I instructed no one was to leave the manor, that also included anyone new being admitted to the house. Yet contrary to my instructions, you have—'

'That would be me, not my niece.' Aunt Violet rose from her chair with as much poise as a duchess. 'I've invited a friend to stay since you have forbidden me to leave the premises.'

'And you are?' Roper's brash confidence dissolved as he watched her approach.

'Edwards. Violet Edwards.' Her expression softened and she batted her eyelashes. 'I wouldn't dream of disobeying you, however, he's already on his way here.'

'Er, that isn't the point, Miss Edwards. My instructions were specific, I—'

'Detective, you're a reasonable man,' Aunt Violet wheedled, slowly closing the gap between them. 'It's almost Christmas Eve. Surely you wouldn't expect a house guest to sleep in the snow tonight?' She regarded him with mock horror. 'And he's hardly a suspect, since he wasn't here when the ruby disappeared.'

'I suppose not, Madam, however, I—'

'I knew you'd understand, Detective.' She stared into his eyes for long seconds, then smiled, patting his shoulder before she swept past him into the hall.

'Miss Edwards is quite a formidable woman.' Roper blinked as a slow flush crept up his face. 'Has she always been that way?'

'You have no idea, Detective,' Madeleine said. 'My sister has experience with police officers. You aren't the first she's left disarmed, bewildered and stranded in the middle of a room.'

'I see, well, um, yes, uh.' He rubbed the back of his neck with one hand. 'Well, good day to you, ladies.' He backed away and closed the door softly behind him.

'Correct me if I'm wrong,' Iris said slowly. 'But was Detective Roper positively entranced by Aunt Violet just now?'

'Why would that surprise you?' Hannah smiled to herself. 'She's been fascinating men since we were children. I wish I was half as accomplished with the male population.'

'You don't need to attract men, Hannah; there's one right in your sightline you refuse to see.'

'Is there any tea left in that pot, Iris?' Hannah asked, reluctant to go down that road, although more tea was the last thing she wanted just then.

10

Making good on her promise to spend an hour with Iris and the children, Hannah called into the servants' hall first to fetch Mr Bartleby and took him to the nursery floor. The aloof, lazy cat had proved fascinating to the three older children, who were more used to excitable and energetic dogs.

Mr Bartleby sat on his haunches beside six-year-old Lawrence, known as Laurie, while the boy built a fort out of coloured wooden bricks. Just as he positioned the last brick on the wall, a black paw shot out and swiped the top row onto the floor.

Far from angering him, this seemed to amuse the child, who collapsed into giggles before he calmly reassembled the wall again, only for Mr Bartleby to repeat the destruction.

Iris occupied a nursery chair with baby Sophie across her lap and attempted to fasten an embroidered cotton dress onto the wriggling child.

'Why don't you like Mr Gates?' Hannah laid out a line of bricks and posed the question that had bothered her since their first meeting on the drive. 'You kept glaring at him at dinner last night.'

'Oh dear, I didn't mean to be obvious. Actually, he does nothing I can legitimately complain about. He's perfectly agreeable. Too agreeable.'

'I have no idea what that means.' Hannah narrowed her eyes and watched as Laurie demolished her carefully laid-out row of bricks, this time without the help of Mr Bartleby.

'All the bricks *need* to be the same colour, Auntie Han.' He dragged out the word 'need' then reduced her meticulous work to an untidy pile before he rebuilt it again to his specifications.

'I'll try to remember.' Hannah secretly hoped Mr Bartleby would decimate those, too.

Laurie shared his brother's physical characteristics, but their personalities were miles apart. He was a quiet, serious child determined in his approach to mundane things. Like fort building.

'I didn't want to include him at dinner last night, but Mycroft insisted.' Iris handed the baby back to Fiona, who bore her away for a nap. 'I'm sure Gates assumed Mycroft only married me because he was over thirty with few options, and I had a pushy mother.'

'The pushy mother part is accurate, but not the rest. Mycroft adores you.'

'I know he does, and I adore him.' Iris sighed, and propped her elbows on her knees, her chin in her palms. 'There are times I'm overwhelmed by being Mycroft Atherton's wife. What with all the staff to organise and keep happy, the tenants to worry about. Not to mention all those committees that make constant unwanted calls on my time. I envy you your little house on the Thames.'

'To refer to my house as little is condescending, Iris. It's a delightful Georgian villa with eight rooms. It might be a good deal smaller than Midwinter Manor, but then most people's houses are. And it's not all fun and fairy stories. Have you tried travelling on the underground on a busy Monday morning?'

'I'm sorry, darling, I didn't mean to patronise you. And no, and I don't intend to go near the Tuppenny Tube.' Iris laughed. 'But you chose your life, despite our parents objecting at every turn. You spent Grandma's inheritance on a *house!*' She raised both hands in a gesture of frustration. 'What woman buys a house when you're unmarried?'

'What did you spend yours on?' Hannah raised a cynical eyebrow.

'Diamonds,' Iris murmured.

Hannah laughed out loud, just as four-year-old Matilda emerged from her homemade tent comprised of a sheet draped over two chairs and made a grab for Mr Bartleby's tail. The cat squealed and darted away, knocking over a boundary wall Laurie had just completed.

'Why can't I make a castle like Laurie?' Matilda whined.

'Because you can't.' Sighing deeply, Laurie calmly built his wall again. Iris ushered the little girl to a desk and handed her a bundle of coloured pencils. 'Why don't you draw something?'

Once the children were reasonably settled, Iris returned to her seat. 'It still surprises me you decided to work in Aunt Violet's bookshop. I didn't even know she owned one.'

'Neither did I. She's enigmatic about how she acquired it.'

'Could it have been a gift from a former lover?' Iris whispered, throwing a wary glance at the children, but neither appeared to be listening.

'I've wondered the same thing myself, but I won't press her. Besides, I enjoy working there and when we had to rebuild it after the air raid last year, she made me a partner.'

'My sister, the business owner. Who would have thought? And such a strange choice.'

'Not for me. I spent hours in Grandfather's library when we were young.'

'He bought those books by the yard.' Iris's lip curled in disdain. 'I doubt he read a book in his life.'

'Grandmamma did. And some of them were fascinating. I'd curl up in the window seat and travel with explorers in the Far East or the Americas. All inside my head, of course. You can go anywhere with a book.'

'Huh! I can go anywhere with Mycroft's money.' Iris giggled. 'And maybe you're right. I've given Gates too much importance. Mycroft believes he's saving me work now Gates is here to help him with the estate. That I no longer have to trouble myself. But I *want* to be troubled!'

'You've just said the estate is a lot of work. Overwhelmed was the word you used to be exact.'

'Oh, you know what I mean.' Iris slapped her arm lightly. 'I'm interested then, but he doesn't bother to tell me much now.'

'Then tell him that. He probably thinks your time is taken up with the children.' Hannah thought for a moment. 'Iris, did Gates have access to where the ruby was kept?'

'I suppose so, but he'd be pretty stupid to steal it, wouldn't he?'

'Greedy people aren't always careful. He might feel he's untouchable.'

'I don't see how could have known the necklace was in Millie's room. He left for the staff party promptly after dinner and according to the staff, he stayed there.'

'*All* evening?' Hannah asked. 'Can anyone swear he didn't leave the servants' hall at all between nine thirty and midnight when the party broke up?'

'No one has said he did, much less Gates himself. Actually,' she dragged out the word as her thoughts processed, 'none of the staff vouched for him being there all the time between the end of dinner and midnight, so he could have slipped out for a while. The servants' hall is more than one room and it's not as if anyone was keeping an eye on him.' Iris sighed. 'For my part. I wish he *was* the thief; it would validate my dislike.'

'You don't need justification, Iris. No one is required to like everyone.'

'Quite the philosopher, aren't you?' Iris wrapped her arms around her knees, her warm smile taking the sting from her remark. 'I put it down to all those books. Ideas and knowledge are osmosing through your skin.'

'Oh, do shut up. And osmosing isn't a word.'

'Actually, it's the present participle of the word "osmosis".'

'Really?' Hannah stared at her in admiration. 'I thought I was the bookish one in the family?'

'I've had four pregnancies to catch up on my reading.' She cast a swift look at a noisy altercation on the other side of the room where Laurie had completed his fort and now sat with his sister at the child-sized desk. 'Oh, do stop squabbling, you two!'

'I'm helping Matilda draw,' the boy said in his defence. If help was the right word, when he was hoarding most of the pencils until his sister punched him for not giving her the one she wanted.

'Where's Xander?' Hannah asked, promising herself that if she and Darius had a family, she would stop at two. Maybe even one.

'In his room reading that *Wolf Cub's Handbook* you brought him. You should have saved it for Christmas.'

'I brought others. Anyway, it keeps him occupied and he seems to like it.'

'He loves it. He recites the Wolf Cub promise to anyone who will listen.' Iris rose and moved to the table and divided up the pencils fairly between the children, accompanied by mild threats to throw them all away if they continued to bicker.

'I'd like to see Dianna Dunleavy as the culprit,' Hannah said, keeping her voice low for the benefit of small ears. 'To punish her for flirting with Darius. And for giving her daughter a name like Sissy and making her dress like a twelve-year-old.'

'She was christened Cynthia,' Iris said, laughing. 'It's interesting she was the only one of us to go outside the morning the ruby disappeared.'

'Technically, it was stolen the night before, though there could be some doubt about that.'

'Dianna and Sissy's room is close to the bedroom the girls occupied, isn't it?'

'Next door.' Iris gasped. 'You don't think Sissy took it, then hid it somewhere outside the house?'

'If she did, Dianna put her up to it. That poor girl daren't do anything without her mother's approval. She watches her all the time.'

Iris seemed to consider this, but then shook her head. 'Dianna moans constantly about money, but her husband didn't leave her a pauper. I doubt she'd sink to robbing her neighbours.'

'She was insistent she stayed the night. It was snowing, but not badly.'

'Hannah, really,' Iris snorted. 'I'm beginning to think you've kept company with policemen and murderers for too long. You see villains everywhere.'

'To be accurate they *are* everywhere. I'm simply throwing ideas around to see if they're feasible,' Hannah replied. 'I don't want Sissy to be the thief either. I quite like her.'

The high-pitched whine of an engine brought Hannah to

the window in time to see a motorcycle turn in at the gate. The rider, heavily muffled in a long dark green riding coat, complete with a leather fur-trimmed hat and goggles, sped down the drive. A pair of leather gauntlet gloves encased both hands, head bent forwards over the handlebars as one might ride a horse. Drawing closer, he eased back on the throttle, brought the motorcycle into a gentle curve and skidded to a halt.

'Is that Aunt Violet's policeman?' Iris peered over her shoulder, wide-eyed. 'He came on a motorcycle.'

'It is, but please don't call him that. And the motorcycle is his favourite manner of transport. They use the same model at the front to carry despatches. Aidan bought one himself to take him around town. Well, that's his excuse. I know Guildford is only ten miles away, but I'll bet it was a cold ride.'

'Is it Santa Claus?' Laurie let out a whoop that sent the cat beneath the nearest chair. He uncrossed his legs from the floor and joined his mother and aunt at the window.

'Let *me* see.' Matilda shoved between them, pinched her brother to make him move then pushed her mop of curly brown hair from her face so she could peer through the glass.

Laurie grabbed his arm and scowled at his sister but offered no complaint.

'It is not,' Matilda intoned with all the disgust a four-year-old could muster. 'He's got no sleigh. But he's got a green coat so he could be an elf?'

Iris suppressed a laugh behind her hand and Hannah debated whether to repeat this observation with Aidan later but decided against it.

'Don't be silly, Matilda.' Laurie elbowed his sister. 'Elves don't ride motorcycles.'

'Ow, that hurt!' Matilda raised a clenched fist towards her

brother's face, but Hannah grabbed her arm before she could make contact.

Fiona's expedient arrival put paid to further discussion. They made their farewells to the children and Hannah elicited a promise from Fiona to return Mr Bartleby to the housekeeper's room when he woke up, then she and Iris left the nursery floor.

'When you and Darius have children,' Iris said as they descended the stairs side-by-side, 'it's imperative you don't talk in front of them. They hear everything and repeat it at the most inconvenient times.'

'What makes you think I'll marry Darius?' Hannah contrived to appear shocked.

'Everyone assumes you will. It appears you're the only one who doesn't.'

* * *

They had reached the lower floor where Aunt Violet was helping Aidan off with his coat, one he wore over a tweed suit which looked substantial, but probably didn't keep out the cold effectively, as he visibly shivered.

'Well, that was a bracing ride.' Aidan shook out his hair flattened by his leather helmet and bent to remove his stout calf-length boots. 'You promised me a murder, remember, so have there been any recent developments, Vi?'

'I said it *looked* like a murder,' Aunt Violet corrected him. 'And not, since this morning, no.' Aunt Violet handed the damp overcoat to the butler who bore it away. 'Our local policeman has started questioning the staff and family, but I doubt he's discovered much.'

'If you could apply your skills to locating the ruby, Norah will be forever grateful,' Hannah said. 'And it's nice to see you, Aidan.'

'Hah!' His left boot hit the floor with a thud. 'I'll do my best. Nice to see you again too, Hannah.' His right boot followed the left, both swiftly removed by a hovering Venables.

'Let me introduce you to my other niece.' Aunt Violet stepped sideways as Iris insinuated herself between them, one hand extended.

'Iris Atherton, Mr Farrell, but do call me Iris.'

'It's a pleasure to meet you, Iris. Aidan Farrell.' He stood to shake her hand, then looked down at his feet and up again. 'And as I'm standing here in my socks, I appreciate the informality.'

'It's kind of you to offer your expertise with our dilemma. I also welcome the opportunity to meet my aunt's gentlemen friends. My husband, Mycroft, is in the billiard room with Darius,' she added, ignoring Aunt Violet's hard glare. 'It's the only place they get any privacy now Roper has appropriated the study. I'll introduce you when you get settled.'

'The study?' Aidan looked up from the hall bench where he sat, sliding his feet into a pair of brogues he pulled from a capacious bag. 'Isn't that a crime scene?'

'When she says appropriated, she meant he's barred everyone from going inside until Mr Ellis's cause of death is official.' Aunt Violet lowered her voice though it was hardly necessary. 'But I'm fairly sure we all know what that will be.'

'Hmm. I doubt this Roper chap would allow a random stranger to poke about in there, then? Pity, I would have liked to examine it.'

'Talk to Darius,' Hannah suggested. 'He was one of the first to see Mr Ellis. He has some interesting observations for you. Although Detective Roper seems convinced the two crimes are linked, even without knowing how Mr Ellis died.'

'Ah, one of those, eh? He's devised a theory and now he's trying to get the evidence to fit. That's how miscarriages of justice occur. Is it possible Mr Ellis was killed because he knew the identity of the jewel thief?'

'If he did, he's no longer here to tell us, so how do we begin to prove it?' Hannah said.

'Do you know what the deceased was doing in the study last night? Weren't the other gentlemen playing billiards?'

'No one really knows. Not even his wife or son,' Aunt Violet said.

Aidan planted both hands on his thighs and pushed himself to his feet. 'Bring me up to speed then Vi. I can't wait to find out what I am up against.'

'You must be frozen to the bone.' Aunt Violet linked her arm with his. 'I'll have some tea sent to the sitting room and tell you everything. I'll also warn you what to expect from Detective Constable Roper.'

'I'm rather impressed with your detective inspector,' Iris ventured as they watched Aunt Violet and Aidan disappear through the sitting room door. 'He's very handsome, isn't he? Not quite what one expects in a policeman. He has this masterful quality about him. Aunt Violet seems quite smitten, though isn't he younger than her? Or is that because men age better than we do?'

'He is. But what's five years when you're forty?'

'Oooh, Hannah. You're treading on dangerous ground.' Iris halted, her smile fading. 'Didn't we just tell Inspector Farrell the study was out of bounds?'

'Yes, why?' Hannah followed her sister's gaze to where a figure emerged from the study. The person had their back to the two women, head bent as they eased the door closed and turned the key in the lock. 'Isn't that Mr Gates? Perhaps Mycroft sent him to fetch something.'

'Perhaps, but no one should be in there. Mr Gates?' Iris strode towards him, Hannah close on her heels.

His mistress's voice acted on the man like a gunshot. He froze, his back still turned towards them. Straightening slowly, he hesitated before swivelling to face them, a smile pasted on his face and a brown cardboard file held close to his chest.

'Mrs Atherton. I-I didn't see you there.'

'Apparently not,' Iris said in her best schoolmarm voice. 'I was under the impression no one was supposed to enter the study on Detective Roper's orders.' His momentary alarm vanished like mist. 'His lordship needed some information about the tenant farm at Hillbrook.' He inclined his head to the papers tucked beneath his arm. 'Mr Atherton sent me to fetch it.'

'Oh, I see. Well, you'd better take the papers to him.'

'Mrs Atherton.' Mr Gates inclined his head again and retreated along the hallway.

'Did you believe that?' Iris asked when the secretary was out of earshot.

'I don't know. But that file he was holding had a label with *Hillbrook Farm* on it, so perhaps he was telling the truth,' Hannah replied. 'You really don't like the man, do you?'

'No, which irritates me, as I like most people. He's always perfectly civil towards me and clearly hard-working. Maybe it's me?'

'You cannot possibly envy a secretary, Iris.' Hannah linked her arm through her sister's. 'Perhaps I'm the one who should envy you?'

'Now wouldn't that be a triumph for me, since I've always known you're Papa's favourite.'

'Nonsense.' Hannah smiled, though silently acknowledged it was true.

11

With over half an hour to kill before the dressing bell, Hannah craved some fresh air that was not laden with pine and wood smoke from the various fires Iris insisted were set daily. She collected her heaviest outdoor coat from the row of hooks in the vestibule. Pulling her velvet cloche hat over her hair, she wrapped the thickest scarf she could find twice around her neck. She slid her hands into a pair of thick gloves found in a wicker basket beneath the hall stand and let herself out through the front door.

Taking the path that encircled the house, she kept her head down to avoid slipping on rogue patches of ice when she heard her name being called. Darius gingerly picked his way towards her on the slippery path, determination on his face to keep upright. Laughing at his careful steps, she waited for him to catch up.

'I saw you leave and hoped you wouldn't mind if I joined you.' He halted, breathless, beside her, his bright smile replaced by uncertainty. 'That is, unless you have an important errand to run and I'm intruding?'

'As if you could.' She slid her hand through the crook of his arm, relishing the feel of his strength beside her. 'And what sort of errand could I be running here unless it's a break for freedom?'

'That's not a kind thing to say about your sister's hospitality.' His eyes sparkled with mischief, their combined breath creating a white mist in the air.

'I heard Aidan has arrived, but I haven't talked to him yet.'

'You'd have to wrestle Aunt Violet to the ground first. She's not left his side.'

'She's probably briefing him on the current situation,' Darius said, chuckling.

'Is that what you call it?' Hannah raised an eyebrow, enjoying this newfound intimacy that apparently included risqué jokes. 'He arrived on his motorcycle, and in this weather, would you believe? I expected him to take the train, but Aidan is adventurous. Matilda thought he might be one of Santa's elves.'

'It's those goggles he wears,' Darius laughed. 'I'd be interested to know Aidan's perspective on the case, but he might find it frustrating to have no authority here. It's not as if he can go around questioning people.'

'He knows how to be discreet.' She hugged his arm to her side as they strolled the terrace. 'Do you wish you'd spent Christmas with your father? You must have disappointed him by coming here.'

'I doubt it. Father has a longstanding arrangement to spend the festive season with friends in Norfolk. On Christmas Day they dine on roast goose, drink whisky, swap shooting stories and try to wangle an invitation to Sandringham. Not my idea of a pleasant time at all. I hate guns.'

'Did you say Sandringham?' Hannah stared up at him, impressed.

'Indeed. Papa has many stories of tramping through the grounds after pheasant with King George.'

'It's going to be worth being married to you just to hear those,' she laughed.

'It galls Father that His Majesty is a better shot. Did you know he was once ranked number six in the country?'

'Your father or the King?'

'The King, of course. Father says he has this peculiar way of holding his front arm straight down the barrel.'

'I imagine a monarch can hold his firearm any way he wishes,' Hannah said, sobering as she relived the gunshot they had heard during breakfast, her pace slowing. After the initial unease, Mycroft had established it was in fact the gamekeeper who had been scaring off a fox.

'You're thinking about Lynford Ellis, aren't you?' Darius asked softly.

She nodded, warmed that he understood her so well.

'That incident at breakfast was unsettling. He seemed genuinely rattled.' Darius said.

'I know so little about High Wood, but it's always mentioned in hushed voices.'

'Only those who were there really know what it was like, which was hellish, from what I've heard. I imagine you've seen chaps like Lynford at Endell Street?'

'Maura asked me the same thing, and I have, yes. At least the condition is being recognised as a sort of breakdown, and not cowardice any more. Although I didn't realise he'd been injured.' Darius paused and stared down at her, prompting her to add, 'At dinner, he informed us that his uniform had been damaged.'

'A shrapnel wound to his shoulder, apparently,' Darius replied. 'But it's his state of mind which received the real battering. When they dragged the survivors off the battlefield, they left almost three-quarters of his men lying dead in the mud.'

'That must have been horrible.' Hannah shuddered. 'No wonder he is still suffering.'

Darius slid an arm around her waist, his breath warm on her cheek. 'He has Millie. With her care, he has every chance to get over it.'

'Can you ever recover completely from something like that?'

'I don't know, but it must be hard for him to see men like Mr Gates, who will probably never pick up a rifle, let alone risk being shot themselves. He gets to live in comfort and draw a salary, while better men are dying.'

'Better men?' Hannah smiled, recalling the same thing was being said about the Belgian refugees who had established their own village in Twickenham with well-paid jobs making munitions and sat out the war. 'Don't you like him either?'

'Not me, I'm ambivalent towards the man.'

'I was too, at first, but Iris's hostility has made me think. And Sissy's question at dinner about him not being in the army unsettled him too.'

'Really? I can't say I noticed that. He had a ready answer, as I recall.'

'Too ready.' Hannah shook off the thought. 'Maybe I'm imagining it. Mr Gates has done nothing other than earn Mycroft's trust. Mycroft used to refer to Iris on estate matters, and she feels shut out since he came to work here.'

'A touch of jealousy, then?' Darius suggested.

Hannah offered no comment, but his words gave her pause. Who was Iris jealous of, Mycroft or Mr Gates?

Having completed a circuit of the house, they climbed the four steps onto the terrace which the gardeners had cleared of ice to reduce the risk of slipping. They strolled past the three sets of

French doors and stopped outside the music room where a two-tier fountain stood. Three spacers, each one smaller than the one below, frozen solid the day before, had shed most of their icicles, but the full basin was still solid.

The surrounding fields lay silent beneath a thick layer of glistening snow. A strip of deep orange rippled and glowed like fire as the late afternoon sun slipped below the horizon. Darius drew her to a gentle halt at the stone balustrade to admire the view when Detective Roper walked around the far side towards them.

He wore a dun-coloured suit that he had paired with a canary yellow waistcoat over an ankle-length trench coat. He walked with a slight swagger, which only stressed the confident ease with which Darius wore his military-style charcoal grey suit and overcoat.

'Ah, Mr Clifford and Miss Merrill. How fortuitous. Taking a perambulation, I see?' His gaze slid pointedly to Hannah's spread hand on Darius's forearm. 'My apologies if I have interrupted anything, er, private.'

Hannah experienced sympathy for him, in his skimpy overcoat, his boots thin-soled and the leather cracked.

'Can we help you, Detective?' Darius remained calm, though unsmiling. 'Or are you also in need of the air? Cold, but refreshing, don't you agree?'

'Have you come to tell us you've found the ruby and have the culprit in custody?' Hannah loaded her voice with sarcasm, which earned a pinch on her inner arm from Darius.

'Not as yet, Miss Merrill, but I hope to do just that soon. I've confirmed your whereabouts with the rest of the company on the evening in question, and Mrs Dunleavy said she saw you out here. I was hoping you wouldn't mind if I asked you a couple of questions.'

'I thought we were to be interviewed individually, Detective?'

Hannah asked, annoyed to think Dianna Dunleavy was apparently tracking her movements.

'I'm confident this encounter will fill in any gaps in my investigation.'

'I assume your search of my room revealed nothing of interest?' she asked, still annoyed that, despite knowing it would happen, she had received no warning and returned to discover several items out of place and had still to locate her favourite shoes.

'A process not intended to imply wrongdoing, Miss Merrill.' Apparently, this was the only apology she was going to get, if it was one. 'How well are you acquainted with Mr Selwyn Atherton and his family?' He slapped his gloved hands together and stamped his feet as he awaited her reply.

'I'm not sure how to answer that, Detective. What exactly are you asking?'

'It's a simple question, Miss Merrill. A general response will suffice.'

'I've known Selwyn Atherton since before my sister married his older brother. As to how well I know them, we meet on family occasions, which are infrequent. The last time was my sister's birthday party in May of '14.' Hannah had missed Sophie's christening because of a bad head cold.

'And you, sir?' Roper pinned Darius with a hard stare.

'Me?' Darius said, confused. 'I barely know them at all.'

'Brief acquaintance doesn't prevent one from forming an opinion, sir. And first impressions are often important.'

'Then I decline to answer on the grounds I might unintentionally disparage the family,' Darius replied, stone-faced.

'I see.' Roper drew the words out slowly. 'Then I'll put it a different way.' His voice held a patronising edge. 'Miss Merrill, at any time has your sister mentioned her brother-in-law's family might be experiencing financial difficulties?'

'No, she most certainly has not!' Hannah snapped. 'And I'm not sure what you're implying, Detective.' Her pulse racked up a notch at his audacity, but she reminded herself if Aidan Farrell had asked the same thing, would she have been equally angry? Probably not.

'Might I ask if either of you have ever seen this famous ruby?' Roper asked, appearing unaffected by Hannah's chilly reaction.

'I saw it for the first time at dinner last night,' Hannah replied. 'But I had never heard of its existence until yesterday.'

'The same for me, Detective,' Darius said.

'How close were you to this ruby during the dinner?'

'Close?' Hannah did not understand the question, but Darius was quicker.

He shrugged, replying, 'No closer than the width of my host's dining table, I imagine.'

'Detective,' Hannah began. 'Are you suggesting the ruby wasn't real?'

'Ah, those are your words, not mine.' He seemed pleased with her reply. 'Did you get that impression?'

'The possibility never occurred to me!' Hannah was unhappy with where this conversation was going.

'Precisely.' Roper's smile held triumph, and with an inclination of his head in mock obsequence, he backed away slowly. 'I appreciate your co-operation and assistance, Miss Merrill, Mr Clifford. I shall leave you in peace – for now.' Turning he sauntered away in the direction he had come.

'Did he really imply Selwyn might have plotted to steal his wife's ruby?' Hannah asked, open-mouthed.

'It's the impression I got. Or he believes Selwyn has already sold the ruby and orchestrated a staged burglary at his brother's house to convince everyone it has been stolen. And don't glare at me like that. It's not *my* theory. I'm simply expanding on what Roper said.'

'Well, don't. I was prepared to like him, but I've changed my mind now.'

'He has an unusual interrogation technique, I'll say that for him.' Darius tightened his hold on her arm and began walking again. 'Have you had a chance to talk to Maura Atherton since you arrived?'

'We've had a conversation, yes. Why do you ask?'

'Has she mentioned her father might have financial difficulties?'

'Well, she has not. And surely you're not taking Roper's idea seriously?'

'Not really, but I can see how he developed the idea. People have done worse things when desperate, and before discarding it, we should consider every possibility.' He placed a hand on the small of her back as they entered the hall and walked into a rush of welcome warmth. 'Having the ruby go missing from someone else's home would certainly look less suspicious than stealing it from his own.'

'Darius, what are you saying?' Hannah halted in the act of removing her gloves and stared up at him.

'No, hear me out. That ruby does no one any good being kept in a bank vault, so if Selwyn is in a tricky financial situation, it might be a temptation for him to sell it.'

'We don't know if there *is* a situation.' She bent to remove her outdoor boots and placed them beneath the bench. 'I refuse to see Selwyn in those terms. He's a lovely man. I've known him since I was at school—' She broke off as a maid crossed the hall and disappeared through a door. 'I can't imagine him doing that,' she continued in a fierce whisper.

'Lovely men can find themselves in tough positions, Hannah.'

'Even so, can you imagine Norah agreeing to that? Even if Selwyn proposed it.'

'If Norah even knows,' Darius said.

'Then where does Basil Ellis come in? If Selwyn had gone into the study to take the ruby, Basil wouldn't think anything of it. And surely, he wouldn't kill his own daughter's future father-in-law?' Hannah checked no one was in the hall who might hear them, but still lowered her voice. 'Anyway, Selwyn played billiards all evening.'

'There is that.' Darius thought for a moment. 'I arrived slightly later than the others, as I was with you. Perhaps Selwyn did too.'

'Could we stop this?' She turned around so he could help her off with her heavy coat. 'I'm uncomfortable being asked to suspect Iris's in-laws of wrongdoing.'

'It was merely an exercise in logistics. I wouldn't dream of repeating.' Darius gently unwound Hannah's scarf from around her neck and hung it on the row of hooks. 'Detective Roper doesn't mind upsetting people; it's how he gets results.'

'Not a very nice way of doing it. To disparage those he's never met before.' Hannah pulled off her cloche hat and smoothed down her disarrayed hair.

'Purely for that reason. Selwyn and Norah give an impression of a content and affluent family, but suppose there are undercurrents which make them less than perfect?'

'Like what?' Hannah frowned.

'I don't know, but if Roper is even slightly suspicious of you, I suggest you make an effort to stay civil with him.'

'Why would he have a negative opinion of me?'

'It's the haircut.' Darius pointed a finger at her head. 'They say only chorus girls and flappers wear their hair short.'

'Cheek!' She planted a well-aimed elbow into his side. He doubled over, laughing. 'Not me. I love the way it frames your beautiful face.'

'Well recovered, Mr Clifford.' She was about to move in closer to kiss him, but just then Venables appeared. Like a ghost. She stepped back quickly and pretended to adjust the sleeves of her dress.

'The dressing bell has gone, sir, Miss,' the butler informed them, mildly offended.

'Thank you, Venables.' Darius inclined his head in acknowledgement. 'We promise not to be late for dinner.'

'I'm sure Cook will appreciate that, sir.' He bowed stiffly and withdrew.

'Strangely,' Darius began, his gaze on the retreating butler, 'I was taken back to the day my former headmaster told me how disappointed he was in me when I sabotaged the rugby match against Harrow.'

'He does have that way about him.' Hannah laughed. 'Why did you sabotage a rugby match?'

'Ah, that's a story I shall save for another time.' He slid an arm around her waist and guided her past the Christmas tree, beneath which an impressive pile of wrapped gifts had appeared.

'I've just remembered.' Hannah halted at the bottom of the staircase. 'Aunt Violet asked if we could get downstairs quickly after the dressing bell because Aidan wants to brief us.'

'Brief us? That sounds like one of my Room 40 meetings,' Darius chuckled.

'Don't mention Room 40!' they chorused, both erupting into spontaneous laughter.

Darius claimed his work in secret intelligence was not as exciting as anyone imagined, much of it spent in one room in the old Admiralty building in Whitehall. Room 40 was where a group of cartographers pored over obscure messages intercepted over the airwaves and deciphered using codebooks captured from the Germans. Room 40 had become a private joke between them.

'Aidan insisted,' Hannah said when their mirth died down. 'He doesn't want everyone in the house to know who he is.'

'Not a bad idea,' Darius agreed as he backed steadily towards the staircase. 'Nothing like a Scotland Yard connection to make people clam up.' He bounded up the staircase, calling over his shoulder. 'Bet I get there first.'

'I'll take that wager.' Hannah hitched the hem of her skirt and ran after him.

12

Determined to win her wager with Darius, Hannah chose a sage green gown for dinner, one which needed no help to fasten, and arrived at the sitting room to find Aidan and Aunt Violet were already there with Iris and Mycroft. But there was no sign of Darius.

Hannah accepted a glass of sherry from the tray a footman held out as she entered and went to join Aidan, who stood beside the sofa Aunt Violet occupied. He wore an immaculate evening suit and crisp unwrinkled white shirt.

'I find it hard to believe you brought that suit with you on the back of your motorcycle,' Hannah said, greeting him with a smile.

'I borrowed this one from your brother-in-law,' Aidan replied, straightening his tie. 'I didn't pack mine for Christmas in Guildford. Not many dinner parties there, so I was unprepared.' He splayed his hands at his sides. 'Excellent fit though, eh?'

'It's perfect,' Hannah said truthfully, taking a sip from her glass. 'So, Aidan, who are you supposed to be?'

'I thought I might pass myself off as an aspiring crime writer.' When Aunt Violet scoffed, he looked mildly hurt, but recovered quickly. 'If that doesn't convince anyone, I could always revert to my previous life as a hotelier, which is something I know a fair bit about. I used to work in my mother's establishment in Kensington when I was younger.' He retrieved his sherry glass from a nearby table and moved behind the sofa where Aunt Violet sat.

'Your mother owns a hotel?' Mycroft said from his position beside the fireplace. 'What's it called?'

'The Brunswick.' Aidan grimaced. 'Although we might have to rethink that due to current circumstances. Mother had to talk down an angry mob last year who were convinced it was owned by Germans.'

'I must take you there, Hannah.' Aunt Violet tapped Hannah's arm affectionately. 'I'd love to show you what an establishment looks like when designed by a woman.'

'I quite like the sound of that,' Mycroft said. 'I may even patronise the establishment the next time I'm in town.'

'Do let me know if you so choose,' Aidan said, 'I'll ask her to give you her best suite.'

'Why is he doing that?' Aunt Violet nodded to where Mycroft toured the room offering refills of sherry from a decanter while a redundant footman stood to attention by the door.

'He seems to like it,' Iris whispered. 'I believe he must have been a waiter in a former life.'

Hannah choked on a mouthful of sherry at the same moment Darius sidled through the door. He gave a small start when he saw Hannah, who watched him from the corner of her eye as he collected a glass of sherry on the way to his seat on the sofa opposite her, from where he mouthed, 'You win' and saluted her with his glass.

'Darling,' Iris said to Mycroft, now returned from filling glasses. 'I was just saying to Hannah, I feel strange keeping our new guest a secret from Selwyn and Norah. After all, they're family.'

'I'm aware of that, my sweet, but the fewer people who know the better. Everyone would be on their guard if they knew. Besides, he isn't a secret exactly; we're just being discreet about how he earns his living. And what Detective Roper doesn't know won't hurt him.'

'Vi has explained the circumstances.' Aidan broke off long enough to acknowledge Darius. 'I doubt an official police report could be so detailed and concise.' He smiled at Aunt Violet who coloured slightly. 'This subterfuge is all new to me but I'm rather enjoying it. I'm interested to see how this chap Roper operates.'

'It's all been very difficult.' Iris's voice hitched and she drooped her gaze to her lap. 'This is supposed to be a party, but everyone is so tense. I'm sure everyone checks their rooms hourly in case something else goes missing.'

'Not to mention any other bodies that might turn up,' Aunt Violet added.

'What's the general opinion of this detective chap?' Aidan asked.

Mycroft's smile faded and his thoughts went somewhere darker. 'In my view, Detective Roper has made himself too comfortable here. He's set up shop in the housekeeper's room and according to Mrs Weberly, he orders food and cups of tea at all times of the day. Let's hope the weather doesn't take a turn for the worse or we'll have to accommodate him overnight.'

'I've been told he's banned Mr Bartleby completely, who has now been relocated to the butler's pantry,' Iris said, taking the opportunity to voice her own resentment.

'Bartleby?' Mycroft frowned. 'I didn't know we had a member of staff by that name?'

'He's Hannah's cat, dear,' Iris explained with an indulgent smile. 'He's been entertaining the children in the nursery. Matilda especially will miss him when he goes home.'

'Ah. I see. My mistake.' He scuffed his shoe against the fire-place like a chastised schoolboy.

'He has an aggressive way of questioning people,' Hannah said. 'He makes a vague accusation and then steps back to see what happens.'

'Not the best method to get someone to talk, but it can be effective.' Aidan stared thoughtfully into the dark liquid in his glass. 'Has he established whether anyone other than the staff and houseguests might be the killer?'

'If he has, he's not imparted it to me.' Mycroft's jaw clenched. 'He's keeping his thoughts to himself.'

'He thinks we're all guilty.' Iris turned petulant. 'He made me recall every moment of the night the ruby was stolen. By the time he finished badgering me, even *I* thought I might have taken it.' She glanced towards the door. 'Oh dear, Norah and Selwyn are here. I need to warn you she's extremely upset about her ruby and is bound to bend your ear about it.'

'Don't worry about me, Mrs Atherton,' Aidan laughed. 'I'm an expert with difficult people and will be suitably sympathetic.' He smiled at their approach. 'They look quite pleasant to me.'

'Oh, they are, which makes it all so horrible.' Iris swept towards her brother-and-sister-in-law. 'Selwyn, Norah, come a meet a friend of my Aunt Violet's.'

Aidan kissed Norah's hand and shook Selwyn's like an old friend, then as Iris had warned, she proceeded to engage them in a dramatic account of finding Mr Ellis and the loss of the Calhoun Ruby.

'Mr Farrell, I don't believe you have met Hannah's parents,' Mycroft said as the couple arrived at the door, ushering them closer. 'Madeleine and Hector Merrill, I'd like you to meet Aidan Farrell, a friend of ours from Guildford who has been kind enough to join us.'

'How lovely to meet you.' Madeleine held Aidan's gaze steadily making no attempt to remove her hand from his. 'I do hope our small drama will not spoil your visit. We're all sure it will be sorted out in due course.'

'I've been apprised of the situation, Mrs Merrill, and believe I can cope.' Aidan bowed and accepted Hector's outstretched hand.

Madeleine moved away and took the last seat beside her daughters.

'Murder can hardly be described as a small drama, Mama,' Hannah whispered.

'Do hush, Hannah.' Madeleine glared at her. 'Do you think I'm stupid? He's Violet's policeman, isn't he? What's he doing here?'

'Er, yes. But don't mention that.' Hannah looked to where Aunt Violet was deep in conversation with Maura on a nearby chair. 'Aunt Violet thought he might help with... everything.'

'You might have warned me he was coming. I don't much like being treated like a suspect.' Madeleine absently took the glass her husband handed her while fingering her necklace with her free hand. 'Though he is rather attractive.'

'Mother!' Hannah flushed and looked away.

'Well I think it's rather fun.' Hector leaned his forearms on the back of the sofa, his face level with Hannah's. 'It will be interesting to see which peeler gets to the finish line first.'

'It's not a race, Papa, and no one was told,' Hannah said. 'Well, no one who didn't need to know.'

'Mads, stop sulking and play along.' Hector pushed off the sofa and settled into his favourite wing-back chair by the fire, his sherry glass tilted towards where Lynford and Millie had engaged Aidan in conversation. 'The happy couple seem to like him, and they haven't had much to smile about today.'

'Poor Lynford, as if he didn't have enough to cope with. And don't call me Mads!'

'Mama, everyone calls you that, except Iris and me.' Hannah left her seat and wandered to where Aidan was exerting his considerable charm on Millie.

'Have you come all the way from London in this weather?' Millie asked Aidan.

'No, I was staying locally, but didn't want to miss this wonderful party.' Aidan turned to Lynford, his features softening. 'Allow me to offer my condolences on the tragic loss of your father, Captain Ellis. This must be an awful time for both of you. Especially combined with the theft of your family jewel.'

'That's kind of you, sir.' Lynford inclined his head. 'And much appreciated.'

'We're all so shocked about Mr Ellis.' Millie exchanged a weak smile with Lynford. 'And Mama is devastated about the pendant, but then it meant more to her than my sister and me.' At Aidan's enquiring look, she added. 'Not that we aren't proud of the ruby, only it's been a shadow throughout our childhood.'

'One with a provenance that's hard to live up to,' Maura added as she and Iris joined the huddle intent on the new arrival.

'You must meet Mrs Ellis.' Frowning slightly, Iris gave the room a brief scan. 'She isn't here yet. Is she on her way down? I could ask Mama to fetch her?'

'Er, no,' Lynford replied. 'Mother asked me to tell you she doesn't feel up to dinner tonight. She asked if she might have a tray sent to her room.'

'Of course, I'll let Venables know.' Iris reached for the bellpull then excused herself to greet the latecomers, among them Dianna, who on being introduced to Aidan almost purred when he bent over her hand.

'Have you any theories about the fate of this famous ruby, Mrs Dunleavy?' Aidan asked.

'Me? Oh, no.' Dianna simpered and fiddled with a curl above her ear. 'I was as surprised as everyone else when it went missing. I was in here all evening between dinner and going to bed. Although Mrs Ellis went upstairs to get a shawl, but then returned without it. You could ask her if she saw anything.' She gazed up at him, her knees slightly bent, as if she had been told gentlemen were protective of diminutive women. Though Hannah thought it made her look slightly ridiculous.

'That's not quite true, Dianna,' Madeleine corrected her. 'A little after Rose returned you left the room. You were gone a little while if I recall. Are you sure you didn't see someone in the hallways?'

'Me? Certainly not!' Dianna snapped, detaching herself from Aidan's side. 'I would have said so if I had. Has Sissy come down yet?'

'She's over there with the girls.' Iris nodded to where the three had gravitated to the window seat. Hannah circled the sofa and approached Darius, who now chatted with Lynford by the window.

No more snow had fallen that day, but the sky was inky black, and a smattering of stars appeared in the dark heavens. The rows of trees lining the drive were softened by a lumpy layer of snow as if someone had scattered meringues along the hedgerows.

'My father wasn't an easy man.' Lynford's comment caught Hannah's attention, so she took a chair within earshot, though pretended to be interested in one of Mycroft's spaniels who had wandered in.

'Was he unsupportive of your recovery?' Darius asked.

'He claimed recovery was not what I needed. That if I returned to service and put it behind me, I would be fine.'

'I assume he didn't know what "it" was?' Aidan added, joining their conversation. 'You were at High Wood, I understand, Captain?'

'Yes.' Lynford inhaled slowly before continuing. 'But I won't burden you with any of it. I carry those images with me as a kind of penance I'd hate to inflict on another human being.'

'That's an odd word to use,' Darius said. 'Penance is for the wrongdoer. I doubt you are that.'

'It will always feel like that to me. The truth is, I knew I was leading my men into a trap. I was more scared of disobeying orders than preserving their lives. I should have had the courage to refuse.'

'Then you probably wouldn't be here,' Aidan said. 'To disobey a superior officer on the battlefield can be punishable by death.'

'I still wish I had refused. And I always will.' He exhaled softly. 'My leave is over soon, and I shall have to return to my regiment. My main regret now is I shall have to leave my mother all alone.'

'You must have mixed feelings about that,' Aidan said.

'That's a tactful way to put it, Mr Farrell.' His smile was guarded. 'To be honest, I try not to think about it too much. But I will cope, when there are others in a worse state than I.'

'I hear doctors are doing pioneering work to treat what is now referred to as shell shock,' Aidan said.

'An odd description for it, but better than being accused of cowardice. However, I'm determined not to subject myself to aesthetics or electricity. It might quiet the demons, but the cost is too high. It turns men into mindless shells.'

This heartfelt speech was the most Hannah had heard Lynford say since she arrived and with a sense she was intruding on a male domain, she considered changing seats. However, all the chairs and sofas were occupied and to move might seem too obvious, so she stayed where she was.

'May I ask, if anything unusual happened the day you arrived at the Manor?' Aidan asked Lynford.

'Not really. Father was annoyed by Mother's insistence we stop at an inn, but to be honest, I paid little attention to his griping.'

'Was he always difficult?'

'Always. But he's been worse since I came home. He couldn't understand how I could be medically incapacitated with a minor shoulder injury. My shattered nerves irritated him, so he referred to it as my... weakness. I forgot he's been like that all my life.'

'He took a second job with the War Office, didn't he?' Aidan asked, showing he had not wasted his first afternoon.

'He didn't say much about it, but to listen to him, you'd think he was running the war single-handedly. He was always on the lookout for what he called "enemies of the country".'

'Did he find many?' Darius asked, smiling.

'Not that I knew of.' Lynford laughed, a full-throated, joyful sound that brought all eyes towards him.

'He wasn't unusual,' Aidan said. 'The country is experiencing a mania about spies that borders on paranoia. Most of which are unfounded.'

'I doubt he meant spies, just unscrupulous people who profit during a time of terror and crisis.'

'It's reprehensible, but there will always be those who benefit from the tragedy and misfortunes of others.' Aidan sighed. 'It's human nature.'

Venables arrived and announced dinner, silencing all conversations. Glasses were placed on available surfaces as the guests joined the exodus towards the dining room.

'How much did you hear?' Darius extended his arm to escort Hannah, who gave the dog a final pat before taking it.

'Most of it. It's nice to hear Lynford talking about it. Maura told me he never does.'

'Recovery is slow, but in his case seems sure.'

'I'm so glad. For Millie's sake. A pity his father didn't give him a chance. All he needed was a little patience.'

'Most people are frightened of what they don't understand.' Darius led her into the dining room, where all the elaborate table decorations and candelabras draped with ropes of dried fruit and holly leaves had been re-assembled. Hannah paid silent homage to the servants tasked with making the transformation each evening.

'I hope Mycroft takes a photograph of this room,' Hannah said. 'It's so beautiful it ought to appear in *Vogue*.'

'Under the heading, "Dinner in the House of Death?" perhaps?'

'Ugh. That's horrible.' Hannah sat on the chair Darius held out for her. 'Forget I mentioned it.'

* * *

On her way to breakfast the next morning, Hannah was descending the staircase, when she spotted Dr Eames in the hall below. He still wore his overcoat but held his hat in one hand, though there was no sign of his doctor's bag.

Mycroft emerged from the dining room with Venables and greeted the doctor with an outstretched hand.

'Did I hear you say post-mortem?' Detective Roper appeared from nowhere, his expression daring Mycroft to exclude him. 'I hope you were about to inform me of this?'

'I wouldn't dream of doing otherwise, Detective.'

Watching from her vantage point, Hannah debated whether to alert them to her presence, but envisaged they would wait until she was out of earshot before continuing, so stayed where she was. Unless someone craned their neck up to the landing, she was almost invisible.

'I assume you have no objection to Mrs Ellis and her son being present?' Without waiting for a response, Mycroft nodded to Venables. The butler disappeared into the dining room and reappeared seconds later with Rose Ellis and Mycroft.

Mycroft must have suggested they go somewhere else to talk, but Mrs Ellis was dismissive.

'He can tell me here, and now,' she announced loud enough for Hannah to hear. 'I have no need for another formal interview. I've had enough of that with this individual.' She graced Roper with an up-and-down stare.

'As you wish, dear lady.' Dr Eames removed his glasses and then replaced them on his nose. 'The mortuary is overstretched dealing with soldiers who expire after being repatriated, so they are working extra hours. As a favour to me, an associate carried out a preliminary examination, although a full and official report needs to be transcribed and will reach you in due course.'

'Dr Eames,' Lynford interrupted. 'Would you kindly get to the point? How exactly did my father die?'

'I understand,' Dr Eames conceded, 'that Mr Ellis died as the result of a subdural haematoma; that is, a bleed to his brain caused by a powerful blow to his left temple.'

'Which could have resulted from a fall where he struck his head,' Detective Roper said. 'An accident?'

'The pathologist thinks not. A curved indentation on his left temple was too deep to result from a simple fall. He concluded that Mr Ellis was struck a fatal blow with something heavy and with a curved edge where his skull was at its thinnest.'

Even from where she stood, Hannah saw Lynford's face drain of colour.

'Did-did he die instantly?' Rose brought a shaking hand to her face.

'I cannot say, Mrs Ellis,' Dr Eames replied apologetically. 'That he did not leave his seat at the desk shows he lost consciousness quickly and expired sometime later. A few minutes or an hour, perhaps. The full post-mortem will reveal more.'

'If we had known about this injury, could we have helped him?' Lynford asked.

'I doubt it, Captain. By the time the alarm was raised, and transportation made to a hospital on these icy roads, there would have been no treatment effective enough to save him. Now, if you'll excuse me, I need to get home.' Dr Eames executed a small bow to Detective Roper. 'No doubt there will be calls to answer from patients with colds or sprained ankles precipitated by the snow. Oh, one more thing.' He removed a large envelope from his briefcase and handed it to Lynford. 'This is a copy of the preliminary report for the officer in charge. A full one will be sent to the police officer in charge of the investigation in due course.'

'Thank you.' Lynford accepted the envelope reluctantly as if its existence signalled the final words on his father's life.

Mycroft signalled to Venables, who, having kept silent vigil by the front door, rushed forward to show the doctor out.

'I'll take that if you don't mind, sir.' Detective Roper took the report from Lynford's unresisting hand.

'I doubt it will tell us what we didn't already know,' Lynford said dully.

'That's where we disagree, Captain Ellis. We have yet to find the weapon which inflicted the injury. Now I know what to look for.' He clicked his heels and sauntered away.

'I don't care what killed him, only who,' Lynford said when there were only the three of them. 'Not that it matters much now.'

'I suggest we return to the dining room,' Mycroft said, holding open the door for them. 'I would understand if you had both lost your appetite, but the guests will wish to hear what Dr Eames said.'

Rose nodded and obeyed, followed by her son. Mycroft remained at the open door, then called out, 'You too, Hannah.'

Hannah groaned, and, abandoning any effort to be quiet, stomped down the stairs and joined him.

'This hall has amazing acoustics,' Mycroft said, grinning.

'I cannot say I've noticed.' Hannah lifted her chin and strolled past him.

Hector looked up curiously as they entered, then applied his cutlery to a sausage, while beside him Selwyn forked fried egg into his mouth and continued while Mycroft summarised what Dr Eames had told them.

'I was so hoping there had been a mistake,' Iris said sadly. 'That it was really a stroke or a heart attack, and therefore no one's fault.'

Lynford murmured something to Millie as he took his seat and Maura appeared near to tears and had to be comforted by Sissy, who seemed the most unaffected.

Dianna's face drained of colour, and she pushed away her newly filled plate.

'Was the person who killed Basil the same one who stole my ruby?' Norah asked.

'I thought it was *my* ruby, Mama,' Millie said with asperity.

'You know perfectly well what I mean,' Norah snapped.

'Norah!' Iris raked her with a hard glare. 'Could we forget about the ruby for five minutes?'

'I've changed my mind.' Rose climbed shakily to her feet. 'I think I'll go back to my room. If I could trouble you for some tea, perhaps, Iris?'

'I'll have some sent up,' Iris said, adding, 'No stay where you are, Lynford. Mama will help Rose upstairs.'

Madeleine rolled her eyes at her daughter but complied.

'Oh, yes, of course. I'm sorry.' Norah flushed, apparently conscious she was showing herself up. Again. 'You do look rather peaky.'

'Those eggs were just the way I like them, too,' Madeleine muttered as she slowly obliged and accompanied Rose from the room.

'Very peaky,' Hannah said, but she was looking at Dianna. Her complexion had turned waxy, and beads of perspiration stood out on her forehead. 'Dianna, you look about to faint. Do you need some help?' Perhaps she was not used to close-quarters death, no matter its cause.

'No. I will be fine in a moment,' Dianna made an effort to control her voice. 'It was a shock to hear – well, we all heard it. Only I didn't expect—'

'Expect what?' Hannah stared at her, waiting for her to fill the silence.

'Nothing. I think I'll go to my room too. I feel a little shaky.' Dianna scraped back her chair and made her way to the door.

'I'm sorry, Aunt Iris, but I'm not hungry any more.' Millie clambered to her feet. 'Are you coming, darling?'

Hannah's gaze shifted to where Lynford now stood by the mantlepiece, a cigarette forgotten in his hand as he stared, unseeing, into the flames.

He frowned, confused, then his face cleared. 'Of course.' He examined the cigarette briefly before tossing it carelessly into the fire and followed her.

Hannah wondered briefly what was going through his head, but Darius's welcoming smile as he held out her chair banished the thought completely.

13

After breakfast, Hannah took a walk in the grounds to clear her head. A low mist still clung to the trees, whilst a slight thaw had made the snow underfoot slushy and melted ice dripped from the branches.

When the damp cold started to bite through her gloves and sting her cheeks, she returned to the house, where the clear, sharp notes of a skilfully crafted melody drew her towards the music room.

At first, she wondered if someone was listening to the gramophone, but when she passed the open door, she saw Maura at the piano. Sadness clouded the girl's face, which held a future promise of real beauty with her well-defined jaw and wide brown eyes.

At first, Hannah was reluctant to intrude, but unwilling to leave her to such heavy thoughts she eased into the room and closed the door behind her.

She had wondered if Darius had overplayed Maura's talent, but she was wrong. The girl's skill was exceptional, and it was tragic her parents seemed not to recognise it.

Maura looked up, her fingers pausing on the keyboard and the room fell silent.

'Please don't stop on my account.' Hannah discarded her gloves and scarf on a nearby chair and leaned her forearms on the piano lid, facing Maura over the shiny black wood. 'But if I'm interrupting your practice, I shan't stay.'

'You aren't interrupting me at all, and I need to get used to playing for other people.'

'I'm sorry your Christmas has been spoiled,' Hannah said. 'It must have been a shock to be told Mr Ellis was killed by someone who stole the ruby. Maybe Detective Roper will still find it?'

'I don't care if it's never found.' Maura picked out notes which sounded like random keys, but as her fingers gained speed, they formed a catchy rhythm. 'Do you think Detective Roper was right and Mr Ellis was killed because of the ruby?'

'I really don't know. Perhaps he saw something which revealed the thief's identity.' She repeated what Aidan had said but without conviction. She was as puzzled as anyone.

'The ruby is more of a burden than a treasure. There was some ridiculous story about a curse once, but I never believed it. Even Mama said some Calhoun ancestor probably invented that to stop people stealing it.'

'Possibly, but then even thieves can be superstitious.'

'True. It didn't work though, did it? And it's such a responsibility.'

'Isn't it kept in a bank vault most of the time?' Hannah said.

'I meant the expectations attached to it. What if Lynford and Millie never have children? The ruby will then pass to me, and I have no intention of producing babies.'

'Why worry about something that might not happen?'

'Do you like Chopin?' Maura asked, apropos of nothing.

'Is that what you were playing?' Hannah asked, taken aback

by her rapid change of subject. 'I couldn't identify the composer, but the melody is familiar.'

'It's "Nocturne Opus 9", a piece he dedicated to his sister. Not that there's any symbolism attached to my choice. Millie has a tin ear.'

'You must have worked hard to perfect it.'

'No, not really. It's an advanced piece, but easier than it sounds, especially if you simplify the chords. Some notes are hard to reach, and my hands are smaller than a man's, but I mastered it quickly.' She paused again, throwing the room into silence. 'I hope you don't think I'm conceited saying that?'

'It's not conceit to be aware of your own ability.'

'My music teachers all said I have talent, but if I'm to be a professional pianist I need to study at the Royal Academy of Music.' Her smile faded. 'Not that it's likely. Mother says music is a useful accomplishment for acquiring a husband, but no career for a lady.' She paused before continuing. 'I've no wish to marry. My dreams are not of weddings but playing the piano in concert halls to enraptured audiences.' She shrugged. 'Well, attentive ones, anyway.'

Hannah was about to say Maura might change her mind in time, then remembered how galling casual dismissal was to a young person still discovering who they were.

'Are you going to marry that handsome Mr Clifford?' Maura asked suddenly.

'Whatever makes you say that?' A slow flush crept into Hannah's cheeks that she wished she could control.

'I might be young, Hannah, but I can tell the difference between a friend and a beau. Not that I blame you; he's very handsome and has the most attractive laugh. Oh, and his eyes, they seem to draw one in and yet are kind at the same time.' She looked up and met Hannah's gaze. 'There, you're blushing. I knew I was right.'

'Could I ask you to keep it to yourself, Maura? Neither of us is ready yet for the family's unbounded enthusiasm when they find out.'

'I like secrets, so I'll not say anything.' Maura grinned.

'I had to fight for my independence, too, you know.' Hannah inclined her head. 'And you've met my mother.'

'I have.' Maura giggled. 'Mothers are challenging, aren't they?'

'How was your interview with Detective Roper?' Perhaps that was the reason for her sullen mood.

'Not something I would volunteer for, as his questions seemed designed to try and trap me. He would ask something quite inoffensive, like what time did I go to bed. Then five minutes later he would ask the same thing again.'

'That's a well-known technique to trip you up. I assume he didn't manage it?'

'What?' Her eyes rounded in panic but softened again so fast Hannah thought she had imagined it. 'Oh, I see what you mean. No, he didn't. But he asked me what my perceptions were about the ruby, which confused me.' She caught Hannah's slight frown. 'It was such an odd thing to ask. But I shall tell you what I told him. That I know my parents are happy, but sometimes I wonder if my mother regrets leaving all that wealth behind in America.'

'Your father is far from impoverished.' Hannah hoped that was still true, despite Detective Roper's implication otherwise.

'Compared to the Calhouns, he is. They have a "cottage" in Rhode Island as big as a palace, and so many servants you don't see the same one from one day to the next. I think I impressed the detective, but he's not a man who is easily read. He wrote it all down anyway.' Hannah silently agreed Detective Roper was an enigma, but she didn't want to talk about him. She was more interested in encouraging Maura in her ambition, not that her musical knowledge was extensive enough to judge.

'Don't abandon your dream to study at the Royal Academy of Music, Maura. Bide your time and let your parents get used to the idea.'

'Huh! By then I'll be too old to be a music student.'

'I broke most of the rules before I was your age. And don't be too harsh with your mother. She's very upset.'

'I couldn't exactly miss it. All she cares about is that jewel and getting Millie married off, so she can pass it on down the family. Like we're European royalty or something.'

Maura slammed her fingers down on the keys making a harsh, discordant sound. 'Mother blames her, you know. But Millie just wanted to have some fun and dance with Lynford, and now she's being made to feel she let the Calhouns down.'

'That's nonsense, I—'

The door rattled, and Norah glided into the room, her noisy entrance making Hannah wonder if she had been listening in the hallway.

'Is that how you view your heritage, Maura?' Norah's lips drew into a thin line. 'When I've spent years preserving it for you and your sister.'

'Preserve it for whom, Mama?' Maura sighed, showing this was a recurring conversation between them. 'The pendant will spend the next twenty-one years in a bank vault.'

'You shouldn't expect to benefit. The ruby is a symbol of our family to be treasured for future generations.'

'We won't ever agree on this, Mama.' Maura rose to her feet and faced her. 'But answer me this: what happens now it's gone? What will you dedicate your life and future generations to then?'

'You're being pessimistic.' Norah snorted. 'Detective Roper told me himself he's close to finding the thief.'

Hannah was about to suggest this was rather optimistic of him when Darius's face appeared at the door.

'Hannah.' His gaze shifted to Maura, then returned to her, completely bypassing Norah. 'Detective Roper wants to interview Millie, but she's refusing to do it alone. I suggested you sit in with her. Would that be acceptable?'

'What does Millie say about that?'

'Why didn't she ask me?' Norah protested. 'After all, I'm her moth—'

'He's waiting in the library,' Darius interrupted, before making a rapid exit.

'I almost forgot.' Maura made a show of addressing Hannah. 'I promised to have tea with the children. I'll walk with you, if that's all right, Hannah?'

'Of course you may.' Hannah pretended not to see Norah's mouth twitch with pent-up resentment as they left.

* * *

Hannah gave the library door a peremptory knock and entered, her gaze going straight to Detective Roper, who lounged in a leather wing-back chair by the fireplace. His feet didn't quite reach the floor, making him look slightly ridiculous. A laugh rose in her throat, and she turned her back to close the door carefully, giving her time to compose herself. Once under control, she crossed the room to join them.

'I really appreciate you agreeing to this, Hannah.' Millie twisted in her chair and watched her approach. 'Mama would have accompanied me, but she'd only keep interrupting and complicating things.'

'I'm happy to help, Millie.' Hannah took the empty chair beside her. 'These things can be nerve-wracking.'

'If you are both quite ready, I'd like to get started.' Detective Roper brought his hand down on the desk blotter in emphasis. 'Now, Miss Atherton, tell me exactly what you did after dinner on the evening before last.'

'I went upstairs to tidy my hair and – well, make myself comfortable.' She took a breath before continuing. 'Uncle Mycroft had set up a gramophone for us in the drawing room. I knew the pendant would get in the way while I was dancing, so I took it off and placed it in the drawer of my bureau.'

'What, loose in the drawer?' He raised a sceptical eyebrow.

'No, I put it in the jeweller's box, then inside the drawer.'

'Did you lock the drawer?'

'It didn't have a lock. But I had no reason to believe it wouldn't be safe there.'

'Hmm, well, we all know what "thought" did, don't we?'

'You don't have to be sarcastic, Detective,' Hannah interjected. 'The house was secure, so why would she imagine a member of the family would take it?'

'I wasn't talking to you, Miss Merrill. My questions are for Miss Atherton.'

'I apologise.' Hannah inhaled a calming breath. No wonder Millie didn't want to do this alone.

'When your family arrived at Midwinter Manor for the holiday break,' he said, consulting the notebook on the desk in front of him, 'I understand the ruby was kept in that cabinet.' He pointed his pencil at the tall black lacquered cabinet decorated with white lotus and red dragons at the far end of the room. 'Why not put it back there, when you stopped wearing it?'

'I intended to,' Millie's voice filled with regret. 'But everyone had split up into various rooms and the gentlemen were in the billiards room, so I would have had to disturb the gentlemen's game of billiards to get the key. I decided to wait until morning and ask for it then.'

'Were you aware Mr Ellis was in the study when you left the ruby in your room?'

'No, I wasn't. But had I known he was there, I would have been reluctant to disturb him.'

'Do you have access to the key to the cabinet where the necklace was kept?'

'No. Uncle Mycroft keeps it. Somewhere. I would have had to ask him for it.'

Detective Roper rose clumsily from the chair, which, due to its height from the floor to accommodate Mycroft's height, required two attempts.

Hannah bit her bottom lip to hide a smile, but Millie appeared too nervous to react.

He circled the far side of the desk and slid open the bottom right-hand drawer, removed a wooden shelf with a thumb and forefinger and held it up like a magician. 'As you can see, the drawer has a false base with the key lodged in a groove on the underside.'

'How clever,' Hannah said, genuinely intrigued. 'So removing that shelf wouldn't reveal the key. You would have to know where it was?'

'Exactly. I gather you were also ignorant of this device, Miss Merrill?'

'Yes, I was. There's no reason for me to know about it. But why is it relevant? The necklace was taken from Miss Atherton's room. The key wasn't needed.'

'Which is an important aspect of this case. The cabinet was still locked the following morning when the butler entered and the key where it should be.'

'What exactly are you saying, Detective?' Hannah asked.

'That the thief might not have come in here at all as he was well aware the necklace was in Miss Atherton's room.' Hannah did not respond, mindful that this suggested someone inside the house must have taken it. But who? All the guests apart from three were family, so that left the staff. None of whom she was willing to accuse.

'Miss Merrill, were *you* aware Miss Atherton was not wearing the ruby during the latter half of the evening?'

'No. I saw it at dinner, but not after that,' Hannah replied. 'And I didn't go into the drawing room at all.'

'You retired at around ten fifteen, I believe? Did you see anyone on the bedroom landing when you retired?'

'I-I don't think so, but I wasn't really paying attention.'

Detective Roper scribbled something on a notebook open at his elbow while Hannah considered mentioning her encounter with Darius, and later her brief chat with Maura but decided against it. Aidan had pre-warned her about volunteering information, which had seemed strange advice for a policeman to give, but she heeded it anyway.

'After you left the drawing room, Miss Atherton, you and Mr Ellis—'

'Captain Ellis,' Millie interrupted him.

'Of course. You and Captain Ellis remained in the drawing room for the rest of the evening?'

'That's right. My sister Maura, and Sissy Dunleavy were there too. We played the gramophone and danced until almost midnight.'

'Why didn't you use the music room?'

'Er, is that relevant?' Hannah asked. 'The fact is, they didn't.'

'These are simply routine questions, Miss Merrill.'

'The drawing room is larger, so better for dancing,' Millie replied.

'And when you retired for the night, Miss Atherton, did you check the necklace was still where you put it after dinner?'

Millie blanched and stared at Hannah, then back at the policeman. 'Er, no. I was very tired. We were dancing, and – drinking champagne, so I went straight to bed.' She hesitated. 'Well, not straight away. Lynford escorted me to my room, and we spent a few moments saying goodnight.'

'Outside your room?'

'N... no. Actually, he came inside. But only for a moment or two.' Millie's cheeks flushed red. 'Maura was sleeping, and we didn't want to disturb her.'

'Did Captain Ellis ask about the necklace at any time?'

'No, why would he? He saw it at dinner. Everyone did. Why would he want to see it again?'

'He might have asked where you put it when you took it off earlier.'

'Well, he didn't!' Millie's cheeks flushed angrily.

'And you heard no one enter the room during the night?'

'Not that I remember. But then I sleep heavily.' Her bottom lip trembled. 'It didn't occur to me that the necklace wouldn't be safe with only the family in the house.'

'The family, yes.' He threw them a look before he held up his notebook as if about to give a speech. 'Along with Mr Clifford, Mr Gates, and Mrs Dunleavy and her daughter, Miss Dunleavy. The butler, Mr Venables, Mrs Weberly the housekeeper, the footmen Benson and Griffiths—'

'I didn't know those were their names,' Hannah interrupted. 'Thank you for the explanation, but you can stop now. I see what you're getting at.' Millie fidgeted in her seat and looked about to cry, and Hannah began to feel nervous herself.

'As I was saying,' Roper said slowly, fixing Hannah with a stare. 'There were also several temporary maids brought up from the village to help with the extra work. Young women whom you might never see again.' He lowered the notebook. 'I appreciate people in your circle regard servants as invisible, Miss Atherton, but any of these names could belong to a thief.'

Hannah was about to refute this but saw the sense in his reasoning.

'You've made it sound as if I purposely let the ruby be stolen.' Millie's breathing quickened and her face flushed a deeper red. 'I would never do such a thing. It means so much to Mama.'

'Your mother, but not you?'

'In that it's a family heirloom, yes. But she treasures it more, as it was acquired by an ancestor of hers.'

'And your sister, Maura? How does she view the loss of this priceless bauble?'

'She was shocked, naturally, though I haven't discussed it with her. You'll have to ask her.'

'Oh, I shall, Miss Atherton. I certainly shall.' His gaze stayed on Millie's face. 'Tell me about Captain Ellis.'

'What about him?' Millie's demeanour changed instantly. Her nervousness dissolved and she lifted her chin and met his gaze in challenge.

'I've been informed he suffers from shell shock caused by his experiences at the Somme.'

'He does, but he's improving. What has Lynford to do with anything?' Millie became defensive.

'Did he get on with his father?'

'I-I'm not sure. They weren't close, but whenever I saw them together, they were civil.'

'Civil,' Roper repeated the word thoughtfully. 'Mr Ellis was, I understand – unsympathetic to his son's condition. In fact, the evening he died, wasn't there an incident at dinner?'

'It was nothing,' Millie swallowed. 'And it was over in a moment.'

'But Mr Ellis was less than supportive. In fact, he displayed impatience. Even anger.'

'I believe so, but again, it was nothing.'

Hannah reached for Millie's hand that lay in her lap and covered it with her own. An action Roper saw but ignored. She wanted to tell him to stop but recalled what Darius said about unsettling witnesses and reminded herself he was only doing his job. Besides, Millie was in no actual danger. 'Might Captain Ellis have resented his father?' Roper continued. 'Perhaps such incidents had become a daily occurrence, and he was pushed too far?'

'What *are* you implying?' Millie turned to Hannah for support, her hand gripping her tighter. 'Lynford would never have hurt his father.'

'I didn't say he would, Miss Atherton. That was your assumption.' He consulted his notebook again and a heavy silence descended between them. 'Is it possible Captain Ellis confronted his father over the scorn he showed at dinner? Might he have stopped by the study before he went to the drawing room and struck him in anger? An uncontrollable impulse that left him with a fatal injury?'

'That's an outrageous suggestion!' Millie sprang to her feet, her eyes blazing but tear-filled. 'You have no proof he did any such thing. I've answered all your questions about the ruby, but I'm not staying here to have you disparage my fiancé. He isn't well.' Giving the policeman a final, furious glare, she turned and left the room.

Hannah was about to add her own protest, but Roper seemed to have forgotten Millie and was engrossed in reading his notes again, one hand softly stroking his chin but with no apparent regret. Deciding he wasn't worth it, she followed Millie from the room.

'Millie, where are you going?' Hannah hurried to catch up with her anger-fuelled stride along the hallway.

'Anywhere away from that man.' She halted as Hannah reached her. 'How could he imagine Lynford capable of such a thing?'

'It's his job. He doesn't have a personal grudge against any of us. He's testing you, that's all. He wants you to get emotional and blurt something out he's not aware of.' Perhaps she had learned more from Aidan Farrell than she'd realised.

'I shouldn't have let him anger me.' Millie pulled a handkerchief from her sleeve and blew her nose noisily. 'I'm worried people might believe the worst of Lynford because he's a soldier. He's killed before.'

'The circumstances are entirely different,' Hannah said, although she silently agreed.

'How did it go?' Aidan appeared from an alcove below the staircase, confirming Hannah's impression he had been waiting for them.

'Not smoothly,' Hannah replied when Millie seemed incapable of answering. 'He implied Lynford may have killed his own father.'

'I suspected that might be his line of approach. He's worked out a theory and now he's putting the pieces together to fit.'

'You don't believe Lynford killed Mr Ellis, do you, Mr Farrell?' Millie turned pleading eyes on Aidan.

'I think nothing, Miss Atherton. I'm here purely as a friend and observer.' Aidan's reply was quietly reassuring, but Hannah suspected he purposefully avoided the question.

14

Leaving a distressed Millie being comforted by Lynford in the sitting room, Hannah headed for the stairs, but as she passed the study, she saw a crack between the door and the jamb. She approached carefully and, having checked both ways to see she wasn't observed, eased open the door.

'Aunt Violet?' She addressed a figure she recognised crouched on the floor. 'What are you doing in here?'

'Good grief, I thought you were Roper for a moment.' Aunt Violet scrambled to her feet. 'Quick! Come inside and close the door!'

Hannah checked the hallway was empty before obeying. 'What are you looking for?'

'I'm not sure. But when Mr Ellis was found, was this cabinet locked?' Aunt Violet approached the black-lacquered cabinet decorated with garish red dragons and flowering white lotuses, the kind popular in the last century when Eastern art and furniture were all the rage. She rattled the catch, but the door would not budge.

'It was. Detective Roper made a point of showing me and

Millie where the key was kept and that it had not been touched. What point are you trying to make?'

'That no one knows for certain the thief came in here looking for the ruby at all. So why did they kill Mr Ellis?'

'Perhaps he didn't intend to?' Hannah shrugged. 'He thought the room was empty and when Mr Ellis surprised him, he panicked and attacked him.'

'With what? And in answer to your question, that's why I'm here. I'm looking for a murder weapon. Dr Eames said it was something curved and heavy.'

'Surely Detective Roper would have already found it?'

'Perhaps, or maybe the killer took it with them?'

'What about the crystal vase that was broken?' Hannah suggested.

'Too small and not the right shape, apparently.' Aunt Violet propped both hands on her hips and surveyed the room. 'I suppose I'm looking for something that isn't here. You've been to Midwinter before. Would you notice if anything was missing?'

'Hmm, possibly,' Hannah said. 'Mycroft is a creature of habit, and this study is a copy of the one at Atherton House.' She circled the desk and moved to an open bookshelf bereft of books but which held a dozen or so trophies, all bearing the name Mycroft Atherton for achievements in cricket, rowing and rugby. She picked up a rowing trophy from Mycroft's university – a model of a narrow scull with the figure of a man holding two oars sitting inside, the base made of a rectangle of hardwood with a brass label engraved with Mycroft's name and the date.

'Detective Roper has examined all of those.' Aunt Violet came to stand beside her. 'They all have hard edges and corners so would have drawn blood or left a gouge. At the very least it would have left behind a hair or a skin fragment.'

Hannah shuddered and replaced it where she found it.

'Do you know how many there are meant to be?' Aunt Violet asked.

'Actually, no. But if it's not a trophy, I can't think what it would be.'

'That's not much help, is it?' Aunt Violet leaned a hip against the desk. 'I've tried to work out what happened in here, but it makes little sense. The thief kills Mr Ellis, then tries to get into the cabinet to get the ruby.'

'How? Unless—' Hannah thought for a moment. 'Maybe he knew where the key was kept, opened the cabinet and when he discovered the ruby wasn't there, returned it.'

'Why bother? He's just killed someone, so wouldn't he be too intent on getting out of the room instead of messing about with keys? Or he didn't need the key. I could do it. I wouldn't leave a mark either.'

'Who taught you how to pick locks, anyway?' Hannah asked. 'You never did tell me. Was he a sweetheart?'

'No, he was a—well, never mind what he was. Anyway, it was a joke between us. And I would appreciate you not mentioning it in front of Roper. Now, forgetting Mr Ellis for a moment, let's concentrate on the theft of the ruby. Only Lynford, Sissy and Maura knew Millie had taken the pendant off. Millie and Lynford spent a few minutes saying goodnight in her room. He could have taken it then.'

'Why would Lynford take it? The pendant was Millie's, and they are getting married.'

'Not owned by Millie. In trust to her. What if he and Millie planned it together? They would have had no chance once it was back in a bank vault. But if everyone believed the pendant had been stolen in the middle of a house party, they could sell it later when the fuss had died down.'

'I don't like that theory.' Hannah pouted. 'I'd feel better if a stranger broke in and took it. Even if you are right, the thief sees the jewel is not in the cabinet he has just picked, so then what? He goes upstairs and searches all the bedrooms? That's pretty blatant.'

'Unless he knew which bedroom to search. Someone who knew Millie had taken the pendant off. It might help to know what Basil Ellis was doing in here that night.' Aunt Violet propped one hand at her waist and tapped a pen against her lower lip. 'The other men were playing billiards, so what was so important he abandoned a game to come in here?'

'Making a telephone call?'

'Who do you telephone that late? It was after ten.'

'Maybe he wrote something?' Hannah circled the desk. 'There are some ink spots on the blotter, but they are faded, so probably old.' She did a quick search through the drawers on either side of the desk, which revealed no more than the mundane objects one might expect. Paper, envelopes, dictionary, together with three rather expensive fountain pens.

'Just to play devil's advocate...' Aunt Violet wandered the room, examining statues, books and artwork. 'What if Mr Ellis was on his way to bed, saw the thief coming out of the girls' room, and challenged him? Millie was his son's fiancée, so he would have been protective. Even angry.'

'If he was attacked on the landing, the killer would have had to drag him down here, unconscious,' Hannah pointed out.

'Or dead.' Aunt Violet added.

'All right, dead, then. They would have to bring his body down a flight of stairs and arrange it here by the desk. Mr Ellis wasn't tall, but he was very solid. It would take someone much bigger and stronger to accomplish that. Or more than one person.' Hannah sighed. 'Oh dear. It sounded much better inside my head.'

'That's that, then.' Aunt Violet splayed her arms in surrender. 'Now, shall we go before someone finds us in here?'

'I wasn't planning on coming here in the first place,' Hannah said, throwing a last look at the Chinese cabinet. 'Aunt Violet, would you show me how to pick a lock?'

'Oh!' Aunt Violet clutched a hand to her chest and fluttered her eyelashes. 'I'm so proud.'

'Very funny. I'm serious. Would you?'

'Of course.' Her aunt grinned. 'All you need is a steady hand.'

The door swung open, making them both freeze on the spot.

'Oh, hello, Hannah. Violet.' Mycroft halted on the threshold. 'I didn't expect anyone to be in here.' He stared around vaguely. 'Am I disturbing you?'

'Not at all,' Hannah exhaled a relieved breath 'We were, uh—'

'Admiring your trophies,' Aunt Violet held up a brass figure cradling a cricket bat. 'They're very impressive.'

'Ah, yes. I was quite a star in my Oxford university days.'

'We apologise for being here if we shouldn't,' Hannah interjected. 'But the door was unlocked, and—'

'Don't worry about it, Hannah.' Mycroft stood back to allow both women into the corridor, pulling the door closed behind them. 'I was only checking to see if Roper had left anything behind. He says he's finished in here.'

'Finished?' Hannah said, alert. 'Has he found the ruby?'

'No, he hasn't. But he's made an arrest.'

'Who's been arrested?' Hannah demanded, her voice sharp.

'The footman, Benson.' A nerve beside Mycroft's left eye fluttered, showing the extent of his frustration.

'He's just a boy, and blushes whenever you look at him!' Violet's voice hitched an octave higher. 'I cannot see that shy young man as a jewel thief.'

'I agree,' Hannah said, her own voice tight, mildly peeved no man had ever reacted like that to her.

'No more than I do, Violet.' Mycroft pinched the bridge of his nose with his thumb and forefinger as if warding off a headache. 'Benson has been with me since he was fifteen. Venables trained him and he's always been an excellent worker.'

'Then why does Roper suspect him?' Hannah asked.

'Let's discuss this in the sitting room.' Mycroft stared pointedly at a passing maid who blushed when she saw him staring at her and darted away. Hannah and Aunt Violet had to hurry to keep up with his long stride, their skirts flapping like two eager chickens hoping to be fed.

'I warn you, Iris is extremely upset.' Mycroft halted at the door with his fingers around the handle. 'She has a soft spot for the lad.' Giving the hallway a quick glance, he pushed open the door and ushered them inside.

Darius sat perched on the sofa arm where Iris sat, his hand on her shoulder offering comfort.

Iris looked up as they entered, her hopeful expression fading into abject misery. 'You've heard, then?' she said, bringing a crumpled handkerchief to her nose.

'What happened?' Aunt Violet sat beside Iris on the sofa. Hannah wandered to the window, feigning an interest in the snow, but her intention was to stay close to Darius without drawing attention to the fact.

'That horrible policeman happened.' Iris blew her nose noisily. 'He picked the first person he could bully and jumped to some ridiculous conclusion.'

Mycroft groaned and Aunt Violet muttered something unrepeatable just as Aidan joined them.

'Detective Roper has arrested a footman for stealing the

ruby!' Hannah blurted, but unexpectedly he showed no surprise. His expression that of a man about to deliver bad news.

'I've just left him and he's convinced Benson also killed Mr Ellis to get it.'

'That's ridiculous!' Hannah reached for Darius's hand but at the last second clenched her fist, aware it would draw unwelcome attention. 'He's made an assumption, that's all. There's no real evidence.'

'*We* know that, but Roper appears to have twisted the facts to suit him,' Aidan began. 'Benson was seen on the bedroom landing that night, and according to Roper's theory, the footman saw Millie enter her room minutes after dinner wearing the ruby. That he waited around for her to leave before going inside and taking it before returning to the staff party to establish an alibi.'

'That works if he had prior knowledge Millie was going to take the pendant off, but she didn't decide until she reached her room,' Hannah said. 'And when was he supposed to have killed Mr Ellis in the study? Before or after he took the ruby? It doesn't make sense. And who told you all this? You've only been here a day!'

'I asked to sit in on the interview with Benson as an impartial witness. Surprisingly, Roper agreed.'

'Huh! Only to show off how clever he is.' Iris sniffed and wiped her wet cheeks.

'It would take someone resourceful to make a plan like that work.' Mycroft strolled to the fireplace, his hands held towards the flames, his head turned to his audience. 'And with all kindness to Benson, he's not the sharpest of lads. But I've employed enough servants to know the ones I can trust. The dishonest ones have a certain calculating slyness about them. They avoid eye contact and keep a veil over their thoughts. Benson does neither of those things.'

'I got that impression too.' Aidan tugged up his trousers at the knees and sat in an armchair, one leg crossed over the other as he relaxed into it. 'You ought to work for the police, Mr Atherton.'

This remark brought a guffaw from Mycroft and a watery smile from his wife.

'Who was the witness?' Aunt Violet got straight to the point. 'The one who saw Benson on the landing?'

'I asked Roper that, but he refused to reveal it,' Aidan replied. 'He seemed focused on the fact Benson left the house before breakfast the next morning, before anyone knew the ruby was missing. His parents live in the village, and he went to visit them as it was his morning off.'

Mycroft rose from the chair, jammed his hands in his trouser pockets and paced the room, evidently too restless to sit.

'Roper's convinced Benson has hidden it somewhere,' Aidan added. 'He's having the footman's room turned inside out and has instructed he be kept locked in the cellar vegetable store until he can be persuaded to reveal where it is.'

'Persuaded?' Aunt Violet gasped. 'I don't like the sound of that.'

'Neither do I.' Iris sniffed into the now ruined handkerchief. 'I told him it wasn't necessary. That Benson wouldn't try to run away, but he wouldn't listen.'

'I'd like to know who this witness is too,' Hannah said. *If he or she even existed. And no one has yet explained why Benson would kill Mr Ellis?*

'Unfortunately Benson had no business to be on the bedroom landing at that time of night.' Mycroft sighed. 'His room is in the attic, accessed by the servants' stairs that bypass the bedroom floor.'

'What was Benson's explanation?' Aunt Violet asked.

'He hasn't one. Or he refuses to give it. Either way, Roper is also going to search his parents' home.'

'How awful for the boy's parents, having their home rifled through by police?' Iris said between sobs. 'I'll never be able to show my face in the village again.'

'Is that even legal?' Aunt Violet's mouth worked, showing her frustration. 'Aren't there rules about keeping people in custody and searching houses?'

'In peacetime, I would agree.' Darius relinquished his perch on the sofa arm and took the wing-back chair Hannah's father favoured. 'But the Defence of the Realm Act has meant the police have much wider powers.'

'Well, I think it's disgraceful,' Aunt Violet said. 'And with no insult to your household, Mycroft, I doubt your cellar will make for comfortable accommodation.' She was still speaking when Detective Roper entered the room without knocking.

'It's customary to knock, Detective Roper.' Mycroft's eyes narrowed with disapproval and mild disgust. 'This is still a private residence, although you appear to treat it as your own territory.'

Hannah noticed he did not offer the policeman a seat.

'There's no need for that tone, sir. I'm only doing my job.' Roper tucked both thumbs into his waistcoat pockets and swivelled towards Aidan. 'By the look of your faces I assume Mr Farrell has revealed my intention to charge the young man with the murder of Mr Ellis as well as the theft of the ruby?'

'He has, and we unanimously feel it's a complete farce,' Mycroft snarled. 'I'd like to know what proof you have of either crime.'

'I am not obliged to explain, sir, but given time I feel sure the whole affair will be sorted out to everyone's satisfaction.' He turned to address Aidan.

'I'm also aware you've been questioning the guests, sir.' Roper's ferret eyes scanned the occupants of the room, none of whom met his eyes apart from Aunt Violet.

'*My* guests,' Mycroft reminded him. 'Most of whom are family. Surely it shouldn't surprise you that what has happened is a matter worthy of discussion?'

'Unless you intend to keep us all locked up in our rooms?' Aunt Violet's eyes locked on Roper's until he looked away. Two bright spots of red burned on his thin cheeks as he discovered being on the wrong side of Aunt Violet could be unnerving.

'I allowed you to be present during the interview, Mr Farrell —' Roper said again, then paused and cleared his throat '— because you expressed an interest in interrogation techniques. What I did *not* ask for, was your unsolicited advice on my methods.'

'Which is quite true, and I appreciate your indulgence. However, might I ask you a question, Detective?' Aidan's tone remained conciliatory but uncompromising. 'Do you listen to the answers your witnesses and suspects give?'

'What sort of question is that?' Roper bridled. 'Of course I listen, but most people I question are either complete liars or are economical with the truth.'

'Most people?' Aidan raised a sceptical eyebrow. 'Which suggests you're pre-disposed to ignore anything anyone says.' Aidan leaned forward in his chair. 'When you questioned Benson in regard to the murder, did you pay attention to his response?'

'He denied it, as I would expect.' Roper snorted. 'He lied, of course.'

'What told you he lied?' Aidan's shoulders lifted in a visual question mark. 'Did you notice his eyes, his voice? What he did with his hands?'

'I don't see what—' Roper began.

'Exactly. You didn't see because you weren't paying attention.' Aidan threw up his hands in a gesture of surrender. 'Mention of the ruby completely blindsided Benson. I doubt he had seen the thing, let alone planned and executed a scheme to obtain it. As to suggesting he had committed a murder, I thought the lad was going to faint on the spot. Doesn't it follow that killers are prepared to be accused on some level and have a story prepared?' When Roper did not respond he added, 'Because they are intent on hiding their guilt. Benson hid nothing. He was genuinely horrified.'

Hannah did not mention that Benson was on duty at dinner, so it was likely he had seen the ruby, but she was enjoying seeing Roper's discomfort. By the self-satisfied look on Aunt Violet's face, she was too.

'Sir, I don't know where you obtain your crackpot theories, but in my experience, the louder a suspect protests their innocence, it's a fair bet they are probably guilty.' Roper's agitation heightened his colour, and his eyes darted around the room without settling on anything. Or anyone.

'Probably, but not certainly.' Aidan kept his voice calm and reasonable, while Roper's agitation increased. 'The possibility of doubt remains but you've allowed none. You've made up your mind.'

'Benson has offered no reasonable explanation for his presence on the bedroom floor,' Roper began in an attempt to reclaim his authority. 'Had the footman's presence in the vicinity of the crime been innocent, he would have revealed it. However, he stayed obdurately silent. Therefore, he must be guilty.'

'Silence isn't always consent, Detective.' Aidan uncrossed his legs and fidgeted. 'Assuming guilt, without actual evidence, presents a weak case. Especially as you haven't found the necklace itself.' He caught the warning look Aunt Violet shot him. 'I apologise, though, Detective. This is your investigation and as a... civilian I'll let you handle it.'

'Thank you, sir.' Roper's condescending tone might have been the final irritant for Aidan had he been watching, but his attention was elsewhere.

'Must you keep him in the cellar?' Iris spoke for the first time since the detective had arrived. 'It seems unnecessarily cruel, and it's almost Christmas.'

'Better than a jail cell at Woking police station, Mrs Atherton. He'll get superior food here.'

'We're allowed to feed him, are we?' Mycroft's sarcasm went over the detective's head.

'Did Benson explain why he killed Mr Ellis, who was nowhere near the ruby when it was stolen?' Hannah asked.

'The young gentleman has explained nothing, but I'll get the truth out of him. Now if you'll excuse me, my chief inspector is expecting a written report.' He sketched a perfunctory bow and left.

'Well,' Aunt Violet said into the heavy pause that followed while everyone absorbed what had just happened. 'It appears he's made up his mind. Does anyone have a suggestion as to how we can change it?'

'I'd love to joke about it with you, Vi,' Aidan stroked his chin thoughtfully, 'but I'm afraid the man has a point. I don't believe in coincidences either.'

15

While most of the servants were busy clearing up after breakfast, Hannah entered the basement through the green baize door and crept past the kitchens where staff were diligently tidying up. The smell of hot soap, bacon fat and the clatter of crockery mingled with muted voices and multiple footsteps crossing the clay-tiled floor.

The storerooms on the garden side of the house were partially underground as the land the house was built on sloped down to the river. The windows overlooked a picturesque stone bridge over the water where Mycroft allowed the village children to fish for sticklebacks on warmer days.

She traversed a long corridor that led into a second, shorter one, at the end of which a metal grate sectioned off a storeroom for vegetables and dry goods. The room, if it could be called that, where she found Benson had been modified with a truckle-bed made up for sleep, a chair and a bucket for use as a temporary latrine.

He sat on the edge of the bed, head down and his arms hanging loose between his knees. His hair was unkempt and instead of the smart footman's uniform, he wore brown woollen trousers and a thick, homemade sweater, the open collar of a shirt visible at his neck.

He glanced up as she approached, a frown appearing on his handsome face. 'Miss Merrill? What're you doing down here?' His inquisitive smile vanished, replaced by wariness. 'I hope you haven't come to ask where I put the ruby, 'cos I'm telling you now, I don't know. And I didn't kill that old bloke, either.'

'I'm sure you didn't, Benson. That's not why I came.' She pulled her shawl tighter around her against the chill damp that permeated the walls.

'What do you want, then?' He rose from the bed and approached the metal cage.

'Mr Atherton doesn't believe you are guilty of anything, Benson. Our friend from Scotland Yard is here and he feels there is more to this than Detective Roper has discovered.'

'Couldn't find his arse with both hands, that Roper man,' he muttered without apology. 'And he don't know the half of it.'

'If you tell me why you were on the bedroom floor that night, it might exonerate you.' *Or not.*

He dropped his hands from the metal cage and returned to the bed a couple of feet away. 'I can't tell you that, Miss. Only I'd ask you one thing. Keep that Gates bloke away from Fiona.'

'Fiona? Has Mr Gates threatened her?'

'Only in the way any upper servant threatens young maids in a house like this. He's been sniffing around her, though she's told him often enough, he won't let up. Now I'm out of the way, he'll think he's got a free pass.'

'You won't be here much longer, I promise.' She hoped it wasn't a lie. 'Detective Inspector Farrell is good at his job. He'll find out what happened.'

'People like you, Miss, in your grand houses and driving

about in smart cars, still believe the innocent don't get punished. Well, for the likes of me, that ain't true. I can't tell Roper where the ruby is 'cos I don't know. And I've never killed anyone in my life. Don't mean I won't hang for it.' He released a derisive snort. 'And I thought going into the army was the worst thing that could happen to me.' He threw up his hands. 'Now look at me.'

'Don't lose heart, Benson.' Though she was fast doing so herself. She had come down here in the hope he might confide in her, but it seemed he knew no more than she did. Apart from Andrew Gates being an unpleasant character. But was he a murderer?

'Do you need anything?' she asked feebly. 'Are you getting enough food? Do you need more blankets? It must be cold down here at night.'

'It's not what you'd call comfortable, but I survived last night, and I can do it again. It's Fiona I'm worried about.' He frowned, as if debating with himself, then his brow cleared as he decided. 'Would you tell her she isn't to blame for anything? And I forgive her if she chooses not to tell.'

'Not to tell what?'

A familiar cough sounded behind her, sending Hannah's stomach into freefall. She swung around to find herself face-to-face with Detective Roper.

'Come to nobble my suspect, have you?' He planted both feet in the doorway, his face dark with annoyance.

'I've no idea what that means, Detective,' she said, despite having been around Inspector Farrell long enough to be more than aware of the common terms. 'I came to see if Benson was being treated properly.' Then she cursed herself for sounding so guilty. Aunt Violet wouldn't have done that. She'd have challenged Roper before he could utter a word and he would have done the apologising.

'As you can see, he's fine. No bruises or cut lips, if that's what's bothering you.'

'It wasn't. But thank you for the reassurance that there won't be any, either.' Her courage returned, along with her anger at Roper's sheer lack of compassion. Anyone could see Benson wasn't a criminal. His first and only concern was for Fiona, not himself. She stepped closer to the metal cage until she could feel the stark chill emanating from the metal. 'If you need anything, tell Venables. I've instructed him to come straight to me.'

'Thank you, Miss.' Benson nodded, and his eyes dulled as he resumed his former position on the bed from when she had come in – head down, hands between his knees.

'I'd appreciate you not coming down here again, Miss Merrill,' Roper said. 'Not without informing me first, if you don't mind.'

Hannah gave him a neutral stare, not trusting herself to speak, then swept past him into the dank corridor and had to stop herself from breaking into a run back through the door that led to the upper floor.

* * *

The chime of the dressing bell had not yet faded as Hannah hurried upstairs to change, hoping to step into the nursery and say goodnight to the children. Matilda was already bathed and prepared for bed and her usual chatty self, while baby Sophie seemed pleased to see her. At almost nine months she had developed characteristics which made her interesting to spend time with as opposed to a small creature who cried, slept and fed at intervals.

Her visit to the boys' room was somewhat livelier, where Xander and Laurie were more intent on bombarding her with questions about London and whether she had seen a Zeppelin than the storybooks she had offered to read to them. When she finally left, it was almost time to go down for pre-prandial sherry and with a sigh of relief, she closed the door behind her.

Fiona was outside the door, her back against the wall and hands behind her back as if waiting for someone.

'The boys aren't asleep yet, but they seem quite settled,' Hannah said, making to move past her towards the stairs. 'So you're safe to enjoy the rest of the evening.'

'Er, no, Miss. I wanted to talk to you if that's all right.' She nodded to the room Hannah had just left. 'If you wouldn't mind, could we go back inside for a moment?'

'Of course.' Hannah followed Fiona into the nurserymaid's sitting room, a small but comfortable space with floral curtains at the dormer window and matching covers on the armchairs, two of which were placed on either side of a small fireplace.

Fiona offered Hannah one of the chairs and took the other.

'Is this about Benson?' In the short silence that followed, Hannah arranged her skirt and waited for the girl to speak.

Fiona nodded. 'You and Mr Clifford are trying to find out who killed Mr Ellis, aren't you? Is it because you don't trust that Detective Roper?'

'I wouldn't put it that way, Fiona. We feel he's so determined to solve this case that he's perhaps not approaching it from the right angle. Some of the guests and I have a certain talent for rooting out villains. It's a sort of hobby.'

'Mrs Atherton told me about the nurse who killed that soldier at the military hospital where you work. That's why I thought I'd ask for your help.'

'If I can.' Hoping she wasn't about to make a promise she couldn't keep, Hannah shifted into a more comfortable position on the hard chair, though it helped little.

'Peter didn't take that ruby, Miss. And he didn't kill Mr Ellis either.'

'I believe you, Fiona. But without proof, Detective Roper isn't inclined to listen to us.'

'I want to tell you something, but if I told Mr Roper, he would say I was just making it up to get Peter off.'

Hannah's pulse raced. 'You can trust me to keep your confidence.'

'That's just it, Miss. I don't want you to. I need you to find out more. Then use it to prove Peter's innocence.'

'I'll do my best. What is it?'

'Well. That day the Ellises arrived, Peter served the guests afternoon tea in the sitting room. Everyone was there. The Athertons, their daughters and your parents, as well as Dianna Dunleavy and her children, Miss Sissy and Mr Freddie. Not Mr Clifford though, he didn't arrive until later that day.'

'Did something odd happen?'

'Not then, but afterwards, when I was clearing the tables, I was on my way back to the servants' hall, when I saw Mr Gates with Mr Freddie Dunleavy.'

'Mrs Dunleavy's son?' Hannah recalled Sissy saying her brother was going to join the army in the New Year.

'Mr Dunleavy has been here a lot recently, hanging about in the garage. He likes the motor cars. Anyway, the way he and Mr Gates were talking seemed, well, odd.'

'Odd in what way?'

'Mr Gates didn't seem interested in talking to him, but Mr Dunleavy was insistent. Mr Gates tried to walk away twice, but both times, Mr Dunleavy stopped him. That seemed to be the end of it until Mr Dunleavy pulled out his wallet.'

'Which is when I assume Mr Gates became interested?'

'I should say so. He took however much he was offered and

tucked the banknotes into a pocket and looked around, all furtive like.'

'There was more than one banknote?'

Fiona nodded again, dislodging a couple of pins from her hair that fell onto her lap. 'Mr Dunleavy looked very pleased with himself when he left.'

'I don't suppose you know what that transaction was about?'

'How could I?' Fiona hunched her shoulders. 'But it seemed dodgy to me.'

'I'm sure it did.' Was Gates selling goods out of the house, or was he involved in something more sinister? 'Fiona, has anything gone missing from the kitchens recently, or anywhere else in the house?'

'I doubt it, Miss. Venables has a tight hold on everything. I told Peter what I'd heard, and he said that when he was serving the tea, he heard Mr Ellis – the one who was killed, not the Captain – asking Mr Atherton about Mr Gates.'

'What sort of things?'

'Like where he came from. Where he had worked last, that sort of thing. After the Dunleavys left, Mr Ellis asked to use the study as he wanted to make a telephone call. It might not have been about Mr Gates, but—'

'I'm pretty certain it was,' Hannah said thoughtfully.

Fiona hesitated. 'There's something else, but please don't tell Mrs Atherton or I could lose my job.'

'Fiona, whatever you tell me, I would never be instrumental in you losing your job.'

'Well, all right then. It was the night of the party. I was checking on the children, but I wasn't there long because they were fast asleep. Peter and I had arranged to meet in the empty bedroom. Y'know, just to have a bit of fun. We're betrothed, you see, and he's going into the army soon. We have little time alone together and wanted to—'

'I understand, Fiona.' Hannah held up a hand to silence her. 'Could we get to the next part?'

'We were only there about twenty minutes, maybe half an hour, and then the maids arrived, saying they were to make up the room for Mrs Dunleavy. Peter is a popular bloke, so the maids promised not to say anything to Mr Venables. That didn't stop them from gossiping about me and Peter when they got back to the party. Someone must have overheard them because I'm sure that's how Detective Roper found out about Peter being seen outside the room Misses Millie and Maura are sharing.'

'Was that what he was told? That Peter was outside their room, or that he was on the bedroom landing?' Hannah pictured the layout of the rooms in her head. Dianna and Sissy's room was at right angles to Millie and Maura's room, with the door to the servants' stairs in between.

'I'm not sure. But Peter's silence convinced Detective Roper he was guilty.'

'Why didn't Benson explain what he was doing there?' Hannah persisted.

'Because of me, Miss. He was protecting me.' Her eyes welled. 'Being accused of taking the ruby is bad enough, but murder! He would never do anything like that.' She twisted her hands into the folds of her apron. 'Please say you believe me, Miss.'

'I do, Fiona, and if I can help, I will. But I cannot promise anything.'

'I understand, Miss. But thank you for listening.'

* * *

Hannah collected a shawl from her room before going down to dinner. She was pulling her door closed when she saw Dianna at the door to the servants' stairs talking to Gates. Or rather, she was doing the talking and Gates simply stood passively, his eyes averted while she pointed a finger at him.

Hannah was too far away to hear what she was saying, but Dianna's tone was low, controlled, almost threatening.

Suddenly, Gates's gaze shifted past her and, seeing Hannah at her bedroom door, he murmured something, then backed away and closed the door firmly.

Dianna swung around, and on seeing Hannah, the fierce expression she had aimed at Gates softened. 'Oh, Miss Merrill – Hannah. I didn't see you there.' She removed a shoe, waving it briefly before replacing it. 'I broke a strap on my shoe and was asking that young man if he would take it to be repaired by a maid. He was quite rude and told me he doesn't run errands.'

'Andrew Gates is Mycroft's secretary, Mrs Dunleavy. I expect he was a little insulted.'

'But I only have the one pair of evening shoes with me, so I need them.'

'I suggest you leave them outside your door this evening with a note explaining what you need. I'm sure someone will oblige.'

'Yes, that's what I should do. Thank you.' She stared past Hannah's shoulder signalling the conversation as over.

'Are you going downstairs for dinner?' Hannah asked. 'We could walk together if you wish?'

'I'll be down in a few moments. First, I need to change these shoes, though it's a shame my others don't match this ensemble. I won't be long.'

'I'll see you there, then.' Hannah had taken three steps down the stairs when she heard a horrified shriek behind her.

She turned and ran back onto the landing, following the

sound but unsure exactly where it was coming from. Seeing a bedroom door lay open, she made straight for it and found Dianna inside, frozen in shock.

Hannah took in her surroundings rapidly – a room similar to her own, though far messier, and with a smaller window. A shawl was draped over the bed coverlet, the dresser sprinkled with face powder, hairbrushes and combs but nothing that would cause such instant distress.

'What happened?' Hannah urged, but all Dianna seemed capable of was pointing to where a cream canvas laundry bag lay on the bed. The drawstring was loose as if it had been opened and then dropped quickly.

'It-it was under the bed,' Dianna squeaked.

Hannah dragged the bag closer, releasing a dozen or so white and brown feathers that puffed in a small cloud.

'What on earth—' She waved them away, still holding the edge of the laundry bag.

'Be careful!' Dianna cried, a hand clamped on Hannah's arm.

Irritated over a harmless bag, Hannah ignored her and tugged the bag fully open to reveal a bolster-style cushion in the same cream and green brocade that matched others scattered on the pillows and armchairs.

Was Dianna filching soft furnishings as a bonus of her stay? What did she think Midwinter was, a hotel? The thought bloomed then instantly dissolved at the look of utter fear on Dianna's face. Puzzled, Hannah tugged the cushion roughly from the bag, then gasped at the sight of a knife protruding from the stuffing. It appeared to be a plain kitchen knife, about nine inches long with a thin triangular blade and a bone handle, slightly yellowed around the bolts that held it to the metal.

'Well, that explains the feathers,' Hannah murmured. 'And you found this just now?'

'Well, no.' Dianna swallowed. Her face was pale and her hands shook. 'It was under the bed earlier, but I assumed Sissy had put her laundry there. I was about to put it outside the door just now when I saw... that.'

What was its purpose? To act as a warning to Dianna? But about what? Who would do something like this?

'Dianna.' Hannah dropped the bag onto the floor. 'Do you have any idea who might have done this?'

'Of course not. Some disgruntled servant, obviously.'

'Unless you've been particularly unpleasant to the staff, I imagine they've dealt with far worse than you.'

'You mustn't tell anyone.' Dianna seemed almost desperate. 'Please, Miss Merrill. I would appreciate it if you kept this to yourself.'

'Whatever for?' Hannah was truly shocked. She had assumed Dianna would be the first person to raise a hue and cry and demand the culprit be sought out and punished. But the woman seemed terrified.

'I would prefer not to make a fuss. It's... embarrassing that someone would hate me enough to do such a thing. And if Sissy found out, she would be distraught. She's a gentle child and I don't want her upset.'

Hannah found this last excuse very hard to believe. 'What if whoever did this murdered Mr Ellis?'

'I think I know why the... person... did this.'

'Go on.' Hannah regarded her steadily and wondered what sort of story she was going to come up with now.

'On the night of the dinner, I told Detective Roper that I saw that young footman hovering outside the Atherton girls' room.'

'How so, if you spent the entire evening in the sitting room with the ladies?'

'I completely forgot, but I did leave the sitting room for a few moments. I came up here to – to freshen up – and that's when I saw him. The footman.' She twisted her hands in front of her. 'Roper must have told him what I said, and it made him angry.'

'A knife through a cushion is way past anger.' Or maybe not if that was the snippet of information which got Benson arrested.

'One never knows how people will react. One of the other servants must have done it in protest.' Dianna seemed calmer now as if she believed what she was saying. 'I know how loyal servants can be to one another.'

And treacherous. Although Benson was courting the nursery-maid, Fiona. Would she do something like this out of spite?

Careful not to touch the knife, Hannah shoved the cushion roughly back inside the bag, collected up the loose feathers, and tossed them on top before pulling the drawstring tightly closed so she wouldn't have to look at it again.

A female voice called from the landing, answered by another, more distant sound, then the rhythm of rapid footsteps followed until the hallway fell silent again.

'All right. If you really feel this was a harmless prank.' Hannah hefted the bag in one hand. 'But I'm going to hang on to this, in case there's another incident. Next time it might not be aimed at you.'

'Thank you, Hannah. I won't forget this.'

Neither will I.

16

Having stashed the bag in the bottom of her wardrobe, Hannah entered the sitting room where Millie occupied the smallest sofa with Lynford, their absorption in each other a clear message not to disturb them. Norah and Selwyn sat opposite Hannah's parents with Iris, while Mycroft handed out glasses of sherry arranged on the sideboard.

Maura and Sissy sat side-by-side on the window seat, their conversation, if not exactly animated, seemed amiable, if slightly forced, making Hannah wonder what article of clothing Maura had been asked to share this time.

The absence of Dianna was something of a surprise after their encounter upstairs, but her recent discovery was too interesting to keep to herself, so having greeted her parents, she approached Darius and Aidan in light conversation by the fireplace.

'You look positively furtive, Hannah,' Aidan said, smiling. 'Have you been looking for clues?'

'Not deliberately. However, I stumbled across one quite by accident which might be of interest.'

'Those words, "quite by accident", suggest something entirely different.' Darius frowned at her over his glass. 'What have you been up to?'

Ignoring him, she gave the room a swift appraisal. Satisfied no one was interested in their conversation, she briefly explained about Dianna's unwelcome gift.

'Are you serious?' Darius lowered his glass, almost spilling the contents.

'Shhh!' Hannah waved him to silence. 'I wouldn't make it up. It's in my wardrobe if either of you would care to look.'

'You took it?' Aidan said, aghast. 'Whatever for?'

'I'm not entirely sure, but I'm not happy with Dianna's explanation as to how it got there.'

'Explain.' Aidan eased closer, listening intently.

'She did scream, but then so would most people at finding something like that. But then she pleaded with me not to tell anyone.'

'Hmm, not quite the reaction I would have expected from her,' Darius mused. 'She's usually an attention seeker.'

'Exactly. It was as if she knew who had done it and was, well, embarrassed, I suppose.'

'Did she suspect anyone?' Aidan took his turn in the back-and-forth questioning.

'No one specific. She believes it's revenge for informing Detective Roper that she saw Benson on the bedroom landing the night Mr Ellis was killed.'

'People – and I don't just mean servants – can be vindictive if they feel someone is the cause of their misfortune.' Aidan gave the room a slow appraising glance, his attention pausing on the footman.

'Whoever it was didn't exactly choose the most dramatic method,' Hannah said. 'If he wanted to scare her, why not arrange the cushion on her pillow so she would see it when she entered the room? Why leave it in a bag under the bed?'

'Timing.' Aidan took a sip from his glass. 'Leaving it hidden means we cannot pinpoint exactly when it was placed there.'

'That makes sense. At first glance, it looked like laundry, and the maids make up the rooms after breakfast. If it was there then they would have taken it with them.' Hannah broke off as Mycroft approached looking distracted.

'No more bad news, I hope, Mycroft?' she asked.

'Not pleasant, certainly. I've fielded several complaints this afternoon about Detective Roper's mode of questioning. Mrs Weberly has reported two housemaids have threatened to quit in tears.'

'He's been quite civil with most of us,' Darius said. 'But I don't like the idea he's flexing his muscles with the servants just because he suspects one of them.'

'It's not a policy I follow,' Aidan said. 'Everyone deserves to be treated well, no matter their station.'

'Mycroft, couldn't you persuade him to allow Benson to be confined to his room instead of the freezing cellar?' Hannah asked.

'Believe me, Hannah, I've tried,' Mycroft replied. 'He's confident his methods will break Benson down and he'll have a confession out of him by tomorrow.'

'Hannah.' Aidan seemed to sense her frustration. 'If you want to do something productive, see if you can find out from Mrs Ellis what her husband was doing in the study that night.' He raised his glass to where the lady occupied an armchair. 'She's reluctant to talk to me and I don't want it to appear to be bullying her.'

'I'll see what I can do.' Glad to be doing something useful, Hannah placed her half-full glass on a nearby table, and made her way across the room, exchanging a word here and there with a guest. Reaching Mrs Ellis, she prepared to offer more condolences but changed her mind. The poor woman had probably had enough of those that day. 'Mrs Ellis.' She sidled up to the lady's chair. 'Might I get you a sherry?'

'That's kind of you, dear. But as you can see, I'm being well looked after.' She raised her two-thirds-full glass and lowered it again. 'But please, do sit beside me.'

Hannah obeyed. 'Would you mind if I asked you a question?'

'You're more than welcome, but I've already been interrogated by that detective chap. Roper, is it?'

'I might have one that Detective Roper has not thought of.'

'Oh, that will annoy him, if true. He's such a pompous man. And please call me Rose. I feel we've all been through far too much to stand on formality.'

'If you prefer not to answer, I will understand. But do you know what your husband was doing in the study that night?'

'Hah, why would he tell *me* anything?' She caught Hannah's surprised start and softened. 'Sorry dear, and don't mind me. Basil was a private man and had secrets. When he started that government job it was worse. I hardly got a word out of him that wasn't about dinner or the weather.'

'Did you ask him about it?'

'Oh, yes, but all he would say was that it was important war work, and he couldn't discuss it.'

'I sympathise.' Hannah smiled but did not elaborate.

'He used to have his own business in food acquisition and distribution, but when the war began the government took over. Instead of foodstuffs, meat and dairy products going through agents like Basil, provisions were being sent directly from farms to the troops overseas. Our income was considerably reduced, and Basil was embarrassed that he needed to seek other work, so I tried not to make it worse for him.'

'Life has become harder for many people because of the war, Rose. He had nothing to be embarrassed about. Which department did he work in?'

'I've no idea. Something military.' She shrugged. 'He travelled into Woking every day, but he did say he was protecting us all from scoundrels.'

'At dinner on the night he died, he mentioned you stopped at an inn on the way here.'

'Of course, dear. I haven't lost my memory.' She placed a liver-spotted hand lightly on top of Hannah's that was surprisingly warm, almost comforting. 'I needed a break and Basil wanted to have a smoke, so I insisted we stop so he didn't stink up the motor car with the smell.'

Thankfully, Hannah would never have that problem with Darius, who shared her aversion to smoking. 'Did something or someone at the inn attract his attention in some way? Did he get agitated or angry?'

'No, nothing as obvious as that.' Rose thought for a moment. 'We sat in the lounge, and I did notice Basil kept looking over into the public bar. He seemed preoccupied, but I'm used to that so took little notice.'

'Did he talk to anyone?'

'Other than to castigate the landlord, no. Not that I saw.' Rose laughed as if she had told a joke. 'He was probably annoyed by someone's lack of manners. Basil was very intransigent with people he felt were not behaving in a certain way.'

'He was judgemental?'

'Exactly.' Rose smiled. It seemed even in death she displayed reluctance to criticise her husband.

'And later, when you arrived at the Manor. Did he say anything?'

Rose studied a picture on the wall, her eyes distant as if deep in thought. 'Whatever it was must have stayed with him. Basil quite rudely interrupted Iris when she was introducing Mrs Dunleavy and her children. He insisted he needed to use the telephone.'

'I don't suppose he said who he was calling?' Hannah expected a negative answer but asked anyway.

'I wouldn't have listened if he had. I was quite annoyed with him by then. Besides, he returned to say the person he wanted to speak to was not there.'

'In your opinion, Mrs Ellis – Rose – would your husband have tried again? The night he died perhaps?'

'I cannot say, my dear. More likely he wanted to smoke another cigar in private and without my complaints.'

'Possibly.' Hannah smiled. 'Well, thank you for speaking to me, Rose. And I hope I didn't upset you.'

'Of course you didn't, my dear and you're very welcome. You know, despite losing my Basil, this has been a very enjoyable Christmas thus far. Iris has been such a wonderful hostess and made us so welcome. I'm delighted Lynford is marrying into this lovely family.' Her eyes lit up and she aimed a bright smile at Hannah. 'Perhaps we'll meet again at Lynford and Millie's wedding?'

'Um, yes. That would be lovely.' Bemused, Hannah moved back to the fireplace where Darius now stood alone. He guided her to chairs on the other side of the room. Iris had carefully arranged the seating in pairs, enabling semi-private conversations.

'Well? Did she have anything interesting to say?' Darius waited until she was seated before asking.

'It's more what she didn't say. She didn't mention Benson having murdered Mr Ellis once. If it were me, I'd be down in that cellar to have it out with Benson and demand to know why he did it. Rose seemed more interested in telling me what a lovely time she's having and invited me to her son's wedding.'

'Hmm. Is the grieving widow not grieving enough?' Aunt Violet said as she joined them with Aidan, apparently hearing this last remark. 'They were married a long time, so she hasn't adjusted to him not being here. She probably expects him to walk in any moment.'

'Or she's still in shock,' Aidan ventured.

'Hmmm, maybe.' Hannah still felt magnanimous toward Rose, despite her odd reaction.

'Or maybe Basil Ellis wasn't an easy man to live with?' Aidan suggested.

'Are any of you?' Aunt Violet raised a sardonic eyebrow at him. 'Why do you suppose I remain happily unshackled? Too many of my friends marry only to discover their husbands are neglectful or downright cruel.'

'Don't write off our entire gender, Vi.' Aidan looked momentarily stricken before his smile returned. 'Not that you're wrong. Married women have few rights and I see too far much violence against women in my job.'

'I didn't mean you,' Aunt Violet said as they exchanged a look of such intensity that Hannah turned away, conscious she was intruding on a private moment.

An image of Eva Ledbetter floated into Hannah's mind. An animated redhead with a winning smile for whom her aunt had risked her own reputation to help divorce an abusive husband. It had taken years to achieve and even then, Eva had to leave London and live in obscurity to avoid the scandal.

'Anyway.' Hannah cleared her throat, demanding their attention. 'I didn't find out much about Mr Ellis's job other than it was something to do with the military.'

'That could be anything, and not necessarily be linked to his murder.' Aidan's brow furrowed. 'I wish we knew what he was doing in the study the night he died.'

'Apart from getting his head bashed in, I really can't tell you,' Hannah said.

Darius glanced past her, gently removed Hannah's empty sherry glass from her hand and placed it beside her aunt's on the mantel. 'Iris has just announced dinner, so we'd better go in.'

'Good, because I'm starving.' Aunt Violet slid her arm through Aidan's and dragged him away.

* * *

'I've spoken to DS Roper, Dianna,' Iris said once the maids had withdrawn and everyone had commenced eating. 'Now he's made an arrest, he says you're free to return home.'

'I'd rather stay if you don't mind.' Dianna's smile over the rim of her wine glass encompassed the table as if daring anyone to show displeasure. 'I feel I ought to support Rose. She needs a friend badly during this terrible time.' She cast a sympathetic glance at the lady beside her, though Hannah half expected to see sharpened teeth.

'We're more than capable of that, Dianna,' Iris said defensively. Not that Iris herself had spent much time with Rose since Basil's death, Hannah thought. She had left Madeleine with that burden. Possibly, Hannah thought, in revenge for her mother's lack of involvement with her grandchildren.

'But you're going to be family, and family can often be difficult at times like this.' Dianna cocked her chin at Norah and Selwyn. 'And Sissy would be delighted, wouldn't you, dear?' The look she aimed at her daughter dared her to correct her, which Sissy did not.

A footman sidled to Iris's chair to impart something in a whisper. Dismissing him, Iris scraped back her chair. 'Excuse me, everyone. It appears I have a small domestic problem to sort out.'

'Well, *I* don't understand it,' Norah snapped when the door had closed on Iris. 'They caught the thief, so what excuse can he have not to return my ruby?' Norah exclaimed.

'Mama, no one believes Benson is guilty, except Detective Roper,' Maura said.

'He's the policeman,' Norah sniffed, refusing to give any ground. 'If he says the footman is guilty, then he probably is.'

'I can't see him as the thief either, Mama.' Millie gripped the stem of her wine glass but shook her head when the footman stepped forward to refill it. 'And I don't say that because he's nice. What would he do with a valuable necklace? I doubt he has contacts in the criminal world.'

'Wouldn't he pawn it?' Norah said. 'Boys like him, from poor households, pawn things all the time to keep food on the table.'

'No self-respecting pawnbroker would risk buying something like that from a footman. It screams stolen goods,' Lynford said. 'Nor would he get nearly as much as it was worth.'

'Which would still be a fortune to someone like Benson,' Dianna added.

'As long as I get it back, I really don't care.' Norah stared at Millie. 'Why are you all championing a mere footman?'

'Mama, could you please stop talking about it?' Maura slapped the flat of her hand on the table, making the glasses jump. 'People are losing relatives, sweethearts, their homes and livelihoods in the hundreds every day because of this war, and all you care about is some necklace. The newspapers say that next year when America joins the allies, your own countrymen will start dying in the hundreds. Have you given a single thought to any of that?'

'Selwyn!' Norah drew herself upright, her thin lips puckered between a pout and a kiss. 'Aren't you going to reprimand your daughter? I refuse to be spoken to like this.'

'In all conscience, Norah, I cannot.' Selwyn tossed his napkin onto the table and sat back. 'She might be a little strident in her opinions, but I cannot fault her reasoning. You have a nephew who will probably have to put on a uniform in a few months. Has that occurred to you?'

'James?' Norah's voice hitched. 'You're talking about James? But... He's just a child!' The genuine horror on her face showed this was the first time she had considered the possibility.

'He's Norah's brother's son,' Selwyn offered the company in explanation. 'He's twenty and old enough to wear a uniform.' Selwyn finally silenced his wife, who seemed to diminish a little in her chair.

Iris returned to the table, a slight flush to her cheeks as she resumed her seat.

'Is everything all right?' Hannah lowered her voice to ask.

'Not really.' Iris replaced her napkin on her lap. 'Detective Roper questioned Fiona rather harshly this afternoon. Then he ordered her room be searched. He had Venables and the footman drag everything into the hall. They were even ordered to dismantle her bed. He dragged her away from the children, so she had to leave them with a housemaid.'

'Why didn't you stay with them?' Madeleine openly eavesdropped.

'I was busy with Cook organising the menus.' Iris glared at her. 'Anyway, that's irrelevant. Roper has concluded that Fiona was in on the robbery all along and only has to prove it.'

'Did he find my ruby?' Norah demanded eagerly, alert to their conversation.

'No, of course he didn't,' Iris snapped.

'Where did he get the idea Fiona was involved?' Hannah asked.

Iris sighed. 'Apparently, the maids who made up Dianna's room walked in on Benson and Fiona together in the bedroom.' She lowered her voice to a whisper.

'You don't sound very surprised,' Madeleine said.

'I'm not.' Iris sighed. 'I've known about them for a while but didn't want Mycroft to find out they were courting. He disapproves of fraternising between the staff and would have sacked one of them. Most likely Fiona and I didn't want that.'

'I see.' Hannah chose not to admit she was already in possession of this information. 'I can see it would be impossible to replace either of them.'

'I doubt you do.' Iris met her gaze. 'And not simply because I might lose my only nurserymaid. Peter Benson will probably be conscripted next year, so it would have been cruel to separate them when that will probably happen anyway.'

'Sorry, I didn't mean it the way it sounded.' Hannah winced.

'Good, because that was something Mother might say, and you're better than that.'

'Excuse me!' Madeleine grabbed her wine glass and turned her shoulder to her daughter.

'Thank you. I think.' Chastened, Hannah asked, 'Has Roper arrested Fiona?'

'Well, no, but I suspect Fiona thinks he will and is terrified. Mrs Weberly caught her sobbing her heart out in the kitchen which is why they sent for me.'

'Iris, dear, are you going to share whatever is going on at your end of the table?' Mycroft's demand caused conversations to break off and glasses halt in mid-air.

'I might as well tell you.' Iris sighed, then repeated everything she had told Hannah before levelling a pleading gaze on her husband. 'I'm sorry, Mycroft, but I didn't want to spoil things for Benson and Fiona.'

'Really, Iris, did you believe me ignorant about those two? And I'm determined that nothing will happen to Benson either. He's innocent.'

'Why didn't you tell me?' Iris stared at him, open-mouthed. 'I've been ducking through doorways for ages to ensure you didn't see them.'

'For the obvious reason. If I admitted to knowing, I would have had to discharge one of them. Despite appearances, I need to seem to be master in my own household.' This remark brought bursts of laughter and a few sniggers from around the table, sending a deep blush into Iris's cheeks.

'Good policy, though,' Hector said between mouthfuls of chicken fricassee. 'Last thing you want is the gel getting in the family way. Most inconvenient.'

'Not always,' Norah said with a triumphant smile. 'My housekeeper was having a liaison with next door's chauffeur, so when she announced her... news, we insisted they get married. Now she works at both houses, and he drives for us too. It's worked out well, what with the terrible servant problem caused by the war.'

'Though maybe not so well for the couple – doing twice the work – or their child,' Hannah pointed out. The only person in the room who acknowledged this remark with anything like understanding was Darius.

17

Dinner broke up early with unanimous refusals of card games, billiards or music in the drawing room. Even Maura expressed reluctance to practise the piano and joined the party in the sitting room for coffee, like threatened animals herding together for safety while eyeing their companions with suspicion. Lynford leaned against the mantlepiece, a cigarette forgotten in his hand as he stared unseeing into the flames.

'Lynford, dear, you're miles away,' Rose said indulgently. 'I've asked twice if you would get me a coffee.'

He frowned as if confused, but then it faded. 'Of course, Mother.' He pushed away from the mantel and approached the sideboard.

'I wonder what's going through Lynford's head.' Darius waited until Hannah was seated.

'I dread to think, but he must be so confused.' She moved aside to make room for him on the sofa. 'He came home hoping for normality after chaos, and it's apparently followed him.' Though she detected no real closeness between father and son when in each other's company. And who could forget

Basil's treatment of what he saw as Lynford's 'weakness' at dinner?

'If we've put doubt in Roper's mind about Peter Benson, perhaps he's turned his interest towards Lynford as Basil's killer. I wouldn't put it past him to goad Millie.'

'For what purpose?'

'To deliberately upset her enough she would run to Lynford and reveal his suspicions about him.'

'Wouldn't that be a bit contrived?'

'He didn't have to believe it. Not if he could make a convincing case against him. Much as he has done for Benson. If he can make the evidence fit, it's enough.'

'That's a cynical view of the police force.' Hannah hoped he was joking but he probably wasn't.

'Ask Aidan if I'm mistaken, then accuse me of cynicism. You have to see it from Roper's perspective. Basil's contempt for Lynford that night at dinner was disturbing. I'm guessing that wasn't the first time he behaved like that.'

'You suspect Lynford might have snapped and attacked his own father?' Maura had described him as kind and understanding, but then any man could be pushed to the edge, especially one affected badly by his experiences at the Front.

'It's not a scenario I'm comfortable with, and besides, Lynford has an alibi,' Darius reminded her. 'He was with the girls in the drawing room all evening, remember? But let's not make a case for Roper. That's *his* job.' He patted her hand briefly and rose. 'I'll get you a coffee.'

'There's something I meant to mention,' Hannah said when Darius returned with two full cups. 'Only that episode with the cushion pushed it right out of my head.'

Darius resumed his seat, followed by a footman who held out a tray that held several glasses of brandy.

Hannah declined but Darius took one, crossed one leg over the other and leaned back, one arm draped over the back of the sofa almost touching her shoulder.

'Don't tell me. You found a signed confession shoved under your door but without a signature.'

'I only tolerate your sense of humour because I cannot think when you're this close.'

'Really?' He grinned, pleased with himself. 'I don't think a woman has ever said that to me before.'

'Oh, please, Darius.' Hannah rolled her eyes. 'There's modestly and there's self-delusion.'

'That's a little harsh. All right, then. You're the only woman that has said it who mattered to me. Is that better?'

'Marginally.' She sliced him a sideways look. 'As I was saying, I had an interesting talk with Fiona upstairs on the nursery floor earlier.'

'Interesting as in a spicy piece of gossip or pertinent to the investigation?'

'You'll have to decide for yourself. She pleaded Benson's case and about their liaison in the bedroom, just as Iris said.'

'Hmm. Could Fiona have been responsible for the cushion thing?'

'I wondered that myself. For about five seconds. She's a sweet girl and more scared than angry. Besides, now we know Dianna isn't the only one who reported it to Roper. Fiona was too scared to explain when Roper questioned her the first time, and now that Peter has been arrested, he would assume she was making it up if she explained now.'

'Yes, I can see that. Which doesn't make Peter innocent.'

'No, it doesn't. That aside – and here's the interesting part – she witnessed a conversation between Mr Gates and Freddie Dunleavy.'

'Goodness, the girl gets everywhere. When does she have time to care for the children?'

'Darius!'

'Sorry, I'm being flippant. Carry on with your story.' He took a thoughtful sip of his brandy, the rich aroma on his breath strangely alluring.

'Fiona couldn't hear what they were talking about, but from what she saw it was an awkward conversation which ended with money changing hands.'

'Now, that *is* interesting.' He thought for a moment. 'When was this?'

'The day the Ellises arrived, Mrs Dunleavy, Freddie and Sissy were here for tea. I would like to know what they discussed. What was Freddie paying for? Information, or something else?'

'I don't know either. Perhaps Freddie wanted something from the estate and offered Gates money for it? What if we search Gates's room? We might find whatever it was?'

'Unless the item has already changed hands.' Darius broke off to decline Mycroft's offer of more brandy.

'I doubt it. Freddie hasn't been here since,' Hannah said. 'Besides, if there was anything to find, wouldn't Roper have found it already?'

'I was thinking of something less obvious but equally incriminating, which if Roper saw, he might not have realised its significance.'

She eased closer and lowered her voice. 'Yesterday afternoon, Iris and I saw Mr Gates coming out of the study.'

'Not exactly suspicious, Hannah. Roper released it back to Mycroft as there was no evidence to be found there. He isn't sure how the vase got broken but assumed the killer did it.'

'Could it have been used to kill Mr Ellis?'

Darius shook his head. 'Too light and small to have delivered a blow with enough power to damage his skull.'

'Gates was definitely shaken when Iris confronted him. I just don't know why.' She absently stirred milk into her coffee. 'I feel so sorry for Iris. Her house party has devolved into a disaster. Norah is upset and Maura is irritated one minute and broodingly quiet the next. Even my mother is tense and not much rattles her.'

'And yet, have you noticed how Selwyn and your father don't look at all bothered?' Darius asked.

'Huh!' Hannah snorted. 'That's because they allow their womenfolk to do all the worrying. Why do you suppose I'm always poking about in other people's business?'

'You said that. I didn't.'

Hannah didn't respond; she was too busy working out how to keep Gates away from his room so they could search it.

Madeleine and Dianna occupied adjoining chairs and had apparently found something to talk about, although there was no sign of either Aunt Violet or Aidan. This made Hannah smile, wondering which of the rooms in the house they had chosen for a liaison.

A whispered but fierce conversation taking place between Norah and Maura caught her attention and shamelessly she eavesdropped.

'I've imagined that prize around your sister's neck since she was born, so I wanted to savour it a little. Losing it was the worst tragedy of my life.'

'Don't be so dramatic, Mama.' Maura failed to hide her frustration. 'Millie isn't even a Calhoun; she's an Atherton.'

'How dare you speak to me like that, Maura. Apologise immediately.'

'At least now I won't have to parade around wearing it like

some museum exhibit,' Millie said, not taking her eyes from her book.

'Leave the girl alone, Norah,' Selwyn muttered. 'Has it occurred to you that your obsession with Millie and that jewel might make Maura feel inadequate?'

'That's ridiculous! I've always tried to show pride in both of them.'

'Mama.' Millie clapped her hand down on her book before tossing it aside. 'If you won't change the subject, I'm leaving.' She gazed around the room. 'Has anyone seen Lynford?'

'I saw him leave the room a moment ago. He could be in the drawing room, dear,' Dianna said helpfully.

'Thank you.' Millie nodded her thanks to Dianna and left without attempting to shut the door quietly behind her.

'Millie was always the more sensitive of my daughters.' Norah broke an awkward silence that followed Millie's departure.

'I don't believe in outdated traditions either,' Maura said, biting into her third petit four. 'If I had the ruby, I'd probably sell it to pay for my piano tuition.'

'You don't need more tuition, Maura. You play beautifully.' Norah raised her chin haughtily. 'Your tutor cost us quite enough and you're more than adequately skilled now.'

'Beautifully is for after-dinner entertainment in drawing rooms, Mama. But not nearly good enough for the Vienna Opera House.'

'Vienna Opera House?' Norah snorted. 'What a ridiculous notion.'

'Hannah,' Madeleine called from across the room, interrupting them. 'You shouldn't monopolise Darius, darling, it's antisocial.'

'It wasn't intentional, Mama, we were, er, discussing—'

'Chopin,' Darius blurted.

'Don't be coy, darling,' Madeleine coaxed, unconvinced. 'We'd all like to hear what you were talking about.'

Several pairs of eyes turned their way in expectant and enquiring faces.

'Well, um...' Hannah searched for a non-committal response but was saved from replying when a maid on her way out of the room gave a squeak of alarm and flattened herself against the open door as a black streak came flying across the carpet and shot beneath the sofa where Madeleine sat.

'What on earth was that?' Madeleine leapt to her feet just as Mycroft's two springer spaniels came barrelling after it, with their flying tails and flapping ears, adding to a general panic as cups were toppled from tables while they barked excitedly.

'Get the dogs!' Iris flapped her hands at the maid who grabbed the collar of the nearest dog, whose paws scrabbled madly at the rug but was too big to get under the sofa.

Darius boldly leapt into the fray and with admirable agility grasped the second dog's collar just as the animal made a leap over the back of the sofa, causing Rose and Dianna to scream in alarm.

'It's just a couple of dogs,' Maura said but was visibly trying to conceal her laughter as she launched into the general chaos.

Footsteps along the hall announced the arrival of Venables, who viewed the frantic scene with alarm. 'I'm so sorry, Madam, but he got away from me.'

'I assume you're referring to the cat cowering under the sofa?' Iris said, one hand hooked beneath the collar of the excited spaniel attempting to get its head in the three-inch gap between sofa and floor.

'Apologies everyone, this is entirely my fault,' Hannah said from where she crouched on the floor and gently tugged the black bundle of fur from beneath the sofa.

Seeing no further threat, the cat snuggled in Hannah's arms, purring and occasionally hissing angrily at the restrained dogs whose excited barks reached a crescendo until two footmen arrived to haul them from the room.

Hannah handed the cat to Venables, who shrugged an apology and made a hasty retreat.

'I cannot believe you brought that animal with you.' Madeleine roughly brushed dog hairs from her skirt before resuming her seat.

'That quite upset my nerves.' Dianna tutted and headed for the sideboard where she poured herself a brandy.

'Whatever was that all about?' Aunt Violet entered the room on Aidan's arm, her skin slightly flushed. 'Did we hear barking?'

'You did. Mr Bartleby paid us a surprise visit, and the dogs objected. Thankfully, no harm was done.'

Darius tugged down his jacket and adjusted his tie before resuming his seat, lowering his voice. He exchanged a teasing look with Hannah. 'Bartleby's timing was impeccable, though.'

Once the dogs were removed, the room emptied as one by one the guests retired to their rooms though it was barely nine thirty.

'Where's everyone gone?' Aidan said as he and Aunt Violet collected coffee and nightcaps from the sideboard and joined Hannah and Darius on the sofa opposite. 'Was it something we said?'

'It's been a difficult day.' Hannah offered them a weak smile. 'I might have an early night myself.'

Hannah gathered her things in preparation to retire just as Venables returned, minus the cat, and went straight to Mycroft's chair.

'Excuse me, sir, but there's a gentleman in the hall, wishing to speak to Mr Ellis.'

'Does he mean Captain Ellis?' Mycroft asked.

'No, sir. He definitely said Mr Basil Ellis. I'm not sure what I should tell him, if anything.'

'Did he give a name?' Aunt Violet asked.

'He declined to say, Miss. He said it was on a matter of importance and he was here in response to a request. Shall I tell him Mr Ellis is unavailable?'

'Can't turn him away on a snowy night.' Mycroft eased out of his chair with a grunt. 'Fellow deserves an explanation. In the absence of our detective, would you care to accompany me, Mr Farrell?'

'With pleasure.' Aidan slid his untouched coffee onto a table and followed him out.

'What do you suppose that was about?' Hannah asked when the door closed behind them.

'No idea, but as the party appears to have broken up, I'm off to bed too.' Aunt Violet placed her brandy glass on the table, nodded a brief goodnight, and left.

'Why didn't Mycroft ask you?' Hannah said, slightly miffed. 'You know more about the situation than Aidan.'

'I suppose he feels having a high-ranking policeman in tow avoids awkward questions.' Darius eased closer, his thigh pressing against hers on the squab. 'And I intend to enjoy this excellent brandy.'

Darius did just that, but he had barely swallowed the last mouthful before Aidan returned and came striding towards them.

'You might want to hear what this chap has to say.' He cocked his finger in a 'come here' gesture. 'We're in the Library.'

Hannah exchanged a look with Darius before the three of them set off along the hallway. 'Your contacts with the War Office might lend some gravitas to the situation,' Aidan said as they walked. 'Being military, this man might be more willing to speak to you.'

'Who is he?' Hannah paused at the library door that Aidan held out for her to enter first. 'What about Aunt Violet? She's not long gone upstairs, and I'm sure she'll want to be here too.'

'Drat,' Aidan muttered, then signalled to Venables who waited in a nearby alcove. 'Please would you go and ask Miss Edwards to join us?'

'Of course, sir.' The butler sped away.

Smaller than the other main rooms in the house, the library curved at one end, the walls crammed to the ceiling with stocked bookshelves so not one inch of wall was visible. Two library ladders ran on rails around the room. A small fireplace and several upholstered chairs were arranged on rugs scattered on the floor to form small reading corners. Hannah inhaled the smell of old and new leather mixed with lavender wood polish and smoke-ingrained carpet, her gaze going to a spare, regal-looking gentleman who rose smoothly to his feet when they entered.

'Good gracious, a committee!' he declared good-naturedly, his amiable smile in contrast to his severe appearance. Every inch of him screamed 'civil servant', from his severe black suit and round horn-rimmed glasses to his sparkling white collar and neat black tie. Even his shoes were immaculate; highly polished despite the snow outside, which suggested he had left a pair of galoshes at the door.

'This gentleman is from the Military Tribunal,' Mycroft said, looking pointedly at Darius.

'Aldershot branch,' the gentleman finished for him.

'Did I hear there was a visitor?' Aunt Violet asked, joining them.

'Allow me to introduce Mr Clifford, who is with the War

Office, and these ladies are my sister-in-law, Miss Hannah Merrill, and my wife's aunt, Miss Violet Edwards. The gentleman who left us in rather a hurry a moment ago is Detective Inspector Farrell from Scotland Yard.'

'Detective Inspector? Goodness, I didn't expect that.' The newcomer adjusted his horn-rimmed spectacles, confused but not yet alarmed. 'Ambrose Featherstone-Haugh.' He returned Aidan's handshake before acknowledging the ladies with a slight nod. 'I was hoping to speak to Mr Ellis. Is he not here?'

Aidan took charge as they took seats. 'I'm sorry to have to inform you that Mr Basil Ellis was murdered here two nights ago.'

'Murdered? Gracious.' Mr Featherstone-Haugh breathed the word. 'That explains the involvement of Scotland Yard. Were you called in to investigate?'

'Ah, no, I'm a houseguest of Mr Atherton's,' Aidan explained. 'The officer in charge of the investigation is a Detective Sergeant Roper.'

'Should I be speaking to him?' Mr Featherstone-Haugh adjusted his spectacles.

'If you wish, although he won't be back until the morning.'

'I see. Well, if he needs to speak to me, he can call my office.' He withdrew a pasteboard card from an inside pocket and placed it on a table at his elbow.

'What exactly is your function at, uh, Aldershot?' Aidan asked.

'I can answer that,' Darius interjected. 'The Military Tribunal's primary function is to deal with men who are unfit for service. They approve, issue and validate exemption certificates.'

'Very precise, sir.' Mr Featherstone-Haugh nodded sagely. 'How was Mr Ellis, er, despatched, if I might ask an indelicate question?'

'A blow to the head, which proved fatal,' Aidan replied.

'How unfortunate, and brutal.' Mr Featherstone-Haugh removed his glasses and peered at them from arm's length before replacing them. 'And has the perpetrator been identified?'

'Not as yet,' Aidan replied. Hannah opened her mouth to correct him, but Darius directed a painless yet firm nudge to her with his shoe, silencing her.

'May we ask why you wanted to speak to Mr Ellis?' Darius asked. 'Was it on Tribunal business?'

'I assume so, but he revealed little in his letter.' He rummaged in a slim leather briefcase that sat at his feet and withdrew a sheet of quality cream bond, handing it to Aidan. 'I received it three days ago.'

Hannah glanced past his shoulder as Aidan read, but the handwriting was difficult to decipher, though the crest at the top was familiar.

'Mr Ellis wrote this on Midwinter Manor stationery the day he arrived.' Aidan slanted the page so both Mycroft and Darius could see the date.

Featherstone-Haugh nodded. 'As you can see, he says the matter is confidential and I should be discreet but does not explain why he wished to talk to me.'

Aidan handed the letter to Darius, who gave it a brief scan before handing it back to its owner, who replaced the letter in his briefcase.

'Did you and Mr Ellis work together?' Hannah asked, forgetting too late she had promised to allow Aidan to do the talking.

'I am his superior, and although our paths crossed on occasion, Mr Ellis worked at the Woking office.' He sighed. 'I was hoping for more information, but it appears I am too late.'

'In your opinion, sir,' Aidan began. 'Could Mr Ellis's death have anything to do with his writing that letter?'

'I cannot say, and it's not as if we can ask him now.' Mr Feather-erstone-Haugh placed a finger against his cheek as an aid to thought. 'One thing has occurred to me since I received it, but it's purely speculation.'

'And what is that?' Hannah and Darius said together.

'Since conscription was instigated in January of this year, large numbers of certificates have disappeared, that is, stolen, from the office. Some young men are desperate not to go into uniform and think nothing of purchasing a forged certificate. It's quite lucrative and go for anything between ten shillings to five pounds. Part of my job is to detect these and prosecute the offenders.'

'Was that Mr Ellis's job too?' Hannah asked.

'It was, but he was less experienced, so he tended to refer suspected cases to me.'

'And you think this is what he was alluding to in his correspondence?' Aidan asked.

Mr Featherstone-Haugh nodded and removed a second card from an inside pocket that he handed to Aidan. 'Should you discover more, I would appreciate you contacting me. This is a serious matter, you understand.'

'I do indeed. And of course I shall,' Aidan said, mildly surprised. 'Thank you for calling, Mr Featherstone-Haugh.'

'It was no trouble.' He pushed his glasses further up the bridge of his nose and climbed to his feet. 'Mr Ellis's death is most regrettable. He'll be a loss to the department, being one of our more diligent officers. I sincerely hope you find the culprit. And despite these events, I hope you all enjoy a Happy Christmas.'

18

'That was interesting, if mysterious,' Hannah said when Venables had been summoned to show their visitor out.

'Mr Featherstone-Haugh described Ellis as one of his most diligent officers,' Darius mused. 'That could be significant.'

Aidan nodded thoughtfully. 'It suggests Mr Ellis might have felt the subject was confidential and should not be committed to paper. Everyone is obsessed with security these days.'

'Like someone carrying a forged exemption certificate?' Hannah said.

'I'm confused.' Aunt Violet drummed her fingers lightly on the arm of her chair. 'Why not write that letter from his place of work or his home? Why here?'

'Because something happened between his home and the manor which he thought was worth reporting,' Darius said.

'How many people on this estate have exemption certificates of service?' Hannah asked of her brother-in-law.

Mycroft thought for a moment. 'The two gardeners are too old, so they don't require one, but my chauffeur failed the medical.'

'You have a chauffeur?' Aunt Violet asked, surprised. 'I haven't seen one since we've been here.'

'Dixon is in Northumberland to spend Christmas with his family, but he'll be back the day after Boxing Day,' Mycroft said. 'I doubt he would do anything to attract the personal attention of a man like Featherstone-Haugh. Oh, and Gates is exempt as he's a chronic asthma sufferer. I've seen his certificate,' he said as if to confirm the truth of it. 'I cannot imagine either of them attracting the attention of someone from the Military Tribunal.'

'That's because you believe the best in everyone, Mycroft.' Hannah leaned over the arm of her chair and gave him a one-armed hug. 'Was Dixon here when Mr Ellis arrived?'

'He was,' Darius said, nodding. 'He admired my Rover, as I recall. I noticed he had a pronounced limp.'

'Which was genuine,' Mycroft interrupted. 'He had polio as a child.' He slapped his palms down on his knees and straightened. 'Well, it's all a puzzle to me. What with Ellis's murder and this ruby business, I don't know what's going on. Now I'm off to bed. Goodnight, all.'

A round of *goodnights* and *sleep wells* followed Mycroft from the room, leaving Aunt Violet, Aidan, Darius and Hannah alone in the library.

'He looks worried, Aunt Violet observed. I don't think he liked us casting aspersions on his staff.'

'I'm not doubting his chauffeur, but is anyone else sceptical of Mr Gates's claim to be a chronic asthmatic, or am I echoing Iris's dislike for the man?' Hannah asked.

'My great-uncle had it, and he wasn't a well man,' Aunt Violet said. 'Even a walk upstairs would leave him wheezing. He had this odd whistle when he breathed and cold weather always left him breathless. He couldn't stand open fires either as the smoke irritated his chest.'

'That sounds like a severe case. Maybe Gates has a milder version? While not affecting him in a civilian job it would still be enough to keep him out of the army.'

'Possibly,' Hannah conceded. 'But Gates looks so, well, sturdy and has a good colour to his complexion. I've never heard him have trouble with his breathing, either. The first day Aunt Violet and I arrived, he had just walked four miles through snow in freezing temperatures, yet he positively glowed.'

'I don't think you should condemn the man on appearances alone, Hannah,' Darius said.

'I'm not condemning anyone, I was only speculating,' Hannah replied.

'She has a point though.' Aidan ran a finger down his nose, thinking. 'A man like Featherstone-Haugh doesn't make house calls on a whim.'

'Could Mr Ellis have been referring to Gates in that letter?'

'Possibly, although I'm not suggesting we confront him. That will get us nowhere,' Aidan said.

'Then what *are* you suggesting?' Aunt Violet suppressed a yawn.

'Gates would need to keep his certificate close in case it's asked for,' Aidan said. 'I wouldn't mind having a look at it.'

'How do we do that?' Darius asked. 'Mycroft has seen it once; what excuse could he use to ask to see it again?'

'Then we won't ask. We'll search his room.' Darius turned to Aidan. 'I assume you'd be able to spot a forged certificate?'

'I'm game.' Aunt Violet straightened, all previous signs of fatigue dissolving. 'But what if it *is* a forgery? It's not as if we could arrest him.'

'Neither could I, officially,' Aidan said. 'Although Detective Roper could. However, I'd rather not tell him until we know for sure. If I'm wrong, we'll make fools of ourselves.'

Darius looked up as the door opened and Mycroft appeared. He strode to a table by the window and retrieved a volume bound in blue leather. 'Forgot my book. Sorry to disturb you.' He started to back away again, but Darius halted him.

'Mycroft, would you be willing to involve yourself in a little subterfuge?'

'Darius!' Hannah gasped. 'You can't ask that of him.'

'That depends on what sort of subterfuge.' Apparently unfazed by the suggestion, Mycroft paused in front of them, the book clutched to his chest.

'Tomorrow evening, I want to search someone's room and I need the occupant to be kept busy for a while.'

'Hmm, which particular occupant are we talking about?'

'Mr Gates.'

'My secretary? Good grief, do you suspect the chap of wrongdoing?'

'I'm not accusing him of anything—' The door clicked again and Venables appeared.

'Oh, I'm sorry, sir. I didn't realise anyone was here. I came to damp down the fire and turn off the lights. I'll come back.' He backed away again.

'No, Venables do come in,' Mycroft said. 'You might be able to assist us.'

'I'd be happy to, sir, if it will help Midwinter go back to normal again. Mrs Weberly and the staff are extremely upset by the goings on. I don't want anyone else to threaten to leave as it's almost impossible to get staff.'

'At some point, would you oblige us by keeping Mr Gates occupied for a little while? We need to take a quick peek inside his room, and we don't want to ask his permission.'

'Ah!' Venables eyes sharpened. 'Might I suggest a Christmas drink in the butler's pantry?'

'Thank you, Venables, but not right now, eh?' Mycroft replied. 'We're trying to—'

'Not you, sir. Mr Gates,' the butler said, mildly impatient. 'Only he's rather partial to a single malt.'

'Oh, I see, yes. Excellent idea, Venables. Get as much down him as you can manage.'

'But don't imbibe much yourself, or you won't be able to control him,' Hannah said.

'That's not likely.' Mycroft laughed. 'Venables was raised on a croft near Inverness. They used homemade whisky to keep out the cold through the bitter winters. His insides are like leather. You can manage a lightweight like Gates, can't you, Venables?'

'*A'd* certainly *gie it a gade try, sor.*'

Hannah blinked. 'Venables, I never knew you were a Scot!'

'He was born Veitch, but we thought Venables was more in keeping with a gentleman farmer's manservant.' Mycroft shared a wide grin with the butler.

Hannah was still processing this revelation when Aidan asked. 'So, who's volunteering to venture into the servants' quarters?'

'I will, as long as you have my back covered,' Darius said. 'We don't want Gates discovering we are on to him.'

'I'm going with you,' Hannah said. 'It will be quicker with two of us.'

'As I'm not being invited, I'll keep watch on the landing in case he leaves the butler's pantry early,' Aunt Violet said.

'Are you sure?' Mycroft aimed a brotherly look at Hannah. 'I don't want to put you ladies in any danger. Iris would never forgive me.'

'It's sweet of you to be so concerned,' Hannah said, 'but Aunt Violet and I have prior experience of searching rooms.'

'Ah, of course.' Mycroft straightened. 'I had quite forgotten. In that case, make it quick and don't come back empty-handed.'

'Mr Gates takes his supper in the servants' hall,' Venables suggested, getting into his stride. 'It's a light meal, so doesn't last long. I could invite him to take a dram afterwards, but cannot guarantee he'll accept, but it might keep him busy for forty minutes to do the deed.'

Hannah sliced the butler a sideways look. 'Venables, why do I have this strange feeling you've done this before?'

'I couldn't possibly say, Miss.' He turned away, but not fast enough to hide a mischievous wink.

* * *

At an hour before the dressing bell was due, Hannah trudged up the last flight of stairs behind Darius to the servants' quarters and along the dimly lit attic corridor. Once behind the door off the bedroom landing, the elaborate silk wallpaper and gold-framed mirrors changed to serviceable brown paintwork below distempered walls of a dull olive green. A thin carpet runner lay underfoot which partly covered bare floorboards.

'This is depressing, and now I feel awful,' Hannah muttered to herself.

'Have you changed your mind?' Darius turned to face her, frowning. 'I could do this on my own if you're nervous?'

'I'm not nervous. It's more that poor Aidan has a room up here while the rest of us enjoy the luxury of the floor below.'

'What do you expect of servants' quarters? Embossed Indian wallpaper and Turkish carpets?' Darius chuckled. 'Aidan won't mind. I imagine he's stayed in far worse.'

'You might be mistaken about that. Aunt Violet told me he

owns a mansion apartment in Chelsea, and he attended Char-terhouse.'

'That's what I meant. Public schools are barely comfortable. Ah, this is the room.' He halted at a plain door set back from the hall beside a linen cupboard. 'Gates always keeps it locked, apparently.' He rooted through his pockets and withdrew some-thing she couldn't see in the low light but jangled.

'You have a key?'

'Better than that.' He inserted a thin metal rod into the lock, then a second rod with the end bent at right angles.

'Does everyone have a set of those except me?'

'What?' He turned his head and frowned. 'Standard equip-ment.' The lock clicked and he straightened. 'Why, who else are you talking about?'

'No one. Forget I said anything. Quick, get inside before someone sees us.' Hannah moved past him and pushed open the door to a room twelve feet square decorated the same as the hall-way, other than a landscape print on one wall of Windsor Castle from the end of the Long Walk. Under the window, there was a single bed and on the opposite wall, there stood a plain wooden wardrobe that had seen better days. A mismatched chest of draw-ers, the nightstand, and a small grate in a corner, with a layer of white ash at the bottom, completed the room.

'Now that's interesting.' He moved the door back, then forward again.

'What is?' Hannah cocked her head, alert for voices, but the floor remained silent.

'How many servants do you suppose oil their bedroom door hinges?'

'How do you know he did it? Perhaps all the servants' rooms have the hinges oiled?'

'Because there's a bottle of oil on the windowsill.'

'Ah, I see. Perhaps he doesn't want anyone tracking his comings and goings?'

'Precisely.'

Hannah was about to click on the overhead light, when she saw a standard lamp on the nightstand cast a dull yellow glow over the sloping ceiling and dormer window from the picture rail down but failed to reach into the corners.

Darius threw open the wardrobe door and stood back, his hands on his hips. 'There isn't much here. Only a couple of suits, a dinner jacket that is probably second-hand and a few shirts and shoes. There's nowhere to hide anything, either.'

'You take the chest of drawers,' Hannah said, moving gingerly so as not to make the bare floorboards creak. 'I don't want to be caught rifling through a man's undergarments.'

Darius smiled broadly as he complied. 'The bottom two hold sweaters, socks, vests and so on.' He held up a burgundy wool jumper towards the light. 'Hmm, not bad quality either. I have a couple of these.'

'Never mind his clothes, is there anything interesting?'

'No, just the usual personal items one would expect of a clerk with few hobbies.' He held up a pack of cards and a shoe cleaning kit, then dropped them back into the drawer. 'Shaving implements, a pack of cigarettes and a lighter. There's a backgammon set here, but no personal letters or a diary that I can see.'

Closing the drawer, he crossed to a shelf over the bed. 'He doesn't even have any books or magazines.'

'Which condemns him in my eyes straight away,' Hannah scoffed, examining a wooden corner cabinet attached to the wall over the black-leaded fire. 'What sort of person doesn't read? Have you found anything yet?'

'Give me a minute.' Darius straightened from his rapid search of the bedside table, from which he took a piece of paper folded in half with printing on it.

'What's that?' Hannah crossed to his side and tried to read over his shoulder, but he flipped the page too fast for her to see.

'His Certificate of Exemption from military service. It seems Mr Andrew Gates does indeed have chronic asthma.'

'Oh,' she muttered, disappointed. 'I don't suppose it could be a forgery?'

'It's been rubber-stamped with the name of the recruitment office, which is practically impossible to fake.'

'Just because one thing is legitimate, doesn't mean he's innocent.' Refusing to accept defeat, she knelt beside the metal-framed bed. A thin horsehair mattress covered with slightly greying cotton sheets and a well-worn blanket covered a set of solid, yet uncomfortable-looking, metal springs. Peering into the dark space beneath she spotted a shape in the far corner. 'There's something under here. It's a box of some sort.'

Flattening herself on the floor, she stretched as far as she could until her fingers closed around a brass handle. She pulled the box into the light and lifted it onto her lap.

'It's a writing case,' Hannah said, keeping her voice low. Beneath the lid were two slim drawers less than an inch deep. The first held a few sheets of poor-quality plain paper, a small blotter and some envelopes, stamps and a grooved area for pens.

'It's quite a nice one.' Hannah ran her fingers over a forest green leather inlay on the folded-out lid.

'Careful,' Darius warned. 'You might leave fingerprints.'

'Tease.' Hannah tutted and slid the top drawer shut. 'There's nothing much here, unfortunately.' She grasped the tiny brass handle on the second drawer, but it was a much tighter fit and moved sluggishly, sticking about an inch out. Impatient, she gave the handle a strong tug, the wood creaking as the drawer came free so quickly that she lost her grip and it hit the floor.

'Steady on, Hannah. Someone might hear. You wouldn't make much of a spy.'

'That's where you're wrong. Look.' She pointed to where the drawer lay in two pieces on the floor. 'It's thicker than the other one, with a false base disguised to make it look like a decoration.'

'That's more like it. What have we here?' Darius scooped up several sheets of paper that had spilled onto the floor.

'What are they?' Hannah asked, her head down as she collected the pieces of the writing case.

'Not drugs, but something just as lucrative: exemption certificates. Blank ones.'

'I *knew* we'd find something.' Hannah grinned up at him from the floor. 'There's something else here.' She bent to retrieve a small square object from where it had rolled under the bed and handed it to him. Darius held up a square stamp with a piece of rubber attached.

'It's the official stamp of the Woking Tribunal!' Darius weighed it in his hand. 'So that's what he's up to. He's selling real certificates but falsifying the contents. I saw a report recently in Vauxhall where a couple of clerks in a tribunal office on the south coast were caught exchanging these for chocolates and cigarettes.'

Hannah tweaked her fringe, that had splayed outwards after her foray beneath the bed, back into place. 'If Gates is selling them, I bet it's not for chocolates and cigarettes,' she scoffed. 'Isn't that treasonous?'

'If it isn't, it should be. I wish we could find out where he's got them from.'

'Darius...' Hannah began, brushing dust from her skirt with both hands as a memory stirred. 'When Aunt Violet and I first arrived, Mr Gates was carrying a brown envelope he said was from the post office. Something was odd about it, and I've just remembered what it was. There was no stamp.'

'So perhaps his contact is local,' Darius said thoughtfully. 'Woking is only about half an hour away by train. Though if he did come by train, his contact could be from anywhere.'

'Sorry. Just trying to help.' Hannah shrugged. 'What's the penalty for submitting a forged exemption certificate?'

'Twelve months in prison and on release being forced to join the army as a private.'

'I can see why he wouldn't want to be caught. I never dreamed there were such things as forged exception certificates.'

'More of this sort of thing probably goes on than any of us realise.'

'Darius?' Hannah said as a thought struck her. 'During dinner that first night, Sissy mentioned her brother Freddie would be joining the army in the New Year.'

'I believe I recall that conversation. She also demanded why we weren't in uniform too. Made me somewhat defensive, actually.'

'Fiona mentioned seeing Freddie talking with Gates, and money changed hands.'

'You think Freddie is one of Gates's customers?'

'It makes sense. Suppose Dianna insisted she stay the night because she planned to collect Freddie's certificate from Gates?'

'Of course. Then Mr Ellis was murdered, so she couldn't leave. Detective Roper's search must have thrown her into a panic in case he found it.'

'Then it's feasible to assume she still has it. But then why didn't she go home when she had the chance?'

Hannah shrugged. 'Roper's search didn't turn up anything, so she got complacent. Or perhaps she thought it would look suspicious if she left?'

'Hmm, well there's no point speculating.' Darius stared around the plain, colourless room. 'Right, well we've been here long enough. Make sure everything is back where we found it.'

'Even the certificates?'

'Especially those. Now, let's get out of here—' Darius broke off as the door swung slowly open.

Hannah froze.

19

'How long does it take two people to search a ten-foot square room?' Aidan's voice was irritation as he poked his head round the door jamb. 'Vi is keeping Gates talking but it's working a little too well. He's beginning to believe she's genuinely interested in him.'

'Violet is?' Darius asked, surprised. 'Venables was supposed to ply him with whisky in the butler's pantry.'

'Gates accepted one drink but made some excuse about having an early night.'

'He's on his way up?' Hannah asked, horrified.

'Not yet. Vi waylaid him outside the wine cellar, but I doubt it will work for long.'

'Quickly, have a look at this.' Darius handed Aidan one of the blank certificates which he accepted casually, but when he peered at it his eyes widened.

'Where did you get this?'

'In that writing desk Hannah is struggling with.' He grinned. 'There are more.'

Hannah sat back on her haunches. 'Don't mock me, this is

harder than it looks.' She prised the pieces of wood apart and slotted the drawer into the runners. Panic made her fingers clumsy, so it took her several tries. 'Ah, that's got it.' She slid the rest of the papers back into the drawer and pushed the writing case back under the bed as fast as she could and scrambled to her feet.

Darius replaced the certificate with Gates's name on it into the bedside table while Aidan held the door open for them.

'Wait!' Hannah halted. 'Can you lock a door with picks as well as unlock it?'

'Good thinking.' Darius delved into a pocket and withdrew the set of picks. 'These are as good as keys.'

The process took a few seconds more than to unlock, after which they clattered down the enclosed staircase and onto the bedroom landing considerably faster than they went up.

'We need to discuss what we do next in private,' Darius said.

'What about the solar?' Hannah said, pushing in front of them.

'The what?' Aidan's eyebrows lifted into his hairline.

'It's a small orangery on the corner of this floor between two bedrooms. And I do mean small – it only holds about six people comfortably. No one uses it much. Iris showed it to me on my first visit. She hides from the children there sometimes.'

'Lead on then, Hannah,' Aidan said, following. 'But I'll have to rescue Violet first.'

'No need.' Aunt Violet strolled along the far side of the landing towards them, tucking thick strands of dark hair that lay curled on her shoulder into its pins. 'Since no one appears to be guarding my reputation, I had to extricate myself.' She swept past Darius who held open the door to the solar. 'Honestly, you only have to smile at some men, and they take it entirely the wrong way.'

'Where is he?' Aidan's jaw clicked and his eyes narrowed. 'Do I need to have a not-so-quiet word with him?'

'Flattering to me, but totally unnecessary.' She raised a sardonic eyebrow. 'I knew my ju-jitsu would come in handy.' She settled into a peacock-backed wicker chair with her hands clasped demurely in her lap. 'Now. What have we got?'

Hannah exchanged a bemused smile with Darius as they selected seats in the miniature conservatory, constructed of wrought iron and full-height glass walls that had been inserted in the corner of the building. During a previous visit, Hannah had established the interior was invisible from the ground because a stone parapet encircled the lower section. It was furnished with wicker high-backed chairs with deep cushions, arranged around a small wicker table used for serving refreshments, and where Darius revealed their find for the benefit of the others.

They had just settled when Mycroft's face appeared around the door. 'Ah, here you are. I wondered where you had got to. How did the search go?'

'Do join us.' Hannah shifted her chair closer to Aunt Violet's. 'We didn't find the ruby, but something equally as interesting.'

'Not part of the contents of my cellar, I hope?' Mycroft eased into the chair, which was a tight fit for his over six-foot frame. 'I must say, when you suggested this escapade, I was somewhat sceptical. I still find it hard to believe my secretary is involved in anything illegal. Any more than I think Benson is a killer and a jewel thief. So, what did you find?'

'Exemption certificates,' Darius said. 'Real ones, but all blank.'

'Good heavens. So, we aren't persecuting an innocent man, after all. I was beginning to worry we were wrong.'

'Is it possible those certificates are the reason Mr Ellis was killed and nothing to do with the ruby?' Hannah asked.

'Let's deal with one crime at a time,' Aidan warned. 'We've established Gates is involved in a certificate fraud, which naturally begs the question he might have killed Mr Ellis to keep it quiet. The letter Ellis wrote to Featherstone-Haugh implies he suspected him.'

'I see.' Mycroft massaged the back of his neck with one hand. 'This is all rather more complicated than I thought. Does Detective Roper know about this find?'

'Not yet,' Darius said. 'I don't want to have to explain how we discovered he had them.'

'Then I suggest we keep this to ourselves for the time being,' Mycroft said. 'At least, until we can hand it over to someone more competent. And I don't mean that as an insult to you, Aidan.'

'Not at all.' Aidan crossed one leg over the other and relaxed against the cushion. 'I have no actual power here while Roper is in charge. Our current advantage is that Gates is ignorant of what we know, so he won't be on his guard. Not against us, anyway.'

'How would Mr Ellis have discovered Andrew Gates's side business? They had never met before he came here.' Hannah asked.

Aidan stroked his chin thoughtfully. 'Unless Gates applied for the certificate at the Woking office and was refused.'

'By Mr Ellis?' Aidan raised a sardonic eyebrow. 'If true, that's quite a coincidence. But why would he keep it to himself?'

'Think about it,' Aidan said thoughtfully. 'He was an invited guest, so perhaps he didn't want to spoil the holiday for his hosts. He may have decided to wait until after the festivities to report him. Gates works here and wasn't going anywhere.'

'Assuming Mr Ellis was as considerate as you, which I doubt,' Aunt Violet said. 'Not if his surly manner at dinner the first night was anything to go by.'

'It's possible Mr Ellis had no authority to detain Mr Gates, which is why he wrote the letter to Mr Featherstone-Haugh,' Aidan said. 'I'm uncertain even I have such authority. I'm not part of the Surrey Constabulary, nor do I work for the War Office.'

'That leaves you, Darius,' Aunt Violet smirked.

'I'm happy to arrest the man, but I'm not sure it would be legal.' Darius smiled wryly.

'Taking Gates out of circulation won't change much.' Aidan took a thoughtful sip of his whisky. 'Finding out who is supplying him with blank certificates would be more useful.'

'You're not suggesting we ignore it?' Hannah said, genuinely shocked. She had believed the hard part was done, and all it took now was to tell someone in authority. Was police work always this complicated?

'What about Dianna Dunleavy? If she is in possession of a fake certificate, she should be arrested too,' Aunt Violet said. 'I shan't be too disappointed to see her carted off, either. She's been a nuisance since got here. She treats Iris like her personal maid and Midwinter like a hotel.'

'She isn't the easiest person, but I suggest we're more discreet than that,' Hannah said. 'Dianna is a guest, and the repercussions could be very embarrassing for Mycroft and Iris. They have to live here.'

Aunt Violet snorted. 'A house where cushions with knives through them get left under the beds.'

'I had almost forgotten about that.' Hannah's thoughts went to the laundry bag in her wardrobe. 'We still don't know who put it there.'

'Cushions and knives?' Mycroft glanced up sharply from his glass. 'What's that all about?'

'Oh, nothing. Someone played a prank, that's all,' Hannah replied. 'No real harm done.' *Not yet, anyway.*

'Let's hope whoever it was doesn't become more inventive and really hurts someone,' Aunt Violet said.

* * *

Hannah parted with Aunt Violet and Darius on the bedroom landing and had almost reached her room when the door leading to the top floor opened and Dianna appeared.

'Oh, Hannah. I thought you had retired some time ago.' Dianna seemed openly shocked to see her, which was enough to stir Hannah's curiosity as the only rooms behind that door were the staff bedrooms.

'Did you get your shoe mended, Dianna?' Hannah braced her hands on the banister rail, recalling this was the second time she had seen Dianna at that door.

'What? Er, yes, yes, I did. I was just—' She glanced vaguely behind her at the closed door and back again at Hannah. 'Did you want something?'

'I'm interested to know what you find so fascinating on the top floor. Or have you found another weapon in a laundry bag in the servants' quarters?'

'I told you, that was just some silly prank. And anyway, I don't see that it's your business.' Dianna moved towards her bedroom door, her bag gripped tightly in both hands.

'There's a murderer in this house, which makes it everyone's business.' Hannah eased closer. 'What were you talking to Mr Gates about the other day?'

'Whatever do you mean?' Dianna raised her chin, but her eyes darted the hallway. 'I told you, my shoes—'

'I doubt it was anything to do with shoes, Dianna.' Her uneasiness made Hannah's nerves prickle. 'From what I saw you were arguing with him. Who argues over mending shoes?'

'You're being ridiculous.' Dianna's breathing quickened, and her face flushed. 'Whatever would *I* have to say to a secretary? Now if you'll excuse me, I have a bad headache and need to take some aspirin.' She opened the door of her room a few inches, but Hannah barred her way.

'If you have nothing to hide, why are you so nervous? And that cushion with a knife through was no prank.'

'How should I know what it was?' Dianna visibly swallowed. 'I-I might have reprimanded a servant who held a grudge against me. And it's not as if you're not so innocent, is it? Did you think you were clever in bringing a high-ranking policeman here from Scotland Yard?'

Hannah opened her mouth and closed it again while Dianna's close-set eyes gleamed in triumph.

'There, you see. I knew it! I've seen him with your outrageous Aunt Violet huddled together in corners when they thought they were alone. Disgraceful behaviour. However, neither he nor you have any authority here and I—'

'Oh, for goodness' sake!' Losing patience, Hannah grabbed the bag from Dianna's hands and yanked it open.

'How dare you!' Dianna screeched. She attempted to snatch it back, but Hannah turned a shoulder towards her and removed a folded sheet of paper tucked into an inside pocket and held it up.

'Is this what I think it is?' She unfolded the paper that was headed *Exemption from Service Certificate*. 'I see it's made out in the name of Frederick Dunleavy.' She read further down the page. 'The poor dear appears to be suffering from epilepsy. Nasty affliction, that.' She scanned the stamp at the bottom which was the same as the embossed block of rubber she had found in Gates's room. 'It looks genuine, but you and I know better, don't we?'

'My Freddie needs that!' Dianna made another grab for the paper but missed.

Dianna watched in horror as Hannah placed the paper in her own bag and clicked it shut and her son's chance of staying out of the army disappeared. Instantly her bravado crumbled. She gave the empty landing a furtive glance, then looked back at Hannah. She seemed to hold an inner debate, then sighed, resigned to her fate. 'Fine, I'll tell you everything, but not here.' She pulled the bedroom door closed gently. 'My Sissy is asleep.'

'Then we won't disturb her. We'll talk in my room.' Hannah led the way along the landing, half expecting Dianna to refuse, but she complied without a word.

She lowered herself onto Hannah's bed, her shoulders slumped and her hands clasped tightly in her lap, the bag discarded on the bed as it no longer contained her lifeline. 'You know why I bought the certificate. To protect my son. You'll understand when you are a mother.'

'I do understand. But what about all those other mothers who have no choice but to send their boys to war? It's the worst insult to them. Freddie must have friends who are away fighting? What will it do to his self-respect to cheat his way through life?'

'At least he'll be alive!' Dianna hiccoughed, close to tears.

'How did Freddie know Mr Gates could obtain an exemption certificate? Or did you find out for him?' Dianna started to protest, but Hannah's steady stare halted her.

'Freddie was in the Barley Mow pub a couple of months ago. He was drinking rather a lot, maudlin about the prospect of being called up. Someone in the bar – and don't ask me who, as I don't know – said when the time came, Freddie could obtain an exemption certificate if he approached the secretary at Midwinter Manor. The Athertons are new to the neighbourhood. We hadn't been introduced, so I cultivated them.' She shrugged.

'Had them to dinner and drinks. Things like that. They became friends, so when Freddie's conscription papers arrived... Well, you know the rest.'

'I'd still like to hear it from you,' Hannah said.

'All right, if you must.' Dianna looked down in an attempt to appear contrite but was unconvincing. 'Freddie paid Mr Gates what he asked, but he said he couldn't get the papers he needed for a week or so – they arrived the day of the dinner when Mr Ellis was killed.'

Hannah conjured an image of her and Aunt Violet's arrival, and Gates holding tightly to the parcel under his arm as he talked to Iris.

'I arranged to meet him in the rear hall after dinner finished that evening,' Dianna continued. 'He-he gave me the certificate and it's been in my bag since.'

Something about her account didn't ring true. 'That's not all though, is it?'

Dianna stared at the door and fidgeted.

'What aren't you telling me?' Hannah demanded, sifting through what she had already said. 'The study. You went inside?'

Dianna swallowed and her face paled, her demeanour going from defensive to conciliatory 'I swear to you, I didn't have anything to do with killing Mr Ellis.'

'Go on.' Hannah's pulse raced, partly with excitement for Benson and herself that she had been the one to extract a confession. It was a heady feeling.

'Mr Ellis was seated in the chair behind the desk but sprawled awkwardly across it. I asked Gates if he was ill and suggested we call someone, but he stopped me.'

'Gates killed Basil Ellis?' Hannah gasped.

'I swear, I didn't realise.' Dianna flinched and hunched her shoulders as if avoiding a blow. 'He said Mr Ellis was only stunned. That he would come to in a moment and we shouldn't be there when he did. I-I believed him.'

'Or you wanted to. Do you know what Gates struck him with?'

'I-I'm not sure. He-he was holding something in his hand. It was small and white. A statue, I think or... No, it was a small bust. The bust of a woman.'

The door opened with a click and Aunt Violet appeared in the doorframe in a champagne-coloured silk negligee, her dark hair flowing down her back that made her look much younger than her forty years. 'Is everything all right, Hannah?' Her gaze went from Hannah to Dianna and back again. 'I heard voices and I—' She closed the door behind her carefully. 'What's going on?'

'It was Psyche!' Hannah said. 'That's what we missed in the study.'

'What *are* you talking about, Hannah?' Aunt Violet looked sceptical.

'The goddess of the soul and inner thoughts. Greek, I think. It's a statuette Iris gave Mycroft on their honeymoon. It's small but heavy and more importantly has a curved base. Gates used it to kill Mr Ellis. We were so busy looking at the trophies we completely missed it.'

Aunt Violet remained calm as she processed this information. 'What now?' She moved further into the room and sat down beside Dianna. 'And you kept all this to yourself?'

'She won't get away with it. I expect the police might call her an accessory after the fact,' Hannah said.

'Police?' Dianna's eyes flew wide. 'You can't tell them. It wasn't my fault. I didn't know Mr Ellis was dead until the next morning.'

'And the ruby? Did Gates take that as well?' Hannah asked.

'The ruby?' Her head moved between them like an automaton. 'I don't know anything about that.'

'I think I believe her,' Aunt Violet said.

'So do I. But we can't keep this to ourselves. You must see that, don't you, Dianna?'

'I-I know I should have said something, but I was frightened. Then that cushion with the knife was left under my bed. I'm certain Gates did it to frighten me. So-so I kept quiet.' She twisted her hands in front of her beneath the weight of their combined stares. 'Then Detective Roper wouldn't let me go home and said our rooms would be searched. I was terrified he would find the certificate, so I carried it around with me.'

'But when Iris said you could leave, you stayed. Why?' Hannah asked.

'For Sissy, really.' Her smile reappeared briefly. 'She so loves it here and there's only me at home.'

Aunt Violet snorted and the smile disappeared. 'Drop the innocent act, Dianna. With Benson arrested, you thought you were safe. You let that boy take the blame when you knew it was Gates who killed Mr Ellis.'

'All right. But it was Gates's idea. He asked me to stay so I could keep an eye on that detective in case he found anything.'

'And did he? Find anything?' Hannah asked.

'I don't know. He's as closed as an oyster. I had nothing to tell him until that man arrived last night.'

'Man, what man?' Aunt Violet sighed. 'Sorry, I forgot for a moment. You mean Mr Featherstone-Haugh?'

'I don't know his name. Gates said he looked official so told me to listen outside the French doors.' She shuddered at the memory. 'Nearly caught my death of cold.'

'You surprise me, Dianna.' Aunt Violet gave her ample figure a slow up-and-down stare. 'I would never have taken you for an eavesdropper.'

'I learned it at boarding school.' Dianna smiled almost proudly. 'Lots of nasty young misses there, I can tell you.'

'But Gates couldn't have known Mr Featherstone-Haugh was here about him. No one did.'

'Which is what I told him.' She drew a deep, shuddering breath. 'But now you know everything. My Freddie will have to join the army and he'll be killed!' She burst into hysterical sobbing that rapidly became a wail.

'Hush, you'll wake the entire floor.' Aunt Violet flapped her hands for her to quiet down.

'I think we'll have to wake up some of it, anyway,' Hannah said. 'You realise you cannot hide this any more, Dianna. It will have to come out.'

'I know.' Dianna released a long, slow breath as the life seemed to go out of her.

'I'll go and get Aidan,' Aunt Violet said, rising slowly. 'Don't worry, Dianna, he'll be discreet and sympathetic. Making sure Gates is arrested and charged is more important than forged certificates.'

This seemed to calm her somewhat though the tears still flowed freely.

Hannah wrapped an arm around Dianna, who was definitely in the wrong but ultimately, she was protecting her son. If Xander were old enough to be conscripted, would Iris do the same? If Hannah were a mother, would she go to such extremes to save her child?

The room grew colder as they waited, huddled on the side of Hannah's bed, her thoughts whirling as she tried to make sense of what Dianna had told her.

She claimed to know nothing about the ruby, but did Gates take that too?

Why did Gates kill Mr Ellis? Had he discovered Gates trying to get into the Chinese Cabinet? Knowing what was kept there,

Mr Ellis guessed what he was doing and threatened to expose him, so Gates snatched up the statue and hit him?

Neither man knew the ruby wasn't there, so it was a plausible theory.

Or was it entirely due to the forged certificates?

Was Gates aware Mr Ellis worked at the Tribunal and had written to Featherstone-Haugh and assumed it was about him? Did Gates assume Mr Ellis had been sent to Midwinter on new evidence and he had been discovered?

Did Basil die for nothing?

Aunt Violet returned a little while later with Aidan, who had clearly dressed in a hurry as his shirt hung several inches below a sweater that had been hastily thrown on over the top.

'Well, Mrs Dunleavy, you have got yourself into a pickle.' His steady stare seemed to pin Dianna to the spot.

'You cannot arrest me.' Her voice was calm but the hand she brought to her neck trembled. 'You're a guest with no powers here.'

'Shall I send for Detective Roper?' Aidan dragged one of the low bedroom chairs closer and sat, his hands hanging loose between his knees. 'It might take a while for him to cycle here and it's pretty cold outside, so he won't be in a good mood being woken in the middle of the night. But it's up to you.'

'No, don't do that. I-I'll tell you.' She clasped her hands together to stop them shaking.

If she thought Aidan would save her from Roper, she was going to be disappointed, but Hannah wasn't going to say so.

Dianna repeated her story haltingly, interrupted at intervals for Aidan to get more detail or to affirm what she had already said. When he seemed satisfied he had everything straight, he pushed to his feet.

'I'll let you get some sleep, Mrs Dunleavy, but you'll probably have to repeat what you have told me to Detective Roper. I advise you to say nothing about this to anyone. We don't want Gates knowing we are on to him, is that understood?'

'How can I sleep with this hanging over my head?' Dianna sniffed wetly. 'What will happen to me now?'

'It's not my decision, although you have no previous record and perhaps a judge would be lenient. You may even get away with paying a fine. However, there's no way around the fact your son will have to do military service.'

'I know.' Dianna whimpered and a tear trickled down her nose onto her dress.

'I promise I will do my best to ensure Detective Roper goes easy on you.'

Hannah hoped he could keep that promise.

20

Despite her late night, Hannah was up early the next morning and was dressed and downstairs before the staff had finished making up the dining room for breakfast.

Detective Roper was in the hall with Mycroft and Aidan, the former looking less than pleased.

'How long have you known about this, Mr Atherton?' Roper demanded.

'Only since last night,' Aidan replied. 'We all did.'

'And when exactly did you intend revealing who you were, Detective Inspector Farrell?' Roper spat the words.

'I apologise, Detective, but I would never encroach on your investigation. I was invited as a houseguest and when the situation was explained to me, I saw the need to remain discreet.'

'Aye, well, that's your story. But encroachment is the least of what has been going on around here. The appearance of this Featherstone-Haugh chap is something else you neglected to inform me about. And you clearly disapproved of my decision to detain the footman.'

'To be honest, none of us thought Benson should have been

incarcerated,' Mycroft interjected. 'And still don't. However, we can debate all that later. Our aim here is to ensure Gates is handed over to the proper authorities.' He sighed. 'I still cannot believe he killed Basil Ellis.'

'Dianna was witness to Gates standing over the body. Or almost. He was holding the murder weapon,' Hannah said.

'What weapon?' Roper sounded sceptical. 'I searched the study and found nothing that could have caused Mr Ellis's injury.'

'I'm afraid it was your bust of Psyche, Mycroft. It wasn't there when we looked.'

'Are you sure? Because it's there now – I saw it this morning.' Mycroft frowned, then thought for a moment. 'Come to think of it, had it been there when we found Mr Ellis, wouldn't Detective Roper have identified it as such?'

'Exactly, and thank you for that, Mr Atherton.' Roper acknowledged this with an inclination of his head. 'Which indicates it was removed and has since been returned.'

'We think Gates must have taken it with him, possibly to remove his finger marks or evidence of how it was used before putting it back,' Hannah explained. 'It's probably why he was in the study when Iris confronted him.'

'Good grief!' Mycroft's eyes widened in horror as the implication sank in. 'My wife's honeymoon gift was used to kill someone?'

'Don't worry, old chap.' Aidan patted his shoulder. 'You'd never know it had been used to batter a man's skull in.'

'Aidan!' Aunt Violet gaped, although it might easily have been her talking.

Aidan's mouth twitched showing he thought the same thing, but the amusement rapidly drained from his face under her aunt's cold stare. 'I spoke to Featherstone-Haugh at his office in

Aldershot. He's going to contact the Aldershot barracks and have the military police send some chaps here to arrest Mr Gates. It will take them over half an hour here from Woking, snow permitting. In the meantime, we say or do nothing that might alert him. I suggest we join the others at breakfast and do our best to act normally.'

'Excuse me, sir,' Venables interrupted, alerting them to his presence.

'Not now, Venables, we're trying to organise something rather intricate.' Mycroft waved him away.

'But, sir, I might have made a grave error.' All eyes swung to the butler, who shuffled his feet. 'When Mr Farrell came out of the study, I spotted Mr Gates was nearby. He may or may not have heard any of the conversation going on within. In fact, he gave no sign at all—'

'Yes, yes, man. Are you trying to say Gates heard us talking?' Mycroft snapped.

'It's possible, sir, but young Bill here—'

'Bill? What's he doing here?' Iris interrupted, nodding to a boy in brown overalls stood by the green baize door, one hand raised to attract attention.

'Who's Bill?' Mycroft frowned.

'The gardener's boy.' Iris rolled her eyes at her husband and gestured the boy forward. A wiry lad of about fourteen with some growing left to do, Bill was barely over five feet tall. His straight brown hair formed a thatch on his narrow head, and his brown overalls were smeared with oil stains.

'Oh, yes, of course he is.' Mycroft peered at him as if he had never seen him before. 'Well, what is it, lad?'

'I was just in the garage cleaning Mr Farrell's motorcycle,' Bill began in a newly broken, slightly croaky voice. 'Lovely machine. It's the new 4hp model, isn't it?'

'Yes, thank you, Bill. It is, but what about it?' The urgency in Aidan's voice showed he had guessed where this was going.

'Mr Gates came running in and asked me how to get it started and how fast it would go, how the gears work and such. He strapped a bag behind the seat and started the engine. I asked what he was doing, but he said you'd lent it to him. I said no one had told me, but he pushed me aside, so I ran inside to tell Mr Venables.'

'Is Mr Gates still there?' Aidan interrupted, alert.

'Last I saw, he took off down the cart track like the devil were after him.'

'Damn and blast it!' Aidan slapped a hand on his head. 'Where does the track lead?'

'It meets up with the Godalming Road two miles away, sir,' Venables interjected.

'He's probably heading for London,' Aidan said. 'He got a head start on us, but we might catch up with him. Darius, could we take your motor car?'

'Mine is faster,' Mycroft said.

'Then what are we waiting for? Can't let the fellow get away.' Detective Roper headed for the front door.

Aidan and Darius exchanged a surprised look with Mycroft before the three of them followed.

Hannah and Aunt Violet reached the drive just in time to see them take the path around the side of the house that led to the garage at a run they had no hope of keeping up with.

'Typical. The men always have all the fun.' Aunt Violet halted beside her, hands on her hips as they watched them pile into Mycroft's Rover. 'I suppose it was too much to ask them to wait for us?'

'The Rover wouldn't hold six of us in comfort, anyway,' Hannah observed just as the Tourer's engine revved, turned in a wide circle, and whooshed past them on the drive, throwing up snow and ice, the silhouettes of four male heads outlining the rear window.

'That's not the way I'd go,' Bill spoke from beside the butler. 'That Tourer's a heavy beast, and once it starts a slide on that icy road, it will be hard for them to control.'

Hannah turned to face the boy, surprised to see he was older than she had first thought, with sharp, intelligent eyes. 'Which way would you go, Bill?' She fidgeted, willing him not to ponder her question too long. He seemed the sort who considered carefully before speaking.

'Wot, me, Miss? I don't never think I'll get to ride any of them—'

'Imagine you were!' Hannah snapped. 'Which way?'

'About a quarter mile down the track, it splits and bears right through the woods. Not big enough for a motor car but a horse or that motorcycle could manage the ruts and fallen branches easily.'

'The main road curves over to the east for a couple of miles before meeting the woodland trail,' Venables said. 'He'll be out of the woods and in Godalming well before the Rover. Then there are any number of smaller roads he could take. You might never find him.'

'Then we'll have to ensure he doesn't get that far,' Aunt Violet said. 'Is there a shortcut that joins up with the main road?'

'Stick to the farm track,' Venables added. 'It circles around the woodland and then joins the main road after a couple of miles.'

'Will my Sunbeam get through the track?' Aunt Violet asked.

'That little red job?' Bill grinned. 'I would say so. It's smaller, lighter and won't mind a bit of snow.'

He hadn't finished speaking before Hannah handed Aunt Violet her coat from the row of hooks in the vestibule, then threw on her own. She followed Aunt Violet outside and almost collided with Lynford and Millie who were coming in, bundled into coats, hats and mufflers, their noses red from the cold.

'What's the rush?' Lynford demanded testily as they barrelled past.

'What on earth—?' Millie stepped back and stared at them.

'No time to explain!' Hannah yelled over her shoulder without stopping.

The garage was close to the house, so in less than a minute Aunt Violet had the Sunbeam's engine running and Hannah had climbed into the passenger seat with the door barely closed before the vehicle lurched forward.

'Aunt Violet, should we have told Lynford what Gates did?'

'I'm more interested in stopping Gates than chatting about it. He'll find out later.'

'I suppose so, and he might have insisted on coming with us.' Their condensed breath filled the tiny interior. The air inside the cab was ice cold from being parked in a garage for three days. Hannah's toes curled in anticipation of cramp, as even with windows tight shut, they were only protected from the freezing temperature by a thin canopy of canvas.

Aunt Violet gripped the wheel and leaned forward to see over the bonnet as they negotiated a single track running behind the row of garages.

'I hope young Bill was right about this track,' she said, just as they cleared the buildings into an open area where the woodland curved away to their right and ran alongside the trees.

'I can't see the main road from here, but I assume Mycroft and the others are over that way.' Hannah indicated a flat snow-covered field to their left.

'Never mind them, they'll make their own way.' Aunt Violet gripped the wheel harder and pressed down on the accelerator.

'Keep your speed down, Aunt Violet, we might end up in a hedge.'

'Don't worry, it's soft going here. There's no resistance on the tyres which means there's no ice. Either that or the steering's better than I thought. Can you see the motorcycle?'

'No. Just trees and more trees. He must have got further ahead of us than we thought.'

'If we don't catch up to him, maybe Mycroft will when he reaches the main road.'

Hannah strained her ears for the familiar high-pitched whine of Aidan's 'Trusty' but all she could hear was their own motor car's engine and the buffeting of the wind through the canopy.

'There's still no sign of him. Oh wait, I can hear it.' Hannah tuned in to the whine of the bike's engine until she could pinpoint its direction. 'There it is!' She could just make out the rear end of the motorcycle, kicking up a small plume of snow behind it. 'He's about a hundred yards ahead.'

'Keep your eyes on him. This track is not straight and at this speed, I need to concentrate.' The Sunbeam's engine kept up a steady hum and chug as it curved around the wood.

'He's stopped! He probably got stuck on something. He's... No, he's cleared it and is moving again.'

'Where?' Aunt Violet followed Hannah's pointing arm.

'Up ahead on that small rise where the trees thin out a little.'

'I see him.' Aunt Violet pressed down on the accelerator, and the car surged forward.

'He seems to be having trouble handling the motorcycle.' Hannah fought to keep the distant figure in sight. 'Do you suppose he's ever ridden one before?'

'Let's hope not. He might oblige us and come off before he reaches the road.' The motor car hit a bump that wrenched the steering wheel out of Aunt Violet's hands.

Hannah made a grab for the door strap and hung on, her knuckles turning white as she watched the motorcycle buck and swerve between the trees.

'There are probably broken branches in the way slowing him down,' her aunt said. Regaining control of the steering wheel, she straightened the front of the motor car.

'He's having to slow down every few feet to guide the bike around them,' Hannah said, narrowing her eyes. 'We've covered at least half the distance between us.'

The main road was visible on the far side of the field where the tourer appeared and bowled steadily along, the space between them closing slightly as it ate up the road.

'There's Mycroft.' She nodded, unable to point as both hands were occupied with holding fast to the door strap. 'He's still a long way off.'

'The road is taking him away from us. Bill was right about the ice.' Hannah adjusted her muffler, now damp from her breath. 'He's swerving all over the place. I hope he meets nothing coming the other way.'

'Let's hope we don't, either; this track is too narrow for more than one vehicle.'

'Bill said the road meets up at some point, so it must bring them back again.' Hannah's stomach lurched as the car rose over a hump and took off into the air before coming down again with a judder that jarred her back.

'How fast are we going?'

'Don't ask. But it's my personal record on snow.' Aunt Violet grinned and rolled her hands on the steering wheel. 'Hold tight, there's a sharp corner coming up and I'm not slowing down.'

Hannah braced her feet against the metal floor, her breath held as they banked hard right, so hard she could swear the driver's side left the ground. The motor car skidded, bumped, but righted itself again.

'We're gaining on the motorcycle.' Hannah switched her focus back to where Gates weaved between the trees, her excitement growing. The engine whined and screamed as it fought obstacles on the forest floor they couldn't see. 'He's having trouble keeping it in a straight line. Wait – I've lost him. He drove into a dip.' Hannah scanned the naked trees frantically for signs of movement but all she could see were bare birch trunks rimmed with a layer of snow in a silent forest floor.

Suddenly a shape appeared between two vertical trunks. 'There!' She took one hand off the strap and pointed, grabbing it back quickly. 'We're gaining on him, Aunt Violet. He cannot be over fifty yards away.' Her breath caught as the line of trees stopped completely as the track ended. 'We're running out of road!'

'I don't need roads.' Aunt Violet swung the wheel to the left through an open gateway and set off across a wide expanse of pristine snow.

'There had better not be a lake under this!' Hannah grabbed the strap with both hands.

'Silly me. I didn't check the map before we left.' Aunt Violet turned her head and grinned before turning back to the road again. 'Don't worry, we can both swim.'

'Aunt Violet!' Hannah's heart leapt into her mouth, but the ground beneath them held. 'It's a field and it ends right where Gates should leave the wood. Hold on.'

'That's not a field!' Hannah pointed to where the ground suddenly fell away into a deep ditch between them and the silvery white ribbon stretching into the distance. 'It's a stream! Tell me you won't try to jump it!'

Aunt Violet did not respond, but just as Hannah thought she

might do just that, the motor car slewed sideways then ploughed on just as the motorcycle, with Gates bent over the handlebars, came out of the wood straight into their path.

'Watch out!' Hannah screamed as the driver's side of the Sunbeam caught the 'Trusty's' rear wheel, turning it full circle. She watched in horrified fascination as Gates was catapulted from the seat in one direction, whilst the motorcycle bounced off a fallen log before landing on its side, throwing up snow, leaves and twigs as it came to a halt.

Hannah froze, half expecting the motor car to slide after it, but they only rolled forward a few feet before coming to rest at an angle, right side upwards. The front driver's wheel had embedded itself in the exposed roots of a tree, which prevented the entire car from ending up in the ditch.

Aunt Violet bent her knees and with a low grunt, positioned her feet into the centre of the door and levered it open.

'Help me out, would you?' Hannah clambered upwards over the driver's seat, fearful that going the opposite way would unbalance the vehicle and send it into the ditch on top of her.

Her aunt grabbed her hand and pulled her through the driver's door onto firm ground. Hannah ran to the edge of the ditch, her feet crunching snow towards the top of the embankment. Her stomach lurched as images of what she might see ran through her head, but she forced herself to look.

Gates lay on his right side about four feet down. He clutched his left shin, his jacket covered in snow, dead leaves, mulch and twigs. The bag he had attached to the motorcycle had been flung clear and lay at the bottom of the ditch. The impact had split the locks and clothes littered the sides and bottom of the ditch. The writing case lay a few feet away, the broken drawer front revealing the stolen certificates.

'I've broken my ruddy leg!' Gates yelled.

'Then we're even,' Aunt Violet yelled back. 'Because you broke my motor car!'

'Well, aren't you going to help me out?' Gates shouted.

'No. You can wait for the police,' Aunt Violet said.

'His leg might actually be fractured, Aunt Violet.' Hannah's experiences at the hospital told her badly broken bones could cause embolisms. 'We don't want him dying on us.'

'He's moving so it's probably only sprained,' Aunt Violet replied just as Mycroft brought his Tourer to a halt on the road on the other side of a rickety gate. The four doors were flung open simultaneously, and the occupants came hurtling towards them.

'Are either of you hurt?' Darius grabbed Hannah by her upper arms and looked her up and down.

'*He* claims to be.' Hannah nodded to the ditch where Gates was struggling to pull himself up, but with nothing to hold on to he was getting nowhere. 'But we're fine, really. Though could you move back a little, I'd rather not end up in there with him.'

'Oh, sorry.' Darius backed away, bringing Hannah with him.

'What were you thinking, woman, chasing after him in this... this contraption?' Detective Roper stomped snow from his shoes in mild disgust and glared at the Sunbeam. The motor car lay keeled to one side, its nose pointed into the ditch.

'It's my motor car,' Aunt Violet replied stoutly. 'And without it, Gates might well have got away.'

'We had everything in hand, Vi.' Aidan's feet slipped in the snow as he approached. 'You didn't have to come racing after him. We would have caught him.'

'That's not very appreciative, is it, Aunt Violet?' Hannah stamped her feet, shivering as an icy breeze sliced through the trees.

'I expected nothing else. And you're welcome!' Aunt Violet

called to Aidan, who grabbed a low tree branch and slid sideways into the ditch, followed by Detective Roper. The two of them hauled Gates to the top of the ditch, and together, half-dragged him to the road and hurled him roughly inside the Tourer.

'I doubt you could drive this back, Violet,' Mycroft said, joining Darius beside the Sunbeam, their hands in their pockets and heads nodding as they surveyed the damage to the roadster. 'The driver's side suspension has snapped.'

'You can blame the tree for that.' Aunt Violet adjusted the pins in her hair that the drive through the wood had ruffled. 'I don't suppose there's a garage open around here?'

'I doubt it, and this close to Christmas, you're probably out of luck,' Mycroft said.

With Gates safely handcuffed to the Tourer's steering wheel, Aidan returned to the edge of the ditch and retrieved his motor-cycle from where it lay five feet from the incline. To everyone's surprise, it was not only undamaged but when Aidan jammed his foot down to kickstart it, the engine burst into life.

'They don't call it a "Trusty" for nothing.' He grinned at them from the seat. 'Mycroft and Detective Roper can take care of Gates. I'll go back to the house to fetch some help to get Vi's motor car back to the Manor.'

'I'll stay here with Violet and Hannah,' Darius offered. 'Maybe Mycroft can come back and pick us up?'

'Or we could walk.' Aunt Violet tossed her scarf over one shoulder. 'I don't relish standing around here in this freezing wood waiting for him. It's only a couple of miles and I want my breakfast.'

Hannah rolled her eyes and surveyed her soaked boots with dismay and prepared for a cold, wet trudge back to the Manor.

21

The last quarter of a mile back to Midwinter Manor seemed further and colder than Hannah had anticipated, but Aunt Violet's unfaltering stride ahead of her kept her complaints unspoken.

Finally, they turned into the drive where two grey-green army vehicles were parked at angles to the house, each with a policeman standing to attention by the doors.

Venables greeted them at the front door and in answer to Hannah's question, informed her Gates was in the study being questioned.

'By the military police?' Hannah shrugged out of her coat and longed to change her dripping clothes as her feet were soaking wet and numb with cold. But after all their efforts she wanted to be there at the conclusion.

'Mr Farrell and Detective Roper asked permission to talk to him first. As they were the ones who apprehended him, it was granted, Miss. Mr Clifford is there too.'

Handing her coat to the butler, she took off down the hall, aware her boots squelched with each step.

'They won't let you in, Hannah,' Aunt Violet called after her. 'They'll tell you it's official business.'

'It won't hurt to try,' Hannah called back, not slowing.

Surprisingly, there was no guard on the study and the door had been left open, possibly so the official-looking man in uniform in the alcove opposite could watch the proceedings.

Gates occupied an upright chair in front of the desk, his hands in cuffs behind him and his three inquisitors forming a trio in front of him. His hair was an untidy mess, with a streak of dirt along one cheek. His shirt was torn, and someone had bound his leg, but despite his previous protests, he had no trouble using it to brace both feet apart.

Hannah paused just inside the door, hoping no one noticed her. Aidan and Roper were too intent on Gates, but Darius looked up briefly and caught her eyes but looked back again without speaking.

'What's the story now?' Gates's Home Counties accent began to slip 'I co-operate and you offer me clemency? Hah! As if I'd fall for that. I know how coppers work.'

'I think you'll find the military police have their own methods, Gates,' Aidan said. 'They don't play games, either. Besides, murder isn't negotiable, so you'll probably have to argue between the High Court and the army. I don't envy you.'

'Manslaughter is. Maybe I didn't mean to kill him?' Gates seemed to search for an excuse. 'He attacked me, so I had no choice but to defend myself.' He winced, struggling against the shackles that secured him to the chair. 'Could you loosen these? They're a bit tight.'

'You might as well tell us,' Detective Roper said, ignoring this request.

Gates looked from one policeman to the other, but seeing no sympathy in their faces, he slumped back in the chair. 'I arranged to meet Mrs Dunleavy after dinner that night to hand over the certificate—'

'The one her son paid you for?' Roper said.

'Yes, that one.' Gates sighed. 'I saw Mrs Ellis come out of the study, so I went in.'

'Why?' Aidan asked.

'Look, if you want me to tell this story, stop interrupting me.' Gates's eyes hardened, revealing the ruthless character that sat behind his mild secretary persona. 'I was in the pub in the village when the Ellises arrived in their motor car. That son of theirs was with them, but he's a bit soft, so didn't notice anything. Ellis did, though. I was talking to the bloke who supplies me with the certificates. I had just paid him and I'm pretty sure the old bloke saw the transaction.

'I didn't think much of it at the time. Just some nosey toff sticking his beak into someone else's business. But when the Ellises turned up at the Manor, it shook me, I can tell you. I avoided him as much as I could, but he tracked me down in the hall before dinner one night and demanded I explain what I was doing at the pub that afternoon. I blanked him and said he must have been mistaken but he wouldn't let it drop. He said something about contacting his superior and I would have some questions to answer.'

'Then Mr Ellis wasn't certain you were involved in the certificate forgery?'

'They weren't forgeries. They were real.'

'Semantics,' Darius said calmly. 'They were still illegal.'

'Look, how was I to know Ellis worked at the Tribunal?' Gates winced and attempted to ease his arms but the bonds held tight and he gave up. 'No, he wasn't sure, but once he was on to my supplier, it wouldn't be long before he connected him to me. And knowing Jack, he'd turn me in for a lighter sentence.'

'Did you plan to kill Mr Ellis, or did things just escalate?' Roper seemed to be trying to give Gates some leeway.

'That night in the study I made a bad judgement.' Gates licked his dry lips. 'I thought I could convince him not to carry out his threat. You see, I don't just deal in exemption certificates. I know this doctor who'll provide a letter to get soldiers invalided out of the army. I offered to get him one for Captain Ellis.' Gates shrugged. 'Anyone can see he's had it with fighting. I thought he'd be grateful.'

'How did Mr Ellis react to that?' Aidan asked.

'He told me I was a disgrace to mankind, a poor excuse for a man with no courage. And all the time he had this smug grin on that bloated face of his. I'd bet he never had to miss a meal 'cos his mam's cupboard was empty. His sort never do. Anyway, I lost it. Picked up that statue and belted him with it. I only hit him the one time.'

'That's all it took,' Roper said. 'And now we come to the ruby pendant. What have you done with that, Mr Gates?'

'You take the biscuit, you lot.' His harsh laugh echoed in the enclosed room. 'I didn't touch it. I'm not interested in women's jewellery and certainly wouldn't nick something that was so easily traced. Not my thing.'

'Well, that's fairly definitive,' Aidan said. 'You'll have to keep looking, Roper.'

'I don't need to. I still have my suspect to the theft safely locked up in the cellar.' He sketched a small bow. 'Now, if you'll excuse me, Inspector, and Miss Merrill, I need to have a word with that officer over there.'

Hannah watched him walk away frustrated that, after all their efforts, Benson had still not been exonerated. If Gates was telling the truth, then who did take the ruby?

* * *

Hannah went up to her room to change her wet clothes and mourn the ruin of her new boots that were wet through and would never be the same again. Relieved to be warm again, she joined the house party in the dining room for a well-earned breakfast, arriving in time to hear Aunt Violet reach the end of her account of their impromptu race through the woods.

'Mr Gates was the killer all along?' Norah interrupted Darius's description of the damage to Aunt Violet's motor car. 'Did he take my ruby too?'

'Mama!' Maura rolled her eyes at her mother. 'Miss Edwards, what about Peter Benson? Has he been released?'

Aunt Violet's fork halted halfway to her mouth. 'I'm sorry, Maura, but as far as I'm aware the ruby is still missing, and the footman is still under detention.'

'It's not right!' Maura pushed back her chair and rose, both hands braced on the tabletop. 'They've got the killer now, and Detective Roper said from the start that whoever murdered Mr Ellis must have taken the ruby.'

'He appears to have changed his opinion, Miss Atherton,' Darius said as he and Aidan arrived together. 'No one has confessed to taking it and Benson is still his prime suspect.'

Issuing a sound between a grunt and a cry, Maura stormed from the room.

'She's always been emotional.' Norah fidgeted with her napkin, using it to hide her face. 'She used to bring birds with broken wings and injured furry animals into the house when she was small. Everyone's suffering is hers.'

'You used to applaud her sensitivity, Mama,' Millie defended her sister as she slowly set down her knife and fork. 'Now you consider it a nuisance.'

'You might have told us what was going on, Violet,' Madeleine complained. 'The first thing we knew was you all rushed off in two motor cars and then the military police rolled onto the drive. We thought we were being invaded. It was quite disturbing.'

'There wasn't exactly time, Mama.' Hannah cut into a fried egg with relish. 'It all happened so quickly.'

'But it must have been very exciting.' Sissy waved her slice of toast, depositing a glob of jam onto the front of Hector's shirt. 'Who would have thought Mr Gates was a murderer? I sat next to him during dinner once,' she added, more thrilled than shocked. 'Does anyone know where Mama is? She was up before me this morning, and I haven't seen her.'

'Er, I believe one of the army officers asked to have a word with her,' Iris replied vaguely. 'I'm sure she'll be along soon.'

Hannah exchanged a loaded look with Darius and bent her head to her plate.

To her relief, Sissy fell into conversation with Maura and seemed to forget her question.

22

When breakfast was over, and the lorries had disappeared from the front drive taking Andrew Gates to his new accommodation at Aldershot Barracks, Darius took Hannah's hand, drawing her along the hall to the deserted music room where they settled onto a bay window seat with an uninterrupted view of the snow-covered lawn leading down to the arched bridge over the river, the border of ancient oak trees just still visible through a low-lying mist.

Hannah sat spooned against his chest, her head on his shoulder with his arms wrapped around her waist.

'Well, we did it again. Another villain in custody,' Darius said, his voice vibrating through her hair.

'I can't believe anyone would do something so reprehensible.' Hannah shuddered slightly. 'Our country is fighting for its very way of life and all he cared about was money.'

'Some people see a crisis and step up to do their duty, while others see it as an opportunity. It's human nature.'

'I'm still worried about Benson.' Hannah pulled his arm

tighter into her middle. 'I have no proof, but I know he didn't take the ruby. He was so worried about Fiona; he didn't seem to care what happened to him. One thing baffles me, though. Did Gates put that cushion with the knife in Dianna's room to make sure she cooperated?'

'Ah, I meant to tell you. Venables told Aidan a housemaid did that. She overheard Dianna tell Roper that Benson was outside the Atherton girls' room that night. Benson is a popular member of the household and when he was arrested, the housemaid decided to get revenge on Dianna.'

'She certainly succeeded in frightening her. Maybe Fiona should be warned. I suspect this housemaid might have her eye on Peter.'

'You could be right, but he only has eyes for Fiona. And don't worry about Benson. He's back on staff and out of that awful basement room. Mycroft has also called a barrister friend of his to represent him.'

'If it gets that far, which I hope it won't.'

'Try to see Roper's point of view. Having a possible suspect in a crime is better than none, even if that person is acquitted. He stepped up at the end, although he scared the life out of us on that icy road. You should have heard him yelling for Mycroft to go faster. At one point I thought he was going to grab the wheel himself. Hopefully, your Aunt Violet's motor car can be repaired in good time for you to get back to London. If not, though, I can give you a lift and come down for it later.'

'That's kind of you.' Hannah laced the fingers of her left hand through his. 'Maybe Mr Ellis's death wasn't for nothing if they can stop the thefts of the certificates.'

'Finding all those that have already been issued might be a fruitless task, but that's someone else's problem now. I intend to enjoy the rest of this Christmas with you.' He stared round the room and smiled. 'I'm getting quite fond of this room. Shall we have one in our house?'

'A music room?' Hannah smiled, liking the sound of the words 'our house'. 'I love my house in Chiswick Mall, but can you imagine my maid, Ivy and your butler, Travis in that small kitchen? One or other would give notice every week.'

'Not Travis. He's a stoic fellow, and I doubt one housemaid would be too much for him.'

Hannah smiled to herself, confident Darius didn't have a clue. Travis might have worked for the Cliffords for over twenty years, but Ivy was a force to be reckoned with – not that this was the time to explain.

'Ilchester Place is my family home, but I appreciate it is possibly not to your taste,' Darius said. 'Would you prefer somewhere else? The country, perhaps?'

'No, I enjoy being in the centre of things. It would also be nice not to have to come into town on the underground every day, as I don't intend on giving up the bookshop. Not for a while, anyway.'

'I wouldn't expect you to. You and that bookshop are intertwined, along with Archie and your Aunt Violet. Especially since the rebuilding after the bomb blast. You've made it very much your own.'

'Does that include Mr Bartleby?'

'That cat is such a character. How can one not include him?' He lifted her hand he was holding and placed a brief kiss on her knuckles. 'This is nice. We haven't sat and talked like this for a long time, if ever. My job is all-consuming right now, but that doesn't excuse my having neglected you.'

'Will you stay with the bureau after the war, do you think?' It would be naïve of her to imagine there would be no need for an intelligence department when the guns stopped.

'Don't let my work impress you too much. It might sound like important, vital work but I seem to spend a lot of my time in Whitehall poring over obscure messages we aren't sure are legitimate or not, so we could simply be spinning our wheels.'

Hannah pulled upright and turned on the bench to face him. 'You suspect the British are being misled with fake information?'

'Possibly. It wouldn't surprise anyone. We have the German codebooks, but who is to say they aren't aware of that and are sending disinformation to distract us?'

'I still believe you're doing important work, Darius. You need to believe it too or you cannot give your best. Keep reading those messages, and one day something will come across your desk which might be the difference between the Allies winning or losing. It might even be you who finds it.'

'That's good advice and thank you for your confidence in me.' He wrapped his arms around her, pulling her back against his chest. 'We just need to keep going. Giving up isn't an option. Oh, and to be accurate, we're called the Military Intelligence Five division now.'

'That's an odd name.' Hannah nuzzled closer, relishing the maleness of him.

He chuckled. 'I suppose it is. I've no idea who came up with it.'

* * *

During the morning, silent, fat snowflakes fell softly from a lowering sky, obliterating the lorry tyre tracks that crisscrossed the drive, the churned-up snow from snowball fights and footprints from the pathways. Determined to make the day a perfect Christmas Eve, Mycroft organised early present-giving for the children and mandatory party games for everyone. With a footman on hand in case of accidents, the candles on the hall Christmas tree were lit and presents handed around with appropriate ceremony. After a flurry of enthusiastic paper tearing and squeals of delight, the children settled on the floor of the drawing room surrounded by a mountain of stuffed toys, wooden soldiers, jack-in-the-boxes and books.

'It's so nice to see them playing quietly,' Madeleine observed.

'Only because they aren't bothering her for attention,' Iris whispered to Hannah.

'It's pointless complaining about her. She won't change,' Hannah replied.

'Isn't that book a bit girlish for a chap?' Hector nodded to where Laurie pored over his copy of *The Secret Garden.*

'Absolutely not.' Hannah narrowed her eyes, daring him to argue. 'Laurie is a compassionate child, so I'm sure he'll love the sentiment of the lonely orphan, Mary Lennox meeting the sick Colin.'

'Allegedly sick,' Hector said.

'You've read it?' Hannah started at him in surprise.

'I might have. I bought a copy for my godson's daughter.' He cleared his throat and retreated behind a copy of *Punch.*

'You didn't buy it from me.'

'That I did,' he said without looking at her. 'Your chap Archie posted it to me.'

Smiling to herself, Hannah looked to where her nephew was reading his copy of *The Wolf Cub's Handbook.* Hannah had also bought him *The King of Ireland's Son,* but for the moment he was fascinated by becoming one of Baden-Powell's wolf cubs.

Matilda sat on the floor almost under the Christmas tree, her legs straight out in front of her and a copy of *The Adventures of Danny Meadow Mouse* on her lap. She couldn't master many of the words, but the illustrations of furry animals kept her occupied.

'What happens to Danny?' Matilda asked.

'Well,' Hannah began, 'he has adventures trying to escape foxes where he gets into all sorts of scrapes. First, he's caught by an owl, then by a snare and even gets trapped in a tin can.'

'Oh.' Matilda pouted, comically crestfallen. 'Couldn't you have got me a book about a clever mouse?'

'Matilda!' Iris snapped, aghast. 'That's extremely rude.'

Hannah bit her bottom lip to prevent a laugh and Darius choked on a mouthful of tea while a low ripple of smothered laughter ran around the room.

'Where is Violet, by the way?' Hector scanned the room but slumped back in his chair, disappointed.

'She and Aidan took a drive in Mycroft's motor car,' Hannah replied. 'Her motor car will be under canvas in the garage until the holiday is over.'

'A drive in the snow? Alone with that Farrell chap?' Hannah's father appeared disconcerted for a moment but then smiled slowly. 'Ah, well, I suppose Violet is old enough to make her own decisions.'

'I could have done with more guidance on that subject, Papa.' Hannah attempted resigned acceptance but was aware she sounded petulant.

'I believe I did some things right.' He leaned closer and lowered his voice. 'I persuaded your aunt to live with you in Chiswick. Couldn't have a daughter of mine living alone. The bookshop was something Violet came up with. She inherited it or bought it for a song from a bankrupt, I'm not sure which. Anyway, the responsibility has done you good. Don't tell your mother, but I'm proud of your self-reliance.' He stroked his moustache with a finger and thumb and stared off through the window. 'It was tragic about Gerald, but unlike Madeleine, I was under no illusion about your affection for him. Or rather, lack of it.'

'You knew? Papa, I—' Hannah began, but he halted her.

'That you didn't love him?' He nodded. 'He was a nice young man and would have made a suitable husband.' He turned towards her and winked. 'But suitable was never what you were looking for.'

'Whyever didn't we have this conversation at the time, Papa?'

'It wasn't my place,' he replied, his brow furrowed. 'Daughters are their mother's responsibility. And Madeleine never welcomed my interference.'

That last day with Gerald came back, with all its embarrassed and conflicted emotions. Gerald, heartbreakingly handsome in his second lieutenant's uniform, his hopeful eyes locked on her face as he issued an awkward but genuine proposal. Her head had screamed no, but she couldn't bring herself to voice it. Instead, she had nodded, hoping he thought she was simply overcome and unable to speak. She had watched the train snake away along the tracks with her heart like lead.

'If it helps at all, darling,' her father said gently as if sensing her thoughts, 'he was happy at the end.'

'I hope so.' Hannah met the wistful smile and the far-away look in his eyes that reminded her he had been a young man once, with dreams outside the life he had been guided into by his parents.

Maybe she could ask him what those were, one day.

'Can we go sledging now?' Matilda shut the book with a snap and scrambled to her feet. 'You promised, Auntie Han.'

Hannah cast an apologetic glance at Darius who was comfortably settled in an armchair by the fire.

'We'd better go now, then. It will be dark in an hour or so.'

With enthusiastic cheers and whoops of laughter, the children discarded their new toys and scrambled to their feet.

Wrapped in woollen coats, hats, mufflers and gloves, and laced into stout boots, the small procession went into the outbuildings – the iced-over puddles in the uneven pathway cracking beneath their feet – to search for sledges that they had stored away the previous year.

Xander swung open the door of a small barn where all the bicycles, sports equipment and garden implements were stored. 'It didn't snow much last year, so I haven't used my sledge at all. It might even be too small for me by now.'

'We'll have to see.' Hannah lined up the three wooden sledges in order of size on the barn floor. 'This one looks almost new.'

'He always gets the new one.' Matilda glowered at her brother from beneath a bright red woolly hat. 'The boys have both used mine so most of the paint has been rubbed off.' She aimed a kick at the smallest sledge.

'It is a bit worse for wear,' Darius observed.

'Perhaps Father Christmas noticed it too and has brought you a new one?' Hannah said, with the confidence of prior knowledge.

'You can use mine if you want, Matilda,' Laurie offered.

'No, it's all right.' Matilda grabbed the worn rope and dragged the sledge across the barn floor behind her. 'If he sees me on this old thing, he might feel sorry for me. Then I will get a new one.'

'He's not watching you all the time, Matilda,' Xander called over his shoulder. 'He's not Jesus!'

Matilda trudged in his wake, her head down dragging the battered sledge behind her.

'That was nice of you, Laurie.' Hannah placed an arm on his shoulder and followed.

They reached the pathway that ran around the bottom of the

terrace where Darius lined up sledges and children ready to take on the sloping lawn.

'Kick off with your feet and when you start moving, pull them on top of the sledge out of the way,' Darius instructed. 'And keep your arms tucked in.'

'We've done this before, Uncle Das,' Xander said scathingly.

'We apologise, but you still need to be careful,' Hannah said, effectively chastened by a child.

After several more rides, all three children were screaming with delight and trying to outdo each other in speed and distance on the slope. Darius kept up with them far better than Hannah could, running up the slope and then down again to make sure they did not collide, his face alight with laughter, if slightly breathless.

Matilda started to tire, a condition she revealed with a prolonged bout of irritation with her brothers. Admitting defeat, Hannah helped drag her sledge up to the top of the slope one last time. She held the rope while the little girl climbed on and gave her a push to set her off down the slope.

Darius was helping Laurie untangle the rope on his sledge where it had wrapped around his ankle and Xander was preparing for his next run when Hannah glanced up at the terrace.

Maura stood beside the fountain, a shawl draped over her shoulders and with her arms clasped across her midriff. Hannah waved, but she wasn't looking her way. Instead, she stared into the distance, a pensive, almost sad look on her face.

Darius came puffing towards her up the slope. 'Is that Maura up there?' He shielded his eyes with a hand against the glare of the snow. 'She looks quite pulled down, poor girl.'

'I imagine she's still worried about Peter Benson, despite Mycroft's promise of legal support for him.'

'Perhaps she has a crush on him?' Darius said, wryly.

'I'm fairly certain that isn't the reason. No, Norah had it right, in that Maura is sensitive and carries everyone's misery.'

'Then let's hope it all gets sorted out and that wretched ruby is found.'

The sound of Matilda's scream brought Hannah whirling around. Matilda had toppled sideways off the sledge. She lay where she fell, her red woollen hat poking out of the snow. She made no effort to move and was yelling at the top of her voice for help.

'That child is going to cause Mycroft and Iris no end of trouble,' Darius said as he trudged down the slope and lifted the child clear.

'Auntie Han! You let go of the rope too soon!' Matilda accused her, pouting. She had lost her hat, leaving her brown curls snow-splattered and bedraggled, and a boot had come off too, as snow rapidly soaked through her sock.

'I'm sorry.' Hannah waded through the soft snow towards her as Darius set the child upright.

'That was your own fault, Matilda,' Xander scoffed, retrieving her bobble hat, which was now a cold, wet mess she refused to touch, let alone wear. 'You don't hold on tight enough.'

'I'm cold, Uncle Das,' Matilda whined, shivering. When she had first begun to talk, the little girl had been unable to pronounce Darius's name, so called him Uncle Das, and thus it remained with the eldest three, and most likely would with Sophie when she was old enough. The thought warmed Hannah despite the creeping numbness that crept through her fingertips and feet.

She hefted the child in her arms, her gaze going to the terrace again. It was empty. 'It's time to go back inside, anyway,' she said with a mental shrug.

They trooped back to the house, clumps of slow stuck to their coats, cold and tired but happy where Hannah handed the children back to a waiting Fiona with a promise of crumpets for tea, provided they agreed to go to bed without argument to wait for Father Christmas.

23

Hannah lingered in the vestibule, pretending to remove her outdoor clothes until Fiona and the children had disappeared onto the floor above.

'Hurry up, slowcoach.' Darius grinned at her and started towards the sitting room. 'Come on, or you'll miss tea.'

'I'll be there in a while. Go on without me.' Hannah waved him off.

'All right, but you'll miss out on the crumpets if the children get there first.'

When he was out of sight, Hannah slipped back through the front door. Daylight was fading fast and above an unbroken expanse of snow, the sky had cleared to a sharp blue with a splash of pink on the horizon.

Taking the path around the side of the house, she climbed the terrace steps and strolled to the far end past the music room from where she could hear the strains of the piano from inside.

A thick layer of snow covered the three tiers of the fountain, and a layer of ice covered the pool of water in the basin. Circling the fountain, she perched on the edge where she had seen Maura standing earlier.

Scanning the terrace for a suitable tool, she spied a small stone figure of a rabbit about nine inches high. Hefting it in her hand, she brought the base down hard on the layer of ice until it gave a satisfying crack.

She eased onto the bottom edge of the fountain, her feet braced to steady herself as she removed her glove and pushed the pieces of broken ice away. Leaning over the edge, all she could see was the murky green, algae-covered base, but unwilling to give up on her hunch just yet, she reached her hand into the frigid water.

The water reached past her wrist as she felt past the curved inner edge where a lip of stone dropped away from the basin at an angle. Her hand started to grow numb just as her fingers curled around something hard and round.

Leaning back, she pulled the object from the water. In her hand sat a blood-red stone set into a plain gold bezel hanging from a gold chain that dripped icy water onto the stone.

Hannah stared at it in the fading light, the stone angled to see the myriad shades of red and tiny clouds of purple beneath the surface, while the sound of the piano played softly behind her. The hiding place was perfect; the shape of the lower bowl hid the necklace from sight. Even when the ice melted it would not have been visible from the surface. Only someone who knew it was there would think to search behind the curved stone lip.

The music stopped suddenly, bringing Hannah back to the present. She hurriedly wrapped the pendant in a handkerchief, patting it dry before slipping it into her coat pocket. She shoved her frozen hand into the folds of her woollen scarf until the feeling returned to her fingers, then stepped through the French doors into the music room.

Maura sat with her back to her, her fingers flying across the keys in a fast, military-style tune. Something must have alerted her as she paused and twisted on the bench, a flash of fear in her eyes that transformed into pleasure. 'Hannah! I wondered who that was.'

'You seem happier than you did earlier, Maura.' Hannah pushed her hand deeper into her pocket and closed the door with the other. 'That's an uplifting melody! Another tune I've heard before but have no idea what it's called.'

'Mozart's *Rondo Alla Turca*. One of my favourites.' Maura's hands stilled on the keyboard and she smiled up at Hannah over the polished expanse of the piano lid. 'You'll not believe this, but Papa has agreed I can enrol in the Royal Academy of Music. Isn't that wonderful?'

'It certainly is. What changed his mind?' Hannah raised one eyebrow. Had that been her agenda all along?

'This past few days, he says Mama has embarrassed him over her obsession with the ruby. That it's gained far too much importance for too long. My display at the dinner table last night bothered him – a lot. He said it's time we followed our own dreams rather than only caring about baubles and trinkets.'

'Your father is a sensible man. What's Millie's perspective on this?'

'She's more relieved than I am. She never cared much for the tradition, and Lynford cares even less about possessions than she does. Especially now. All he wants is a quiet life in the country and to live in peace, raising babies with my sister.' She broke off, frowning. 'Hannah, whatever have you been doing? Your coat is all wet.'

Hannah removed her hand from her pocket, the ruby hanging from the fingers she held out.

Maura's face paled. 'You... You found it?'

'I did. But it wasn't lost, was it? Or stolen?'

'How-how did you know where it was?' Maura closed the piano lid and rose, circling the piano slowly.

'Why else would you have been outside in the snow that night? It always bothered me you were so skimpily dressed for a stroll.'

'I thought if it were gone, we could all stop talking about it.' Maura wrapped both arms around her midriff and stared at Hannah with pleading eyes. 'Can't you just put it back in the fountain? It will be safe there, and only the two of us will know.'

'I can't keep a secret like that, Maura. And what about Benson? If the police find it, they'll assume he put it there to collect later. He could be sent to prison.'

'Uncle Mycroft said he'll get him a lawyer, so he'll be let off.'

'That's a naïve thing to say, Maura. What about his good name?'

'I don't know what I was thinking.' Maura slumped onto the piano bench. 'I didn't realise Millie had put it in the dresser after dinner, but when I saw the jeweller's box lying there in the drawer, this wave of resentment overcame me. I did it for Millie, though. She hates the whole idea and has enough to worry about, what with Lynford's illness and their wedding. You saw how uncomfortable she was that night, being paraded around in a room full of people. Mama claims it's just youthful shyness she will grow out of. It's not, she's always been like that. I just slipped the pendant into my pocket and went outside for a breath of fresh air. I walked as far as the fountain, and it seemed the perfect place. Then I started shivering and saw you through the window of the music room.'

'What did you think would happen then? That everyone would simply forget about it?'

'It sounds pathetic, and stupid put like that.' She lifted her hands and let them fall to her lap again. 'If I thought at all, it was that without it, my parents might pay attention to what Millie and I wanted.'

'Like your music?'

'Yes, like my music. Like Millie's wedding, too. But then Mr Ellis was found dead, and when Detective Roper said it must be connected to the pendant, I panicked and wanted to own up about the ruby, but I just couldn't.' Her eyes found Hannah's. Her smile dissolved and her lower lip trembled. 'I'm going to have to put this right, aren't I? Will Mama ever forgive me?'

'In time, I'm sure she will.' Hannah imagined it might take a while but decided not to make things worse.

Her anger that Maura had caused so much trouble instantly dissipated in the face of her distress. She was merely an immature girl trying to make things easier for her and her sister but with no concept of the consequences.

The door opened on a wave of noisy laughter as Selwyn, his arm around Norah's waist, burst into the room. Behind the pair Millie entered, holding Lynford's hand. Norah smiled up at her husband in a way that Hannah had never seen before, and Lynford teased Millie, pretending to chase her round the piano, and in seconds, Hannah was surrounded.

'Hannah!' Selwyn released his wife and rushed towards her as if he hadn't seen her for a year and gave her a quick but firm hug. 'Have you come to attend our little concert?'

'Concert?' Hannah frowned and released the pendant back inside her pocket.

'Hasn't she told you?' Lynford appeared at his shoulder, his expression relaxed, and he had lost the haunted look he usually displayed. 'My future sister-in-law the pianist is going to play Chopin for us instead of us hearing snippets from behind closed doors.'

'And I agreed to come as long as it isn't Mahler; he's so dreary.' Millie giggled to show she was joking.

'It will be a proper performance.' Norah's proud smile banished her permanently sour look.

'It's a lovely idea.' Hannah eyed the door, eager to make herself scarce, conscious of the weight in her pocket.

'Ah, well done, Lynford.' Selwyn beamed at the young man, who had begun moving chairs from the walls, arranging them into a semi-circle around the piano.

'Won't you join us, Hannah?' Millie asked, her smile genuine.

'It's very kind of you, but I can see this is a family occasion.' Hannah edged towards the door. 'Perhaps next time, when everyone can come and hear?'

'You'd be very welcome.' Selwyn regarded her with affection. 'Maura has been practising specially.'

'Perhaps you could bring Darius with you.' Norah gave a teasing smile.

'Thank you, but... um—' Hannah backed towards the door. 'I'll bear that in mind.'

* * *

Hannah closed the door of the music room behind her and leaned against it, as the chatter and laughter died down and Maura began playing.

'Hello, dear,' a low, slightly cracked voice said, from a chaise, one of several positioned to give visitors a stopping point on the long walk through the hallway.

'Oh, Rose, I didn't see you there,' Hannah said, startled.

'She plays beautifully, doesn't she?' Rose cocked her head to where one of Chopin's *Nocturnes* drifted through the door.

'She does. I'm quite envious of her skill.'

'Young Maura aspires to be a professional pianist, you know?' Her gaze met Hannah's. 'If her parents refuse to help her, I've decided I'm going to. But don't tell them that.'

'You are?' Hannah detected an inner strength in the older woman she had either missed or had not been there before. 'Are you all right, Rose?'

'I will be.' Rose turned and stared straight ahead. 'I can see in your eyes what you're thinking, dear. But there's no need to concern yourself about me. I'm not at all sad.'

Hannah was about to say her loss was too new, and that grief would come in time, but it seemed trite and inadequate.

'Basil's death left me horrified, guilt-ridden and numb.' Rose seemed to sense what Hannah was thinking. 'When that Dr Eames told us he had been murdered, do you know what my first thought was?' Her head swivelled towards Hannah, pinning her with a steady stare.

She shook her head.

'That it served him right.'

Intrigued, but strangely not shocked, Hannah eased down onto the bench beside her and waited for her to continue.

'When the war started and the government took over most of the food distribution to send to the troops, our profits plummeted,' Rose said, her voice devoid of self-pity. 'Basil took the job at the Tribunal. But it wasn't enough, and we were struggling badly. The first we knew about the ruby and its tradition was when Norah invited us to dinner. She wanted Millie to wear it at their wedding next year.' She brought a hand to her throat as if gathering strength to continue.

Hannah waited as Chopin continued in the background.

'Basil came up with a plan, you see,' she said after a moment. 'He was going to replace the ruby with a fake. He said the substitution wouldn't come to light until Lynford and Millie's daughter, if they had one, came of age. Plenty of time for our fortunes to reverse.'

Hannah longed to pose questions, but resisted, unwilling to interrupt.

'We argued about it constantly,' Rose continued. 'Basil said I was being short-sighted. After the wedding, the ruby would be returned to a bank vault and stay there for years. When it was finally brought out again, if anyone questioned it, who could say it hadn't always been a fake?'

So, Basil Ellis was content to rob his daughter-in-law of a valuable possession but baulked at keeping his son out of the army with a false medical certificate? Strange how some people's moral compass could be skewed.

'What happened the night he died, Rose?' Hannah asked gently.

'I left the sitting room to fetch my shawl after dinner. Basil said he was going to play billiards with the other gentlemen, but then I saw him enter the study. Norah had told me that the ruby was kept there, so I suspected he might be about to take it.'

'But the ruby wasn't there. Millie had left it in her room.'

'Something neither of us was aware of at the time. How could we be?' Rose sighed. 'I confronted him, begged him to reconsider. I said I would rather be poor than rob our own son and his wife-to-be. As always, he refused to listen to me. Told me to stay quiet, and he would see to things. I called him a selfish, greedy man. He smirked at me and ordered me to get out. I've never been so angry. All these years I've had to put up with his arrogance, his bullying and parsimonious ways.'

'What did you do?' Hannah's voice was little more than a whisper.

'I grabbed a glass vase from the desk and threw it at him. Then I ran out. I didn't even stop to see where it hit. I heard him yell out in pain and the vase smash, but I didn't go back. I was so shaken, I just stood in the hallway like a terrified rabbit.' Her pale eyes met Hannah's calmly. 'That's when I saw you, dear.'

'You told me you had got lost when you went to fetch your shawl. I wondered why you had returned without it.'

'I didn't get that far.' She chuckled quietly. 'When the doctor mentioned a curved injury in Basil's head, I thought I had done it with the vase. It was a heavy vase.'

'You believed you had killed him?'

Rose nodded. Her eyes welled with tears and she blinked them away. 'I convinced myself I couldn't have hit him hard enough, but what if the argument had stressed him enough to bring on a heart attack? Then Detective Roper said Mr Gates had admitted killing him and it was such a relief. Will Lynford and Millie ever forgive me, do you suppose?'

'Forgive you for what, Rose? You've done nothing wrong.'

'Some people believe that to think about doing something is as bad as carrying it out. And at that moment, I truly wanted to kill Basil. He was about to ruin everything, for himself, me, and the children.'

'No, I don't. And if you hope for a contented life watching Lynford and Millie's children grow, you won't repeat what you have just told me to anyone. Ever.'

'Really, dear?' A tiny frown appeared between her watery blue eyes. 'I'm not wicked?'

Hannah shook her head, tempted to say her husband certainly was but chose not to.

'Thank you, dear. I feel much better now.' Rose released her breath in a long sigh. 'I could do with a little rest before dinner.' Accepting the supporting arm Hannah held out to her, she eased herself to her feet.

Hannah watched her totter along the hall, saddened that she

was only in her sixties and yet old before her time. Was that what being married to a domineering man did to you?

She remained on the bench, the pendant a heavy weight in her pocket in more ways than one. Chopin continued to play as she debated what to do with it.

Despite Detective Roper's arrogance and clumsy methods, he had been partly right, in that the theft of the ruby had been an inside job after all. Would Maura have stepped up at the last moment to put things right if Peter Benson had been convicted? Hannah hoped so, but the answer to that question would have to remain a mystery.

As these thoughts crowded her head, slow steady footsteps approached. A pair of immaculate black brogues entered her eyeline and halted beside her.

'Is that Maura playing?' The newcomer cocked his head at the door behind them, his fingers gently drumming against his thigh in rhythm. 'That girl will end up on a stage somewhere, I'm sure of it.' His eyes filled with concern as they settled on her face. 'You seem troubled, Hannah. Anything I can help with?'

'It's certainly a dilemma,' she responded with a wan smile.

'You could do worse than to confide in me.' He tugged up his trousers at the knees and sat beside her, close enough so she could smell the sandalwood and rosewater of his cologne. A very different fragrance to the one Darius wore, but just as pleasant. 'I'm the epitome of discretion,' he said with laughter in his voice. 'My father always said I should have converted and become a priest because I'm so closed mouthed.'

'Really? What are you like with confessions, Mycroft?'

EPILOGUE

Hannah dressed in her best gown that evening for dinner – a sapphire-blue silk gown pinched in at the waist, with an under-bodice decorated with seed pearls, and an asymmetrical overskirt in cobweb black lace attached to one hip and draped across the front in soft folds.

Darius was waiting on the corner of the staircase when Hannah emerged from her room and he closed the space between them, taking both her hands in his. 'It's been an exciting few days, but I anticipate a more relaxed dinner this evening. Not to mention an enjoyable Christmas.'

Detective Roper's superior, on learning he had located a murderer and a fraudster, had sent no less than four officers in a police van to remove Gates to Woking Police Station. Dianna Dunleavy had been relieved of the fake certificate made out for her son and let off with a stern warning. She'd returned home under a cloud, dragging a protesting Sissy with her.

'It's a shame about Aunt Violet's motor car,' Hannah said. 'She only bought it a month ago.'

'Mycroft will sort that out for her. Although I doubt they'll both be returning to London on his motorcycle.' His teasing smile faded. 'And after all this, we still don't know who took the ruby.'

'Er, about that...' Hannah began. 'No, I can't tell you yet. Would you mind waiting?'

'I'll trust your judgement.' His gaze roved her face for long seconds. 'And I'm known for my patience.'

She linked her arm through his and together, they descended the staircase into the hall where two footmen flanked the closed dining room doors, though not Peter Benson, as he had been released from the gloomy basement store and sent to spend Christmas at his parents' home in compensation for his recent ordeal.

'I'm glad we could fulfil your wish for this evening,' Hannah said.

'I trust it's as much your wish as it is mine?'

'I already have mine. I'm wearing this.' She lifted her hand, on which the diamond and emerald ring glinted in the overhead lights.

At a signal from Darius, the footmen grasped a doorhandle each and swung open the doors onto a fairyland of crystal, lights, flowers, glowing candles and the beaming faces of Hannah's family.

Darius covered her hand on his forearm with his and squeezed. 'Are you ready?'

Hannah lifted her chin and took a deep, calming breath. 'I'm ready.'

HISTORICAL NOTE

In January 1917: the Royal Navy intercepted a coded telegram sent by the German Foreign Secretary, Arthur Zimmerman, to Johann Von Bernstorff, the German Ambassador in Washington. The telegram stated that if unrestricted submarine warfare threatened to bring America into the war, then he should approach Mexico to enter the war on Germany's side.

The telegram was decoded by Room 40's cryptologists, with a stolen copy of a German diplomatic code obtained in the Near East and the Russian admiralty sharing a copy of the German naval codebook it had obtained. Thus by 1917 British Intelligence could decipher most German messages.

However, Britain needed a way of informing the Americans without the Germans knowing their codes had been broken and without the US being aware communications to their country were being read by British intelligence.

Britain solved this dilemma by handing over a decoded version sent via the German Embassy in Washington to Mexico so that it would appear the document had been leaked in Mexico.

The ploy worked, and President Wilson released the contents to American newspapers which led to a public uproar. On 4 April 1917, America declared war on Germany.

Acknowledgement to the Military Intelligence Museum
https://www.militaryintelligencemuseum.org/

ABOUT THE AUTHOR

Anita Davison is the author of the successful Flora Maguire historical mystery series.

Sign up to Anita Davison's mailing list for news, competitions and updates on future books.

Visit Anita's website: www.anitadavison.co.uk

Follow Anita on social media here:

 x.com/anitasdavison

 facebook.com/anita.davison

 goodreads.com/anitadavison

ALSO BY ANITA DAVISON

Miss Merrill and Aunt Violet Mysteries

Murder in the Bookshop

Murder at Midwinter Manor

The Flora Maguire Mysteries

Death On Board

Death at the Abbey

Death of a Suffragette

Death by the Thames

Death on a Train

Poison
& Pens

POISON & PENS IS THE HOME OF
COZY MYSTERIES SO POUR YOURSELF
A CUP OF TEA & GET SLEUTHING!

DISCOVER PAGE-TURNING NOVELS FROM
YOUR FAVOURITE AUTHORS &
MEET NEW FRIENDS

JOIN OUR
FACEBOOK GROUP

BIT.LYPOISONANDPENSFB

SIGN UP TO OUR
NEWSLETTER

BIT.LY/POISONANDPENSNEWS

Boldwood

Boldwood Books is an award-winning fiction publishing company seeking out the best stories from around the world.

Find out more at www.boldwoodbooks.com

Join our reader community for brilliant books, competitions and offers!

Follow us
@BoldwoodBooks
@TheBoldBookClub

Sign up to our weekly
deals newsletter

https://bit.ly/BoldwoodBNewsletter

Printed in Great Britain
by Amazon